DEAD GOOD DETECTIVES

Ghost Rescue

For magical **Lyn** and Maria

First published in Great Britain 2023 by Farshore

An imprint of HarperCollins*Publishers*
1 London Bridge Street, London SE1 9GF

farshore.co.uk

HarperCollins*Publishers*
Macken House, 39/40 Mayor Street Upper,
Dublin 1, D01 C9W8

ISBN 978 0 7555 0335 3
Printed and bound in the UK using 100% renewable electricity
at CPI Group (UK) Ltd
1

A CIP catalogue record for this title is available from the British Library.

DEAD GOOD DETECTIVES

Ghost Rescue

JENNY MCLACHLAN

Illustrated by Chloe Dominique

CHAPTER ONE

I'm cleaning seagull poo off the roof of Mermaid's Ice Cream Café when my best friend, Zen, comes hurtling into the model village.

'Sid!' he calls, waving his phone above his head. Then he dashes past my dad, who's sitting at the entrance kiosk, and runs towards me, his cloak billowing out behind him.

Wait . . . *what*? Why is Zen wearing a cloak? Before I can ask, he skids to a halt, shoves his phone in my face and blurts out, 'My Stormchaser app says lightning is hitting Fathom in *one hour*, and you know what that means, don't you?' He doesn't give me the chance to reply. He throws back his head and yells, 'IT'S GHOST-FREEING TIME, BABY!'

I spin round and look out to sea.

Zen's right. While I've been doing jobs for Dad, a storm has crept in. Already waves are crashing against the Cockle, Fathom's curving harbour, and the sky is the colour of an angry bruise.

Thunder rumbles and my stomach squeezes tight with excitement and nerves.

Zen grabs my shoulders. 'Sid, in one hour we could have another ghost wandering around Fathom!'

'*Another ghost . . .*' I whisper.

Amazingly we aren't playing a game. A few months ago I really did free a ghost from Fathom graveyard – a pirate and then his crew of ghostly shipmates – and I might be about to free another one.

It all began when I found a headstone belonging to a man called Ezekiel Kittow. The headstone was hidden under ivy and straight away I knew I had to add it to my map. I shoved the Crunchie I was holding on top of the grave, rested my map against it and started to draw.

I was adding the initials EK to my tiny headstone when lightning crashed to earth. Minutes later, the mausoleum in the corner of the graveyard started to change.

First a door appeared where there should have been bricks, followed by two windows, a lantern and then a sign that said 'Halfway House'.

The next thing I knew, the door creaked open and a gigantic pirate ghost stepped into the graveyard.

It was Ezekiel Kittow himself, or Bones as I learned to call him, and right now he's squeezed in the kiosk with my dad watching him paint a model of a labradoodle.

I turn to look at Bones as he hovers behind Dad's shoulder like a dark shadow.

Except for being a bit shimmery around the edges, he doesn't look like a ghost. He has messy black hair, a beard that's tangled with seaweed, and he's wearing a leather coat and a battered tricorn hat. Oh, and he's soaking wet. Drops of water fall from his beard and ooze from his sodden clothes only to vanish seconds later. Bones is wet because he drowned three hundred years ago when his ship sank and he's never dried out. Even from over here I can smell his damp, smoky pong.

Bones looks up and sees me watching him. A smile spreads across his sunburnt face and the scars on his cheeks crinkle. 'Ahoy there!' he bellows. 'You should see this little dog your father is painting, Sid. He has given him a wagging tail!'

Bones might be loud, smelly and very big, but Dad hasn't got a clue he's standing behind him in the kiosk. That's because, unlike me and Zen, Dad hasn't got *the gift* to see ghosts.

We're not sure where I got *the gift* from, but I passed it on to Zen the night I saved his life by pulling him up a cliff. When this happened I felt something hot, like electricity, shoot from my fingers into Zen's, and from then on Zen could see ghosts just like me.

Suddenly an explosion of green bursts through the wall of the model village and Bones's parrot, Elizabeth, swoops past us and flies into the kiosk, landing on Dad's head.

'*RUM! BUM! BULLY! RUM!*' she squawks.

Dad might not be able to see or hear Elizabeth, but he can obviously feel her icy claws because he shivers and pulls on a hat. A ghost's touch is freezing, even to people without *the gift*.

Bones gently lifts Elizabeth on to his shoulder then strides through the kiosk wall, coming to join us.

'Ho ho, young 'uns,' he says. Then he notices Zen's cloak.

'I say, that is a mighty fine garment you are wearing, Zen. What might the special occasion be?'

Zen swishes his scarlet-lined cloak through the air. He often borrows clothes from his mum and dad's Museum of Curiosities, but I haven't seen him wear the cloak for a while. 'The special occasion is us freeing a ghost,' he says. 'Haven't you noticed the weather, Bones? There's a storm coming and there's going to be lightning. Sid can free another ghost!'

Bones's dark eyes narrow as he looks out to sea, then he sucks in a deep breath. 'God's hat, you are right, boy! Which ghost will you free next, Sid?'

'I don't know,' I say. Then to buy myself a bit of time I walk over to the corner of the model village where Dad has recreated Fathom graveyard.

I crouch down so I can get a better look at the tiny graves. Most of the model village is neat and tidy, but Dad has let the grass grow wild here, just like it does in the real graveyard. He wants everything to look as realistic as possible, which is why he has also included a miniature version of my mum's grave and a river filled with real water.

My eyes follow the little river upstream until they rest

on the model of a building with bricked-up walls. Everyone in the village calls this the mausoleum, but Zen and I know that really it's the Halfway House, a pub where ghosts have been held prisoner for hundreds of years.

I think of the ghosts trapped inside: Peg Tiddy, the witch, with her wild red hair and hundreds of freckles, and Little Will who is always slipping his cold fingers into mine. I think about Dai, Mei Huang, Holkar, Olive, Emma and Beau; all of them are desperate to escape from the Halfway House so they can solve their unfinished business and cross over to the other side.

And then, of course, I think of Old Scratch, the man who trapped the ghosts.

When most people die, they cross over straight away and find peace, but the ghosts in the pub all had unfinished business and found they couldn't leave our world. As they tried to sort out their problems they began to fade away and that's how Old Scratch was able to tempt them into the Halfway House. He told them that time stood still in his pub, and that if they signed their names in his book and stepped inside, they would be able to rest for a while.

This was true, in a way. What Old Scratch didn't tell the ghosts was that there was a spell carved into the doorstep. I know the words by heart:

LOST SOUL,
step forth into this
timeless tavern
And surrender thyself to me,
by order of the Innkeeper

The moment the ghosts walked over the spell, the door slammed shut and they were trapped.

The wind has picked up. It whips through the tiny streets of the model village. Thinking about the Halfway House has made the excitement I felt a moment ago slip away. Now I feel cold inside, and scared. Old Scratch told me that it wasn't him who carved the spell into the doorstep. If he was telling the truth, it means someone else is the Innkeeper and whoever they are they must hate me. I've already freed loads of their ghosts, and I'm about to free one more.

But it's not just the thought of the Innkeeper and

Old Scratch that's making my chest squeeze tight. I'm also worried that I won't actually be able to free a ghost. I'm not one hundred per cent sure how I did it before.

Bones nudges me with an icy boot. 'What might the matter be, Sid? Why do you look so glum?'

I stare hard at the model of the Halfway House. 'What if I can't free any more ghosts, Bones? What if I let the other ghosts down?'

Bones crouches next to me and I see a ghostly shrimp wriggling in his beard. 'Listen close,' he says in his deep growl. 'It was you who broke the spell keeping me and my crew trapped in the Halfway House. If you did it before, then you can do it again!'

'You really think so?'

'I do,' he says. 'And you know why, don't you?' His eyes bore into mine, daring me to say it.

'Because I'm magic,' I whisper. Straight away a blush creeps over my cheeks because I don't feel magic at all. I feel like an ordinary twelve-year-old girl who always wears a stripy jumper and glasses, and who still doesn't know her times tables.

Bones grins, showing his crooked brown teeth. 'That's right. A spell can only be broken by someone more powerful than the one who cast it. You broke the Innkeeper's spell, Sid, and that means you must have mighty powerful magic running through you!'

His words make the glow of excitement come creeping back. Perhaps Bones is right. Perhaps I *can* do it again!

I jump to my feet. 'I need to get my map and a red gel pen,' I say.

'Yes!' cries Zen. 'I'll ask your dad for a Crunchie.'

'And I shall go ahead to the Halfway House,' says Bones, 'to check that Old Scratch isn't lurking about.'

'Who are you going to free, Sid?' asks Zen.

I point at a small headstone shaped like a guitar. Dad carved it out of soapstone and it's smaller than a matchbox. 'I'm going to free Dai Hughes,' I say.

CHAPTER TWO

While Bones goes to the graveyard and Zen asks Dad for a Crunchie, I head towards the cottage where Dad and I live. The model village is in our back garden so it only takes me a moment to run inside and up to my bedroom.

Usually I keep my map in a holder round my neck, but this morning I left it spread out across the floor.

I kneel down and reach for a pen. I know I should be going to meet Zen, but instead I find Dai's grave and start to doodle leaves around it.

My map is massive. It's made up of lots of pieces of paper Sellotaped together and I've drawn all of Fathom on it. And I've not just put the real stuff on there, like roads and houses, but I've added memories and feelings too.

That's why Zen's mum and dad's museum has a rainbow roof – because it makes me happy – and why there are gold stars dotted over the graveyard. Each star shows a place where Zen and I have played one of our best games.

As I draw, I think about Dai. If I free him, then straight away Zen and I are going to have to help him sort out his unfinished business, just like we did with Bones.

Bones needed to find his lost treasure, and Dai has

to finish singing 'Suspicious Minds', the song he was performing on the Cockle when he was electrocuted by his microphone.

After they died, not only were the ghosts trapped in this world, they only had one cycle of the moon – thirty days – to sort out their unfinished business. But as each day passed they realised dust was pouring off them and they were fading away. I saw this happen to Bones. First the feathers on his cap vanished, then the tips of his fingers, finally his whole body began to disappear. I found his lost treasure seconds before his thirty days were up. If I hadn't, he would have turned into a wraith: a miserable, invisible spirit trapped in this world for eternity.

My pen finds its way to the Halfway House where I scribble more leaves alongside the hundreds I've already drawn.

All the ghosts were terrified about turning into a wraith and Old Scratch used this fear to trick them into entering the Halfway House. And that's where they were all trapped, some for hundreds of years, until I came along and broke the Innkeeper's spell.

Wind rattles my window frame as I stare at the tiny

doorstep I drew in front of the Halfway House. I haven't written the spell on it, there's not enough room, but I don't need to. I know the words by heart. '*Lost soul, step forth into this timeless tavern,*' I whisper, still drawing my leaves. '*And surrender thyself to me, by order of the Innkeeper.*'

Rain patters against the window and I grip my pen tighter as I consider the question that's been on my mind for weeks: who really is the Innkeeper? The obvious person is Old Scratch. After all, he's the one who tricked the ghosts into going into the pub, plus he's the only person who ever visits them, stomping up the stairs from the cellar. But he told me it wasn't him, and I believed him.

I hear the back door slam, then Zen shouts up the stairs, 'Sid! What are you doing? We need to go!'

I put my map in its holder and hang it round my neck.

Just as I'm leaving the room I spot my toy microphone. It's neon pink and has rainbow lights that flash around the sides. I picture Dai, his hair slicked back and his tummy straining under the white satin of his jumpsuit. He would love this microphone.

'Coming!' I call, as I slip it in my bag along with a red gel pen. Then I run downstairs to join Zen.

CHAPTER THREE

Thunder rumbles as Zen and I hurry through the gates of Fathom graveyard.

Trees thrash above our heads and rain drips through the leaves. The stream gushes down through the graveyard and waves crash just beyond the sea wall. I can smell and taste the sea. I feel jittery and on edge, like something is about to happen.

'We need to get a move on,' says Zen, as we tread a familiar path towards the Halfway House. 'My app says we've got fourteen minutes.'

We pass my mum's grave, then push our way through waist-high weeds until we reach the stream. Usually we can jump over it, but today the water is flowing so high we have to use the stepping stones. Once we're safely on the other side, we duck under a branch and squeeze between two headstones.

Now we are in the darkest, loneliest corner of the graveyard. Up ahead, half hidden by brambles, is the Halfway House. I take in the pub's lit-up windows, creaking lantern and huge oak door. Zen and I can only see all this because we've got *the gift*. If someone else was standing next to us, they'd think they were looking at an abandoned mausoleum with bricked-up windows and doors. They definitely wouldn't be able to see the shadowy figures drifting around inside.

'The Halfway House looks more hidden than ever,' whispers Zen.

He's right. Overnight more ivy seems to have grown over the walls. It covers the roof and loops in front of the windows.

Suddenly Bones emerges from behind a tomb and beckons us forward, hissing, 'All clear!'

Zen and I creep forward and join him below one of the windows, then I peer through the thick glass. It's like looking into a secret world!

Ghosts move around the candlelit room. Some look solid and almost alive, while others, the ones who walked into the pub just before their thirty days were up, are almost invisible.

One of the palest of the ghosts is a little boy called William Buckle and right now he's turning in circles trying to make himself dizzy. His ragged clothes flutter and his dirty hands fly out as he wobbles around. A teenage girl with a smiling freckled face watches him from a bench. This is Peg Tiddy, the witch. Pressed against her skirts is her familiar, a goat called Radulfus. Sitting next to them is Olive Buckmore, a land girl who died during the Second World War. Olive has bright red lipstick that shines in the darkness of the inn and I can hear her confident voice urging Will to 'Go faster! Faster!

There are other ghosts too. Dai, the Elvis impersonator I'm planning to free, is staring miserably into the fire, and there are two other men sitting on a bench. One has a curly wig and frilly white shirt – Beau Fiddler – and the other man is Mr Holkar. Slumped on a stool at the very back of the inn is a woman wearing a battered leather flying suit. Her name is Mei Huang. She's the quietest of the ghosts and the one I've talked to the least. She used to hang out with the pirates, but since they left, she's kept to herself and only talks to me or Zen if we ask her a question.

Luckily for us, Old Scratch is nowhere to be seen.

'Will's picking his nose,' says Zen.

'Nope. He's stopped,' I say. 'What's he doing now?'

Will is bobbing up and down and wiggling his hips from side to side.

Zen laughs. 'He's doing the Swagg Bouncee! It's a TikTok dance that I taught him last time we visited.'

Great. A hundred-year-old ghost knows more dance moves than me.

'Oi, you two!' hisses Bones. 'Stop rabbiting on about bouncies. Can't you hear that thunder? The lightning will be here any minute. We need to let Dai know we're going to set him free!'

Before I move, I take a long, careful look at a door that's tucked away at the back of the pub. It leads down to the cellar and is how Old Scratch gets in and out of the pub.

Old Scratch is a bony, gaunt man who is as white as chalk and smells of damp clothes and dusty attics. According to the ghosts, he's been visiting the pub for over four hundred years, only he's not a ghost or a weak old man. In fact, he looks younger than my dad and he's strong. He once grabbed hold of me and threw me to the ground as if I didn't weigh a thing.

I push the thought of Old Scratch from my mind. If I'm going to free Dai, then I can't be worrying about him.

'Come on,' I say, tearing my eyes away from the cellar door. 'Let's do this.'

CHAPTER FOUR

I push open the door to the Halfway House and freezing air sweeps over us, along with cries of 'Hello!', 'Felicitations!' and 'Bloomin' heck, you gave us a fright!'.

The ghosts rush to the doorway, a smiling, jostling group. The man wearing the wig, Beau Fiddler, stands at the front and flashes me a foxy smile, but only for a second because then Olive Buckmore, the land girl, steps through him and says, 'Afternoon, chaps. Rotten weather!'

She's quickly replaced by Dai Hughes in his tight white jumpsuit. He raises his chin and in his fake American drawl says, 'Uh-huh?'

Little Will pops through Dai's flares and presses his scabby face against the invisible barrier that keeps the

21

ghosts trapped inside the pub. The barrier doesn't exist for me, Zen or Bones – it only works on lost souls – so I can reach through it and squeeze Will's fingers. But only for a second. Will is freezing, and soon the icy chill creeping up my arm is so painful I have to let go.

Then the ghosts all start talking at once.

'Have you brought comics?' asks Will.

'Now *that* is a fine cloak, Zen!' says Beau.

'Why didn't you come yesterday?' demands Peg.

'I think there's lightning on its way,' says Olive. 'Sid, darling, please say you're going to free one of us?'

'Quiet, you lot!' booms Bones. 'That's what she is here for, if you will let her get a word in edgeways. Tell them, Sid.'

'I'm going to free Dai,' I say, then I blush because it sounds grand and big-headed, plus I'm not even sure if it's true.

Dai clutches the gold medallions hanging on his bare chest. 'Me? Really?' For a moment he forgets to put on his American accent and sounds very Welsh indeed, but then he pulls himself together and croons, 'Why, thank you, darlin'.'

'Why not me?' asks Will, tears brimming at his eyes.

'We would free you, Will,' I say, 'but the second we let you out you'll start to fade away and your unfinished business is tricky to solve. Dai just wants to sing "Suspicious Minds" on the Cockle. That's easy to do.'

'But I only want to stroke a kangaroo!' Will wails.

Peg crouches down and attempts to put her arm around him. 'There ain't no kangaroos in Fathom, Will. How many times do we 'ave to tell you that? If Sid sets you free and there is no kangaroo for you to stroke, then you'll just turn into a wraith and disappear. You don't want that to 'appen, do you?'

Face wet with tears, Will turns to look at the back of the pub where a shape is floating backwards and forwards and wailing, '*WAAAYYNNEEEE!*'

This is Emma and she looks like a proper ghost: white, wispy and with black gaping holes where her eyes and mouth should be. She's so invisible that sometimes I forget she's even in the pub. Emma stepped, or rather drifted inside the Halfway House moments before her thirty days were up. If she'd left it a second or two longer she'd have turned into a wraith and disappeared entirely.

'*WAAYYYNNNEEEE!*' she howls again. It's her one and only word.

Will shakes his head violently. 'No fear! I don't want to be no wraith. I want to stroke a kangaroo then cross over to the other side and see my mum again.'

Bones tuts. 'No one is going to be going anywhere if we all stand around chitter-chattering. Get a move on, Sid! I'm sure the lightning is close.'

I sniff the air. He's right. I can smell sparklers, which means lightning is seconds away.

The three of us leave the ghosts standing at the doorway and push through the weeds towards Dai Hughes's headstone. Of course the ghosts can't follow us, although they would dearly love to. Instead they make do with pressing against the invisible barrier.

I kneel in font of Dai's white marble guitar. *Our Big Hunk o' Love, Dai Peter Hughes, 1930–1974* is engraved on it, although the words are almost hidden by ivy. The plant grows everywhere in the graveyard, but it's extra thick here. I pull some strands away then take out my map and pen. Zen hands me the Crunchie, which I shove into the ivy just like I did when I freed Bones.

A clap of thunder echoes through the graveyard making me jump. Quickly I press my map against the wet marble of Dai's headstone. Bones crouches next to me. Elizabeth is on his shoulder, watching me with her beady eyes. 'You know what you're doing, don't you, girl?' Bones says.

'No!' I reply.

'Course you do.' He does one of his toothy grins. 'Do your magic like you did the day you set me free.'

'But I didn't *do* any magic,' I say. 'All I did was write your initials on my map!'

'And in so doing you broke the Innkeeper's spell,' he says firmly. 'And today you shall do the same for Dai.'

Zen gives me a nudge. 'Just do your best, Sid.'

The ghosts must sense that my confidence is slipping away because they start calling to me from the doorway of the Halfway House.

'You can do it, Sid!'

'God's grace be with you, child!'

'Just scrunch yer face up and force all the magic out of your fingertips like yer doin' a big poo!' This useful advice comes from Peg Tiddy, the witch.

Zen bursts out laughing as a massive flash of lightning fills the sky.

'You missed one!' Will shouts helpfully.

There is another clap of thunder. With trembling fingers I rest my pen on my map.

'Do it now!' says Zen.

I start to trace over Dai's initials. I don't rush. I breathe in and out, nice and slow, and I watch as the letters become thicker. I'm writing the H for Hughes when I hear a crack, and a flash of lightning fills the graveyard. The trees, headstones and statues leap out, as white as bone, and electricity prickles the air. Then it's gone.

The silence that follows is broken by a whoop from Zen. He's always been scared of lightning, but he's so excited right now he's forgotten his fear. I can hear laughter and shouts coming from the Halfway House too.

'Has it worked?' I say.

'Just finish writing!' urges Bones.

I write the H, then Zen pulls me to my feet. Leaving the Crunchie where it is, just like I did with Bones, we run back towards the Halfway House.

When we get there the ghosts have fallen quiet and

taken a few steps back from Dai, who is standing behind the barrier with a look of nervous excitement on his face.

'Courage, man,' urges Bones. 'I know it must feel impossible, but if Sid has broken the spell, you can walk out a free man.'

'I'm just going to go for it,' says Dai, all trace of his American accent gone. He stands tall in his white jumpsuit and sucks in his tummy.

Then he steps forward.

I'm expecting him to smack into the barrier and shoot back again – I've seen this happen so many times to Will and it's always awful – but instead he half falls out of the pub and into the long grass of the graveyard.

The ghosts gasp and I let out the breath I didn't realise I was holding.

Dai pulls himself together. He drops into a crouch, points one hand at the sky and makes the other tremble in front of his face. Then he looks at me through his fingers and croons, 'Thank you, darlin'.'

Back in the pub, the ghosts start to cheer and clap.

Dai straightens up and turns to face them. The rhinestones on his jumpsuit glitter with tiny rainbows.

Sparkly dust floats off him too, drifting towards the trees. This happened to Bones. The moment the ghosts leave the Halfway House their time starts to run out and dust drifts off them, making them fade away. Dai doesn't seem to care. He's just happy to be free.

Like a rock star leaving his adoring crowd, he bows deeply, raises both hands in the air and says, 'We'll meet again. God bless. *Adios!*' Then he blows them a dusty kiss and, without a backward glance, strides towards the graveyard gates.

'Blimey,' says Peg. 'You only went and did it, Sid. You must have really squeezed that magic out!'

I open my mouth, ready to explain that I didn't really do anything except write on my map, but before I can say a word, the door at the back of the pub comes flying open.

CHAPTER FIVE

Old Scratch stomps into the room, his tattered coat swirling around his ankles and his straggly hair flopping over his domed forehead. His face is gaunt, the colour of bone, and he has dark purple shadows under his eyes.

'What is going on?' he hisses, then his bulging eyes fly to the open door and he sees me and Zen standing there. He lets out a cry of rage then lurches forward, hands outstretched.

I just have time to be grateful that Old Scratch's dog, Snout, isn't with him, before I yell, 'RUN!'

Zen, Bones and I turn and throw ourselves through the long grass. We dodge between headstones and jump over twisting roots. I tell myself that if we can get to the seafront, we'll be OK. There will be people there. Old Scratch wouldn't dare hurt us in front of other people . . . would he?

But the sound of snapping branches and feet thudding on wet earth tells me that Old Scratch is still chasing us and he isn't giving up. I force myself to run faster. The rain has stopped, but the stream is still full. There's no time for stepping stones now. I jump the stream, landing on muddy grass.

'Keep going!' Zen cries, as he crashes down next to me.

Bones runs straight through the water with Elizabeth flying over his head. 'Hurry!' he bellows.

'*RUM! BULLY!*' shrieks Elizabeth.

The graveyard gates are just ahead of us. I don't dare look back as we fly through them. We keep running until we burst out on to the seafront.

Now that the rain has stopped, tourists are emerging from cafés and dog walkers are already on the beach. My heart is still racing as we weave between them. We only stop when we reach the railings above the beach.

Panting, I ask, 'Has he gone?'

'For now,' says Bones, looking over his shoulder.

'The villain wouldn't dare follow us here, not with all these folk about.'

Next to me, Zen starts to laugh. '*That* was epic!'

''Twas quite the caper,' agrees Bones with a chuckle.

'Fair play to Old Scratch,' says Zen. 'For a guy who's over four hundred years old, he can move.'

But I can't laugh about what just happened. Not yet. 'That was *terrifying*,' I say. 'He could have caught us!'

'But he didn't,' says Zen with a grin. 'Stop looking so worried, Sid. We got away, didn't we? And have you forgotten what you just did?'

I think about the moment Dai walked free and the surprise and happiness that shone on his face. 'I freed Dai,' I say.

'Didn't I say you would?' says Bones. 'And look, here he comes now.'

Dai strolls towards us along the seafront. He passes tourists in waterproof anoraks and old ladies clinging to umbrellas. He looks ridiculously glamorous in his white jumpsuit and large sunglasses. It's a shame no one except us can see him.

He beckons impatiently, and glittering dust trickles

from his fingers. 'Come on!' he says. 'My show is about to begin.'

In the excitement of the last few minutes, I'd forgotten about Dai's unfinished business. I might have got him out of the Halfway House, but he's still trapped in this world until he finishes the song he was singing when he died.

We hurry after him. The sea on the far side of the Cockle is still rough and it slaps on the curving wall of the harbour. Elizabeth soars above us, a brilliant pop of green against the grey sky.

'My band was supposed to be the finale of Pirate Day,' Dai calls over his shoulder. 'Pete, my drummer, said the fireworks were the true finale, but he never did love rock and roll like the rest of the band.' Dai is so excited that he keeps forgetting to do his Elvis impersonation. 'I never got to do my big knee tremble,' he says, pausing to demonstrate what he means. He goes up on his toes and wobbles his whole plump body. 'See? I was famous for doing this.'

'God's hat,' mutters Bones. 'He looks like a sea creature floundering on the sand.'

Dai either doesn't hear him or doesn't care. He keeps up his knee wobble, dancing his way to the end of the Cockle where he spins round to face us, his hair flopping over his sunglasses. 'I'm ready,' he says, striking a pose. 'Hit the music!'

Zen has come prepared. He gets out his phone and finds 'Suspicious Minds'.

Then I remember my microphone. 'I thought this might help,' I say. I turn it on and the disco lights start to flash. Dai is thrilled. He tries to grasp it, but his fingers slip through it.

'I'll hold it for you,' I say, thrusting the mic under his nose, then Zen presses play and Dai's concert begins.

Dai gives it everything he's got. He croons the words of the song, gazing deep into the eyes of his audience of three: me, Zen and Bones. Zen whoops encouragingly while Bones taps one boot in time to the music.

My eyes are fixed on the horizon. A ghost ship made of clouds came to take Bones's crew away, but I don't know what will come for Dai. Right now there is nothing there except the last traces of storm clouds. Dai said that singing 'Suspicious Minds' was his unfinished business so how come dust is still pouring off him and why is he still so see-through?

Dai swings one arm through the air and for a moment his whole fist disappears. Then I notice that his rhinestones are vanishing one by one.

'Dai!' I have to shout to be heard above the music blaring out of Zen's phone. 'Why are you fading?'

He stops singing. 'Because this doesn't feel like a concert. Back when it happened, I had a crowd, Sid. They were cheering and dancing. I need an audience!'

'But we're your audience,' I say.

'Then start acting like one!' he cries, as he launches back into the song.

Zen doesn't need any encouragement. Not caring that there are people down on the beach watching us, he starts to throw himself from side to side. 'Dance, Sid!' he shouts. 'You too, Bones. If Dai is going to cross over to the other side, then you need to start moving!'

Zen has no problem with going wild, but I do. I'm shy. Bones growls his displeasure but starts to jig up and down on the spot. Now they're just waiting for me to join in.

'Do it for Dai, Sid!' says Zen, spinning round on the wet stone.

So I start to dance. I know how strange we must look – two children dancing on our own at the end of the harbour wall, one holding a toy microphone, the other a phone, but suddenly I don't care. Dai's hand has come back! And his rhinestones are starting to appear again. Plus I've just spotted a large white cloud drifting down from the sky and it looks like it has wheels.

I watch as the clouds billow, bunching together until they form the shape of a sleek open-top car. The cloud-car settles on the horizon, bobbing up and down on the waves. I'm sure I can hear its revving engine.

'Nice wheels, Dai,' says Zen. 'It's a Mustang!'

Dai sings the last line of the song then bows deeply. His audience of two children, one ghost pirate and one ghost parrot go wild, cheering and squawking and bravo-ing!

'Thank you very much!' says Dai, and colour floods through him. His hair becomes black and glossy and his cheeks glow pink from pleasure and all the hip thrusts he's just done. His white jumpsuit is as bright as the foam riding on top of the waves.

Dai gives me my very own special bow, then trots down a set of stone stairs that lead into the sea.

Without pausing, he steps confidently on to the choppy water and walks away from us, his arms raised above his head. Then he breaks into a run. We don't see him climb inside the Mustang. Just as he reaches it, a beam of sunlight breaks through the clouds and Dai vanishes into a glittering ball of light. I squeeze my eyes shut, dazzled by the light, and when I open them again, the Mustang and Dai are gone.

'Elvis has left the building,' says Zen.

CHAPTER SIX

Dai seems to have taken the last traces of the storm with him.

As we walk back along the Cockle, the sea on either side of us is calm and the wind has dropped to a gentle breeze.

'There is nothing quite like watching a fellow cross over to the other side, is there?' says Bones, breaking the silence. 'I wonder where Dai is now?' He glances up at the sky as if the answer might lie there. 'We talked about what might be on the other side often enough in the Halfway House, but none of us truly knows.' His voice sounds wistful.

I glance up at him. 'Does it make you want to go too?' I ask.

Bones could have crossed over to the other side with his

crew, but instead he chose to stay here to help me and Zen free the other ghosts and fight Old Scratch.

He laughs. 'Some day, but you're not getting rid of me that easily, Jones. We still have work to do!'

'I wish we could free them all right now,' I say, thinking of the ghosts still trapped in the Halfway House. 'Now they know I've done it again they must be even more desperate to get out.'

'We've got to wait for more lightning,' says Zen.

'And we need to make sure we can complete their unfinished business,' I say. 'Did you see how quickly Dai faded once he was out of the Halfway House?'

'The dust was pouring off him,' says Zen, 'but remember we're ghost detectives, Sid. Solving unfinished business is what we do.' He takes out his phone. 'I'm going to put an alert on my Stormchaser app. I don't care if it's the middle of the night, the next time there's lightning heading towards Fathom we are going to be ready and waiting in the graveyard!'

'And I'm going to start mentioning to Dad that I'm really into kangaroos,' I say. 'Perhaps I can persuade him to take me to a zoo and then Will can come too.'

When we reach the seafront, we start to look for Old Scratch again. We can't see him, but that doesn't mean he isn't lurking somewhere. To be on the safe side, Bones and I walk Zen to the museum where he lives.

'You don't need to worry about me,' says Zen. 'I'm not scared of Old Scratch.'

'He'll be furious I let Dai out,' I say.

Zen shrugs. 'Yeah, but what's Old Scratch ever really done to us except send his ghost dog after us – a dog we haven't seen in ages – and crunch up that model of your dad?'

Just thinking about that moment in the model village when Old Scratch dropped the crushed model of Dad on the floor makes me feel sick. Afterwards Old Scratch told me that people would get hurt if I didn't stay away from the ghosts and the Halfway House. Nothing happened to Dad, but less than a week later someone rearranged the stones we were following on the cliff, and Zen nearly fell to his death.

'Old Scratch is dangerous,' I insist. 'I know he said he didn't move the stones, but someone did. Perhaps it was the Innkeeper . . .'

'If there even is an Innkeeper,' says Zen.

'The boy's right,' says Bones. 'I know what Old Scratch told you, Jones, but believe me when I say you cannot trust a word the fiend says.'

I think back to Pirate Day, when I went to the Halfway House to confront Old Scratch, and he told me he wasn't the Innkeeper.

'You didn't see the look on his face,' I say. 'I'm sure he wasn't lying.'

But Zen shakes his head, unconvinced. 'It's like when you're at school and someone says they're going to get their dad on to you. It's a load of rubbish, but they say it to scare you. I bet that's what Old Scratch was doing, and it's worked, hasn't it?'

He's right. Old Scratch's words have scared me.

'It's the not knowing that's the worst thing,' I say.

An unpleasant prickling sensation runs down the back of my neck and suddenly I'm sure I'm being watched. I fight the urge to turn round because this has happened to me quite a lot recently. The last time, I came face to face with a little girl on her scooter. I'm not sure who was more surprised, me or her.

But still the uncomfortable feeling grows and in the end I have to glance over my shoulder.

The seafront is still busy, but only two people are looking our way: a tourist who is glancing from her phone to the museum entrance, and Mrs Ferrari who is busy cleaning the fibreglass ice cream that stands outside her café. She waves when she sees me looking and I force myself to smile and wave back.

'Don't you see?' I say to Zen and Bones. 'The Innkeeper could be anyone. It could be someone we know!'

Zen puts a hand on my shoulder. 'Or it could be Old Scratch. After all, he is the *keeper* of the *inn*, otherwise known as an *innkeeper*. You're freaked out, Sid, and it's not surprising. Old Scratch is a seriously creepy dude, but don't see problems where there aren't any. Today is a good day: you freed another ghost!'

I nod. Zen's right. I should be celebrating not wanting to run home.

'Tomorrow we should work out which ghost we free next,' I say. 'The moment lightning comes we need to be ready.'

'Absolutely,' says Zen, then he remembers that he's hungry and he's got macaroni cheese for dinner. 'See you tomorrow!' he says, letting himself into the museum.

Bones walks me up the hill then leaves me to go to the Black Spot Cat Café to listen to Pirate FM.

Quickly I step inside the model village.

It's quiet. There are no tourists about and Dad isn't in the kiosk.

The door to the cottage is locked. I've got a key, but instead of letting myself in I stand and look around the model village. It's strange. Dad usually turns the electrics off if he goes out, but the lights are switched on in all the little shops and houses, and music is coming from the still-turning roundabout. I decide to see if Dad is in the shed that's tucked away at the bottom of the model village behind a row of bushes.

I'm walking past the model of Mermaids Café when I notice something odd.

Dad has made models of everyone in the village – me, Zen, Roundabout Tommy, Sally from the Black Spot Cat Café – and the last time I looked he'd arranged me and the model of himself outside Mermaids. Mini Dad was buying me an ice cream and I was reaching towards it.

Only now my arms are reaching towards nothing

43

because the model of Dad has gone.

Panic rises inside me. Old Scratch has crushed Dad's model once before. Has he done it again? I look around for the model, but I can't see it anywhere. I drop to my knees and feel around at the bottom of the pretend sea. Sometimes children throw models in there. Just when I'm starting to panic, Dad comes strolling into the model village with a newspaper tucked under his arm.

'What are you doing?' he says when he sees me with my arms plunged in the water.

'The model of you is gone!' I blurt out. 'I was looking for it.'

Dad shrugs. 'Don't worry about it. A kid will have taken it. You know how many models we lose. Mrs Ferrari has gone missing four times.'

It's true. Dad is always having to replace the models, but it seems like a strange coincidence that on the day I free another ghost, his model goes missing.

'It must be here somewhere,' I say, pushing my hands deeper into the cold water.

Dad crouches down next to me and puts a hand on my shoulder. 'Sid, it isn't a big deal. I'll make another one tonight.'

'But it's *you*!' I say.

'No, it's a model of me. I'm right here. How about I shut up early and we go and get you a real ice cream? Mrs Ferrari told me she was trying out a new flavour: Jaffa Cake.'

I nod and get to my feet. Dad's right, models are always going missing. What did Zen say? I'm seeing problems where there aren't any.

Even though I'm twelve I take hold of Dad's hand and say, 'Can I get two scoops?'

'And hot chocolate sauce,' he says, leading me towards the exit.

CHAPTER SEVEN

Over the next few days, Zen, Bones and I talk regularly about the ghosts' unfinished business, arguing about whose will be the easiest to solve. Sometimes, if Bones comes to school with us, we do this on the bus, or at break time, otherwise we go to my grandad's fishing hut after school and have a meeting. We keep an eye on Zen's Stormchaser app too, but the weather is unusually pleasant for October.

Every day is sunny and people are still swimming in the sea and playing on the beach. Dad says we're having an Indian summer, although he doesn't seem to be enjoying it much. He has a cold and spends each day huddled in his kiosk, wrapped up in scarfs and sipping Lemsip. His sniffling has even put Bones off from hanging out with him.

I start to think that it's going to be weeks until we can free another ghost, but on Friday morning we have a breakthrough.

'I'm a genius!' says Zen when I meet up with him at our usual place by the fibreglass ice cream.

I sort of already know this. Zen's built a computer and reads books for adults *and* enjoys them. Mind you, he can be pretty stupid too. For example, right now he's eating a cheese toastie and using his tie as a sort of oven glove. Melting cheese is dripping all over it.

'I guess you're going to tell me why,' I say.

'Last night it came to me in a flash,' he says, as we walk towards the bus stop. 'We don't need lightning to get ghosts out of the Halfway House!'

'Yes, we do,' I say. 'We had lightning when I freed Dai and Bones.'

'I know, but there's another way we can do it. Remember what happened with Bones's crew?'

I think back to the brilliant day a few months ago when the pirates who were trapped with Bones ran out of the Halfway House. They got out because Bones's unfinished business was also *their* unfinished business; the moment

47

I found his treasure they weren't lost souls any more and could walk free. The spell on the doorstep clearly says that it's only lost souls who can be trapped: *Lost Soul, step forth into this timeless tavern . . .*

'You're right,' I say, excitement building inside me. 'There wasn't any lightning. I didn't even write their names on my map. They got out because I sorted out their unfinished business for them so that's what we need to do for the other ghosts. You *are* a genius, Zen!'

'I know,' he says, pulling a strand of cheese off his tie and dangling it in front of his mouth. 'We'll tell Bones after school.'

'You'll tell me what?' Bones has stepped through the wall of a house on the high street. A quick glance through the window tells me that he's been watching *Thomas the Tank Engine*. Bones loves Thomas.

Quickly I explain what Zen has worked out: that we can sort out the ghosts' unfinished business for them, without freeing them first. But Bones shakes his head. 'I believe it will be mighty difficult to solve a ghost's unfinished business without the ghost by your side. Remember, my crew may have got out without lightning or names being written down, but you had me helping you hunt for my treasure. And young William Buckle wants to stroke a kangaroo. You can hardly stroke one for him, can you? It wouldn't be the same thing at all!'

But I refuse to give up on the idea. 'It might work for some of the ghosts,' I say. 'At least until we get lightning again. It can be our Plan B, and we can try it out on the ghost whose unfinished business is the easiest to solve.'

'I suppose there is no harm in seeing if it works,' admits Bones. We've reached the bus stop and the bus is already there. 'Let us climb on board and discuss who the lucky fellow will be.'

'Are you coming to school with us?' asks Zen, excited.

'I should think so! Sid has design technology today and she needs my help making a pair of salad servers. Her attention to detail is shocking.'

It really isn't, but I don't complain because having Bones at school is fun. He chats to us during the boring bits of lessons, makes people cold if they're mean to us and helps us with our work. Although he doesn't always get things right. Last week in geography he told me that in the middle of the North Pole there is a giant magnetic rock with a whirlpool surrounding it. When I put up my hand and told the class, I soon discovered it was a load of rubbish.

We take our normal seats on the bus at the front and well away from the other Penrose Academy kids who might notice us talking to an invisible person. As usual, Bones takes the seat in front of us. If someone sits on his lap, they quickly move away when they realise how cold this particular spot on the bus is.

As the bus trundles up the hill and out of Fathom, I get out my notebook where I keep a list of the ghosts and their unfinished business. I read them out loud and we soon agree that the ghost we should try Plan B on is Olive.

'All she wants to do is find out what happened to her fiancé, Ginger,' says Zen. 'That should be easy. Olive last saw him in 1944, which is recent history compared to some of the ghosts' pasts.'

'We'll go to the Halfway House after school and interview her,' I say. 'We'll find out everything we can and then do some research of our own.'

Then, feeling like a proper detective with a proper plan, I put my notebook away. Just then the bus comes to a juddering halt on the coast road. I look up, surprised.

We don't usually stop here. The only buildings are a bungalow and, at the end of a long drive, a stately home called Orlig House.

The bus doors hiss open and a girl with dyed red hair climbs on board. She looks about our age and her Penrose Academy uniform is unmistakably brand new. She has a big rucksack on her shoulders that threatens to topple her over when she leans forward to pay the bus driver. She takes her ticket then fiddles with it as she looks for somewhere to sit. She has big, unblinking owl-like eyes.

'New girl alert,' whispers Zen.

And that's when I realise that I've seen this girl before.

'That's the girl from Orlig House,' I say to Zen and Bones. 'Don't you recognise her? She was standing at the window wearing the same fluffy white hoodie. You waved at her, Zen.'

'Oh yeah!' says Zen. 'I remember. I thought she was a ghost.'

'She's definitely real,' I say, and we watch as the bus lurches forward and she stumbles, clutching at her rucksack straps. Behind us, Owen Kidd, a horrible boy from our year, sniggers and calls out, 'Loser!'

Perhaps this is what makes me smile at the girl and the next thing I know she's plonked herself down in the seat in front of us, right on top of Bones. But she doesn't shiver or complain about the cold, instead she turns and stares out of the window.

With a tut, Bones moves to an empty seat across the aisle.

Suddenly the girl starts waving and I see that a lanky man has wandered into the garden of the bungalow.

He is barefoot and holding a cup of tea, but he doesn't wave back. He's too busy staring up at a tree.

'Is that your dad?' says Zen who is never shy about asking strangers questions.

The girl nods. 'He's not ignoring me; it's just that he's really into plants.' Her voice is so quiet that I have to lean forward to hear her. 'He thinks that tree has got a fungus.' Then she bursts out laughing. It's a surprisingly big laugh for such a quiet girl. 'Sorry, but Dad told me not to say anything weird on my first day and I just said "fungus" . . . and now I've said it twice!'

And, just like that, I like her.

Zen starts quizzing her about why she's starting school late and why she's got an accent.

'Zen, you can't ask stuff like that,' I say, but the girl doesn't seem to mind.

She tells us that her name is Mo, short for Morgan, and that she moved here from Wales just before the summer holidays. 'There were no spaces at Penrose Academy, but now there are so . . . yay!' she says with fake enthusiasm.

After a moment Zen laughs and says, 'You don't recognise us, do you?'

A flash of uncertainty crosses her face. 'Should I?'

'We saw you in Orlig House a few months ago,' I say. 'Zen waved a spade at you.'

She frowns, looking worried, but within seconds her smile is back in place. 'I remember! I was so bored back then and you two looked like you were having fun.'

'Hang on,' says Zen. 'Do you live in Orlig House? Is Molly Noon your mum or something?' Molly Noon is Fathom's one and only celebrity, a rich YouTuber who does yoga and sells candles. My dad starts every single day by doing one of her yoga videos.

Mo laughs. 'No, my mum is a teaching assistant, but Dad is the gardener at Orlig House. That's why we live in the bungalow. It comes with the job.' Mo drops her voice and whispers, 'Listen, please don't tell anyone you saw me in Orlig House or Dad could get in big trouble. Molly Noon is hardly ever there, but we're still not supposed to go poking around. Dad let me in a couple of times so I could see inside.'

'What's it like?' I ask. From the outside Orlig House looks like something from a fairy tale. It sits at the top of the cliff, a huge gothic mansion with windows facing the sea. It's even got a tower, complete with turrets and pointy windows.

'It's *amazing*!' says Mo, her eyes wide. 'It's got a massive indoor pool that's kept warm even when Molly isn't there, a sauna, a fridge that spits out perfectly round ice cubes, and there's a chandelier in the hallway. I mean, it's all a bit blingy – she's got gold taps – but it's still pretty cool.'

'Have you ever met her?' says Zen.

Mo pulls a face. 'No. I've just seen her go down the driveway in her Range Rover. Mainly she lives in Ibiza.'

Zen flops back, disappointed. 'And I thought I'd just made friends with a millionaire.'

Mo laughs. 'I do get five pounds pocket money a week!'

I don't care that Mo isn't a millionaire. She's fun, and when we get to school it seems like the most natural thing in the world to show her around. Bones follows us like a grumpy shadow.

As we're taking her to her form room, he mutters, 'When are we going to discuss Olive's unfinished business? We can't speak freely with this Mo character sticking to us like glue.'

I wait until a loud group of Year Eleven boys are

bundling past, then whisper, 'After school I promise we'll go straight to the Halfway House and ask Olive to tell us everything she can about Ginger.'

Bones groans like this is an unbearable amount of time then says, 'Well, at least I shall have your atrocious salad servers to distract me.'

When we reach Mo's form room she doesn't seem to want to go in. First she has a big drink of water, then she blurts out, 'Can I meet you at lunchtime?'

She looks very small standing in the doorway, clutching her water bottle.

'Course you can,' I say, making Bones bellow with frustration.

CHAPTER EIGHT

I keep my promise to Bones and after school we go straight to the graveyard.

It's a warm evening and the setting sun is lighting up the grass and making the wonky headstones glow. A blackbird sings as we walk towards my mum's headstump.

We call it a headstump because it's made out of a tree stump. Dad carved it himself, adding all Mum's favourite things: beetles, shells, a tiny handprint (that's supposed to represent me). There's even a shark's fin poking out of the top and a lightsabre. Mum was a big *Star Wars* fan.

'Watch out for that there wood pig,' says Bones, pointing at a woodlouse that is curled into the J of the *Laure Benoit-Jones*. 'They look innocent enough, but they will have a nibble at old wood, given half the chance.'

Carefully I move the woodlouse. Then I pull up a couple of weeds and give the shark's fin above her name a squeeze.

'May the force be with you, Laure,' says Zen, and then we head over to the Halfway House.

Visiting Mum's headstump has left me feeling calm. Ever since I freed Bones and dressed up in Mum's pirate costume for Pirate Day, I've felt a little bit closer to her. I might not be able to remember her, but stepping into her clothes and feeling so comfortable in them made me feel that she wasn't quite as far away as I thought.

We push our way through the weeds, then, after checking Old Scratch isn't inside the Halfway House, we open the door.

As usual the ghosts rush forward – they love the view from the doorway and the cold salty smell of the sea.

'Are you coming in?' Will asks hopefully.

I look at Bones. He hasn't been inside the Halfway House since the day he walked out because the pub holds too many unhappy memories for him. He glances at the church clock then says, 'You two young 'uns go ahead. Sally at the Black Spot Cat Café will be taking her flapjacks out of the oven round about now. I'll go and have a sniff of them. Make sure you report back to me as soon as you are done.' Then he walks away.

Zen smiles nervously. 'Ready?'

I understand how Zen feels. We've both been inside the Halfway House lots of times, but it never stops feeling incredible, and a little bit frightening. After all, we never know when Old Scratch might decide to visit.

'Ready,' I say, and together we step into a dark, bitterly cold room.

It's like we've entered another world. The room is large, much bigger than it looks on the outside, and it's crammed full of benches, tables and stools. A wooden bar takes up one wall, lined with dusty bottles and glasses, and the air is heavy with the smell of smoke and the sea. Candles flicker on each table, slowly melting into dripping puddles of wax, and coals shift in a fireplace

'Awesome,' whispers Zen, his breath misting the air.

Perhaps the strangest thing about the Halfway House is the clocks. They belong to Old Scratch and they fill every scrap of space on the walls. Carriage clocks, grandfather clocks, pendulum clocks . . . There's even one with Snoopy on

59

it and another with its face set in the wheels of a London bus. All the clocks jostle for space, endlessly ticking and tocking, clicking and whirring. But their hands never move forward because time stands still in here. It doesn't matter if Zen and I spend five minutes inside the Halfway House, or an hour, not a second of time will have passed in the real world.

Straight away, Zen runs over to check the cuckoo clock by the cellar door. This is our Old Scratch early-warning system. When Old Scratch stomps up the cellar stairs his heavy footsteps make the clock tremble. Zen noticed this, brought some tools from home and tinkered with the clock. Now when Old Scratch is approaching, the cuckoo pops out, giving us time to get away. So far Zen's invention has never let us down.

I feel icy fingers slip round mine and look down to see Will holding my hand.

'Sit next to me, Sid,' he says, leading me to a table.

The other ghosts follow. As they move, specks of golden dust swirl in the air like fireflies. When I freed Bones this dust poured off him like smoke, and the same happened with Dai, but in here it leaves the ghosts slowly . . . at least it usually does.

I watch as the glittery specks land on my clothes. 'Is it my imagination or is there more dust than usual?' I say.

'Yes!' says Will. 'I said that, but no one believes me.'

'Because it isn't true,' says Olive. 'There's always more dust floating around when we gather by the door, Will, you know that.'

With a sigh, Will plonks himself down on a bench and pats the space next to him. The moment I sit down he whispers in my ear. 'There is more dust, I'm telling you!'

I don't want to get drawn into an argument about dust – I've got important detective work to do – so I say, 'I'm sure there is,' then get out my notebook.

Zen and the other ghosts take the remaining places round the table. Holkar, the man who says he used to be a detective and an Indian prince, sits slightly apart, crossing his legs then pulling on the creases in his trousers. Peg and Olive squeeze next to each other. The only ghost who doesn't join us – except for Emma, who is moaning '*WAAAAYYYYNNNEEE*' and drifting backwards and forwards over our heads – is Mei Huang, the aviator.

Mei used to hang out with the pirates, but now they've

61

gone she keeps to herself and is slumped at the back of the pub, close to the door that leads to the cellar.

Quickly we tell the ghosts about our Plan B. They're excited that we might not need to wait for lightning and immediately ask whose unfinished business we will try to solve first.

'We're going to try and free Olive,' I say.

'Why not me!' cries Will, just like I knew he would. Once again we explain how kangaroos are hard to come by in Fathom.

'But I've told my dad that I want to see one,' I say, 'and he said he'd think about closing the model village for the day so we can go to Torquay Zoo.'

This cheers Will up and I can ask Olive about her fiancé Ginger.

She clasps her hands in front of her and sighs with happiness. 'He was a smashing chap. Tall, ginger – obviously – and the best dancer in Fathom. His real name was Ron Clark and he was a pilot based at Kervean airbase. Now, on the day it happened –'

Will nudges me. 'She means the day she died.'

Olive ignores him and carries on. 'I left the farm where

62

I was working and ran up to the cliffs to watch Ginger's plane fly in. You see, flying was such dangerous work that I liked to know he had come home. Anyway, it was a beautiful evening and I was lying in the grass because I felt tired. You see, I had a dicky ticker –'

'What's that?' I say.

'My heart wasn't quite right,' says Olive, tapping her chest. 'It was like that from the day I was born. So there I was, looking at the sky, when I felt a pain. It was like a knife being twisted in my chest, but the funny thing was I wasn't scared. A lark hovered above me. Its sweet song filled my ears and I thought, "Well, old girl, it looks like there isn't going to be a wedding for you. What a waste of a lovely frock!".'

I stop writing and look up. 'Olive, you don't sound like you had unfinished business when you died. You sound almost *happy*.'

She raises one of her perfectly plucked eyebrows. 'Ah, well, you see, Sid, although I could accept that this was the end of the road for me, I had to know that Ginger was safe. I was desperate to see his plane fly in, only I couldn't wait that long. Tiredness washed over me, I closed my eyes and . . .' She sighs. 'The next thing I knew it was night-time and it was cold and the lark was silent. I wandered around Fathom wailing, "Ginger! Ginger!" and I must have stumbled into the graveyard because this polite gentleman suddenly appeared, asking if I'd care to step inside his pub and rest a while.'

'Old Scratch,' I say. 'And you signed your name in his book?'

She nods. 'A great leather thing it was. Then I walked over the doorstep and BANG!' She claps her hands. 'The door slammed shut and I was trapped. I never knew if Ginger came home. Find out for me, Sid. *Please!*'

The blissful look on her face has been replaced by one of desperate anguish.

Zen does a little cough, then says, 'Olive, you do realise that *if* Ginger is alive, and it really is a big "if", he'll be ancient by now, over a hundred.'

Olive blinks then smiles one of her big, beaming smiles. 'Of course I do, Zen. I'm not a total onion!'

For a moment we're all quiet. It's always like this when one of the ghosts talks about their unfinished business. It doesn't matter how many years have passed, they are all still desperate to sort something out.

'It's so unfair,' I say. 'If Old Scratch had left you alone you would have found your way to the airbase and seen Ginger. You might have been able to cross over to the other side that same evening!'

Olive glances at the door at the back of the pub. 'I can't tell you how often I have thought that, Sid. That man has stolen something very precious from me.'

Suddenly Zen speaks up. 'What I don't get is why Old Scratch wanted to trap you all in the first place.' He looks around at the ghosts. 'I mean, no offence or anything, but it's not like you're useful, is it? All you do is make the place dusty. You can't even tidy up after yourselves.' He bangs his hand down, sending a cloud of sparkly dust up into the air. 'And it can't be because he loves your company because he's hardly ever here.'

'And when he is 'ere he just shouts in our faces,' says Peg.

'He likes collecting things,' says Holkar, his clipped voice ringing out. 'Like his clocks, we are another of his collections.'

'Perhaps he is like your father, Sid, with his models,' muses Beau Fiddler, the highwayman, 'or Zen's mother with the objects in the museum.'

65

I think for a moment then say, 'No, Old Scratch is nothing like them. They love their collections and care for them, but Old Scratch seems to hate you . . . So why is he so desperate to keep hold of you all?'

And that's when a cheery 'Cuckoo!' rings out, and a wooden bird pops out of the cuckoo clock.

'Cuckoo! Cuckoo!' it calls, and we hear the steady thud, thud, thud of footsteps.

CHAPTER NINE

'Old Scratch!' cries Will.

Zen and I jump to our feet.

'Come on,' Zen says to me. 'Let's get out of here!'

But I don't move because Will has wrapped his icy fingers round my wrist and is holding tight. A chill seeps through my arm. Will stares at me and says, 'Don't go.'

I could pull away – Will, like the other ghosts, can't actually hold on to me – but I don't move.

'Sid, *hurry up!*' hisses Zen. He's standing by the door to the graveyard, waiting for me.

I've got to get out of here. Old Scratch knows we freed Dai, but he doesn't know we've actually been inside the Halfway House. It's one of the few advantages we've got over him.

'I need to go, Will,' I say.

The footsteps are getting louder and the cuckoo clock is shaking on its nail. Any second now and that cellar door is going to come flying open.

'I don't want you to go,' says Will in a rush. 'It's not just the dust, Sid. Something funny is going on, I know it, but the others just say I'm talking codswallop.'

Thud, *thud*, go the footsteps, and then they stop.

I want to ask Will what he means, but there's not time. So I make a snap decision. I tear myself away from him, but instead of running out of the pub, I go to the cupboard by the fireplace. It's a sooty space where coal used to be stored, but right now it's empty and big enough for me to hide in.

There is a scraping sound on the other side of the cellar door and the doorknob starts to turn. The ghosts' eyes fly between me and Zen who is still standing by the open door.

'*Go!*' I hiss, but instead of fleeing into the graveyard, Zen pulls the door shut and runs to join me.

'I do not know why we are doing this, Sid,' he says, as we squeeze into the cupboard. 'But you'd better have a good reason.'

We pull the door shut just as the cellar door crashes open.

My heart hammers as I try to stay as still as possible, but it's hard. My whole body is trembling, plus I'm sitting on lumps of coal and Zen's foot. At least we're not in total darkness. A beam of light seeps through a crack in the door and when I lean forward I realise I can see into the pub.

Old Scratch is standing in the middle of the room.

His long, frayed coat brushes the floorboards and his white hands hang limply by his sides. He looks like a giant moth as he stands there, his grey hair moving in a hidden breeze coming from the cellar.

Slowly he turns, his pale eyes sweeping the room. 'What has been going on?' His voice is cold and dry. It sounds like paper being torn.

Zen shifts forward and whispers in my ear, 'What about Snout?'

In my rush to hide I forgot all about Old Scratch's dog! My eyes fly to the cellar door, but I can't see Snout's muscly shoulders or her long, pointed nose. Once again Old Scratch has left her behind.

Suddenly he turns, kicks the cellar door shut,

then starts to pace around the pub. He doesn't speak. He barely blinks. He just walks, glaring at the ghosts and filling the room with his sickly scent of cloves and damp earth.

When he is back where he began, and staring at Mei Huang, Zen whispers, 'Explain why we are doing this, Sid.'

'I couldn't leave Will,' I say, as quietly as possible. 'He seemed scared. He said something has changed. Plus you asked why Old Scratch keeps the ghosts trapped in here. Maybe this will give us a clue!'

Zen snorts. 'So no real reason just lots of little ones.'

'We're detectives, Zen. Hiding and looking for clues is what detectives do!'

'But he could be in here for hours,' Zen's whispered voice rises with panic. 'And I need a wee! And what about my dinner? It's veggie sausages tonight!'

Suddenly Old Scratch turns and glares in our direction. I wait until he's staring at Mei Huang again to whisper, 'We're in a timeless tavern, Zen. You'll get your sausages. Now please *shut up* before Old Scratch finds us!'

I press my face back against the crack in the wood and watch as Old Scratch crouches down to stare at Mei Huang.

She lifts her chin and gazes into the distance, stubbornly ignoring him.

Bones has told us that over the years all the ghosts have tried to stand up to Old Scratch by shouting or shoving their hands through him, or calling him names, but whenever they've done anything like this he gets his revenge. Usually he nails up the shutters on the windows, sometimes for years on end. All the ghosts have learned that it's best to keep quiet when he's visiting.

He walks over to Will and my chest squeezes tight as I see the small boy staring at his feet, his hands twitching nervously.

I remember what Will said and try to see if anything has changed in the pub, but as far as I can make out, except for the extra dust swirling around, everything is the same.

Old Scratch shoves his face close to Will's and I see the boy shrink back.

Suddenly I hate Old Scratch more than anyone or anything in the world. He might have told me he wasn't the Innkeeper who made the spell that trapped the ghosts, but right now I don't care. Because it's him who is scaring Will so much that his feet are trembling on the flagstones, and it's him who is making Holkar, usually so proud and upright, sit hunched over on a stool.

I want to burst out of the cupboard and slam my hands into him, but I force myself to stay where I am and to watch every single thing he does, like a proper detective.

When Old Scratch has finished staring at the ghosts, he pulls a silk handkerchief out of his pocket then moves around the room wiping dust off his precious clocks. The dust might drift off the ghosts slowly, but there is still enough to coat every surface in a golden shimmer.

I watch Old Scratch swish his handkerchief over each clock, making sure he gets into every nook and cranny. At first I think he's just fussing over his clocks, but then I notice something. Every now and then he takes a bottle from the pocket of his coat, unscrews the lid, pokes the handkerchief inside, then whips it out again. Slowly the bottle fills up with dust until it gleams like a tiny lantern.

Once he's finished dusting, Old Scratch tucks the handkerchief back into his pocket, pushes a cork into the bottle and slips it back into his pocket too. Then he takes a final walk around the Halfway House. When he reaches the fireplace and the cupboard where we are hiding, he stops.

Next to me, Zen holds his breath and I do the same. Old Scratch is standing so close to the cupboard that he's blocking the light. His musty smell fills the tiny space. Has he heard us? Does he know we're here?

Suddenly his rasping voice says, 'What *do* you think you are doing?'

For a moment I think he's talking to us, but then he steps away from the cupboard and I see Mei Huang has got to her feet. Slowly she bends backwards, and she keeps going, stretching further and further until her hands land on the floor by her feet. She flips over, and she does this again and again, making her way around the room in a series of back flips.

Mei might be dressed like a pilot, but before she flew

planes she was a trapeze artist. She told me about her life in the circus when I quizzed her about her unfinished business. Watching her now, it's clear that she hasn't lost any of her skills.

Old Scratch gives a snarl of annoyance. 'I said, What are you doing? Answer me!'

'I'm stretching,' Mei says in her husky voice.

Will bursts out laughing and starts to clap.

'Cor, you aren't 'arf bendy!' says Peg admiringly, and then all the ghosts are clapping and commenting on her stretchiness.

'Shut up!' shouts Old Scratch, striding away from our hiding place and across the pub. 'I said, SHUT UP! And you –' he jabs a finger at Mei – 'sit down!'

Oh so slowly she flips upright then strolls back to her seat, her leather flying suit creaking. It's only when she glances in our direction and winks that I realise she's done all of this to get Old Scratch away from the cupboard.

Meanwhile Old Scratch is still shouting at the ghosts. He crouches in front of Will who is still laughing and clapping. 'I'd stop doing that if I were you, William Buckle, or I'll nail planks across those windows!'

Immediately Will stops.

Old Scratch grins, his papery skin stretching back to reveal yellow teeth. 'You'd hate that, wouldn't you? Not being able to see the sky or the sea, or the little birds that hop around the graveyard?'

Will can't take it any more. 'I wish I'd never come into this stinking inn!' he yells. 'I should have let myself fade away and become a wraith. Anything would be better than being stuck in here with you, you rotter!'

A strange look comes over Old Scratch's face, then his smile stretches wider. 'Be careful what you wish for, William Buckle,' he whispers, then he turns and bangs out of the pub, slamming the door behind him.

We listen as he clomps into the cellar, then Zen lets out a long drawn-out breath and says, 'Well, that was a waste of time. I nearly weed myself with terror just to watch a four-hundred-year-old man do some dusting!'

'It wasn't a waste of time at all,' I say. 'I found out why the ghosts are trapped in here.'

CHAPTER TEN

Once we've tumbled out of the cupboard we leave the Halfway House straight away.

'But I need to talk to you!' Will says, grabbing hold of my hand again. 'It's bloomin' urgent, Sid!'

'We'll talk later,' I say, pulling away from his icy fingers then shutting the door with a firm click. Will's idea of urgent is wanting to see a picture of a naked mole rat.

'Are you going to tell me your big discovery?' asks Zen, as we hurry through the graveyard.

'We need to find Bones first,' I say. 'He needs to hear this too.'

76

The moment we step into the warmth of the Black Spot Cat Café, cats of all colours start to wind round our ankles. It's a colourful, noisy place. Fairy lights hang from the ceiling, strung between dreamcatchers and crystals, and Pirate FM is blaring out of the radio. Sally, the owner, is behind the counter, piping bright blue icing on to cupcakes. Bones is at our favourite table that's hidden behind a display of pot plants.

Both Sally and Bones give us a wave when they see us at the door. Sally hasn't got a clue that a ghost is already sitting in her café, keeping her company.

'Hello, my lovelies!' she says, her brown face crinkling. 'Are you havin' yer usual?'

'Yes, please,' I say. 'Two kids' hot chocolates and a cupcake to share.'

'We should sell the Castile Cross,' says Zen, as we go to join Bones. 'Then we won't need to share a cupcake.'

'It doesn't belong to us,' I say, stepping round a fat ginger cat. The Castile Cross is a solid gold cross covered in emeralds that we found when we were helping Bones sort out his unfinished business. It's probably priceless, but right now it's wrapped in a Minions T-shirt and shoved

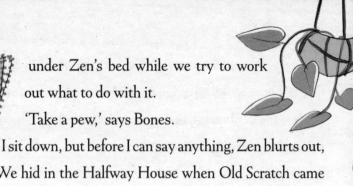

under Zen's bed while we try to work out what to do with it.

'Take a pew,' says Bones.

I sit down, but before I can say anything, Zen blurts out, 'We hid in the Halfway House when Old Scratch came in and Sid says she knows why the ghosts are trapped!'

Bones looks furious, but only for a second because then he catches up with what Zen has just said. He swings his big head towards me, showering me with icy drops of water that vanish seconds after they land on me. 'What? Is this true, Jones? Tell me!'

'I've definitely worked out part of it,' I say.

Then I look at them both and I can't help smiling. 'It's got something to do with Old Scratch's dusting!'

Bones looks confused. 'His *dusting*?' He shakes his head. 'No, there is nothing special about that. The old swine likes to keep his clocks spick and span, that is all.'

'He wasn't just dusting,' I say. 'He was collecting the dust and putting it in a bottle!'

Like Bones, Zen doesn't seem impressed by my theory. 'Perhaps he was collecting the dust because he didn't want it floating around and making his clocks dusty again.'

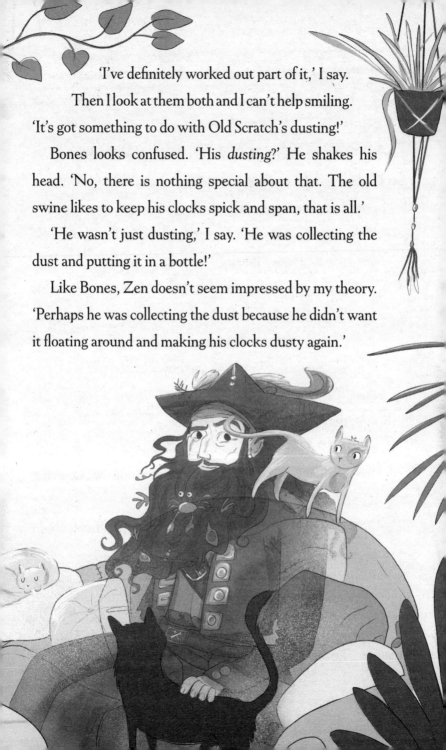

'You don't do much dusting, do you, Zen?' I say.

'Nah, I'm more of an emptying-the-dishwasher type of guy.'

'Well, I know a LOT about dusting. We have over five thousand and seventy-two models in the model village and one of my Saturday jobs is dusting them. I've been doing it for years, but one thing I've never done is put all the dust I've collected into a bottle.'

Bones scratches at his shaggy beard. 'I have seen Old Scratch with a bottle, but I assumed it was oil for his clocks. Are you saying he was putting the ghosts' dust inside it? It makes no sense. What on earth would he want with our dust?'

'I don't know,' I admit, 'but I bet the answer lies in the cellar. We need to find out what's down there.'

Bones's eyes widen. 'Don't even think about going down there, Sidonie May Jones!'

I open my mouth to reply, but have to shut it again because Sally has arrived with our order.

'Here we are,' she says, putting our mugs and a cupcake down on the table. She's already cut the cake in half. 'I popped a surprise ingredient into your hot chocolate!'

'Cat hair?' suggests Bones, as one of Sally's many cats leaps on and through his lap.

'It's a humbug!' announces Sally.

I look down at my drink. I can't see a humbug, but I can see the leaf pattern Sally always draws in the frothy milk. The pattern looks familiar, but I'm too busy thinking about the Halfway House, or rather its cellar, to work out where I've seen it before.

The second Sally has gone, I say, 'But we need to go into the cellar if we're going to find out what Old Scratch does with the dust.'

Bones shakes his head. 'No, you do not need to go into that cellar. It is far too dangerous. What we need to do is talk about Olive's young man, Ginger.'

I know there's no point arguing with Bones. He already feels bad that Old Scratch knows who I am and has threatened me. He was always going to say going into the cellar was too dangerous. So for now I push the idea from my mind, and we spend the next five minutes coming up with a plan to hunt down Ginger, aka Ron Clark. We agree that after tea tonight I'll go round to Zen's so we can do some research at the museum when it's closed, and Bones has offered to spend the evening in the Admiral Benbow.

'I'll see if any of the old boys in there happen to be called Ron,' he says. 'Maybe he stuck around Fathom after the war.'

'We're going to crack this case,' says Zen, and he's feeling so confident that he takes a big swig of his hot chocolate, then splutters, pulling a face. 'Bit minty!'

CHAPTER ELEVEN

When we're leaving the café, Sally hands me my change and that's when I catch sight of the leaf pattern again. This time it isn't drawn in frothy milk, but tattooed on the inside of Sally's wrist.

'What is that?' I ask, pointing at the three loops joined by a line. 'Is it leaves?'

Sally glances at her wrist. 'What, this old thing? It's just a symbol you will find all over these parts if you keep your eyes open.' She points at the circles in turn. 'Each of these represents an element: earth, water and fire.'

'What about the line?' I ask.

She grins and her blue eyes twinkle. 'Oh, that's a wand,' she says. Then she picks up a cheese straw and starts looping it through the air. '*Earth, water, fire,*' she says in a dreamy voice. '*Hear my spell.*' Then she closes her eyes and gives the cheese straw a flick.

She opens her eyes and smiles. 'There. My charm's wound up.'

Zen laughs. 'Sally, did you just do a spell on us?'

'Well, not on you, as such, but whoever eats this cheese straw is in for a surprise!'

'You're joking, aren't you?' I say.

She bursts out laughing. 'Of course I am, yer daft sausage. I'm interested in the old stories about magic and suchlike, and so was my mother before me, but spells and wands are make-believe. Now off you go, I need to brew some of my cobnut beer. There's not a drop of alcohol in it. I'll let you try some next time you visit.'

With that not very tempting offer, we leave the café and walk home.

Sally's words stay with me as we drop Zen off and carry on towards the model village.

I thought spells and magic were make-believe too, but that changed when I freed Bones. To be honest, I'm disappointed by what Sally said. I'd love to talk to someone about magic. I know that I broke the Innkeeper's spell, but how did I do it? And is there any other magic I can do? If I could make lightning happen then we could free the ghosts straight away. The thought that I might be able to control the weather with a spell is both frightening and exciting and it makes a shiver run down my back.

Before I go into the model village, Bones puts his hand on my arm and keeps it there. He knows how cold this makes me and he only does it when he really wants my attention. 'Listen close, Jones. You must promise me that you will not put one foot in that cellar. Do you hear?'

I know why Bones is saying this – he's my friend and he's worried about something happening to me – but I'm sure the answers to so many of the questions we have lie in the cellar. I don't want to make a promise that I can't keep, so I say, 'Don't worry. Right now, what I care about is freeing the ghosts.'

He nods, satisfied. 'Good lass, and now I shall get down to the Benbow and see if Ron Clark is enjoying a pint. See you on the morrow, Sid!'

I watch him go, then let myself into the model village.

It's getting dark now – the nights are drawing in – and I have to tread carefully as I walk along the tiny roads. Imagining my foot crunching down on one of Dad's delicate models makes me pause by the door to the cottage. I think about the model of Dad that went missing, and then I think about two other models Dad has made: the ones of me and Zen. Quickly I run down to the miniature harbour to check they are still there.

I'm relieved to see that the miniature me is still outside Mermaids, my arms reaching towards nothing. Despite what Dad said, he hasn't got round to making a new model of himself. Zen's there too, sitting on the steps of the museum eating a piece of toast. Zen's model is one of my favourite ones in the whole village. Dad's even put a smear of marmite on the toast – Zen's favourite – and given him a little bowler hat.

The models look so fragile, on their own in the darkness of the coming evening, that I pick them up and put them in my pocket. I'll tell Dad that I've taken them to play with. He'll believe me. I used to do it all the time. Then I let myself into the warmth of the kitchen, feeling much happier knowing that the little Zen and me are safe for now.

CHAPTER TWELVE

Later that evening, I find myself sitting next to Zen inside an air-raid shelter in the Second World War room at the museum. Zen's turned off the siren that's usually wailing, but it still feels strange to be inside a tin hut surrounded by gas masks, shop dummies dressed in mud-coloured uniforms and, hanging from the ceiling, a patchwork mermaid made by Fathom's Women's Institute in 1943.

On the bench between us is a pile of newspaper clippings and photographs that Zen's mum gave us. We told her that we had to do a history project on Kervean airbase, which wasn't really a lie.

'Hey, this could be something,' says Zen, pulling out a photograph. It shows a group of men with their arms thrown round each other's shoulders. They're standing in a field full of planes and the caption below reads: *RAF personnel, Kervean airbase, 1945*. Zen turns it over, but there are no names written on the back.

'The one at the end has freckles,' I say. 'He might be Ginger. We should take it to the Halfway House tomorrow and show Olive.'

'Good idea,' says Zen, putting it to one side, then we go back to sifting through the pile.

After an hour we haven't found any mention of a Ron Clark, but we're not massively disappointed. This is just day one of our investigation and we know we'll find loads more stuff online.

Soon we hear my dad out in the lobby talking to Zen's mum, Abigail. He's come to take me home. Now that it's getting dark in the evenings Dad doesn't like me walking around Fathom on my own. I could tell him that a three-hundred-year-old pirate ghost is always with me, but I don't think that would reassure him.

We find Dad and Abigail trying to decide what to call their pub quiz team this week. They can't choose between the Miniaturists or the Stuffed Weasels. Zen gets drawn into the conversation, which means I get to take a quick look in one of my favourite rooms in the museum: Witchcraft and Magic.

I slip into the small red room. Abigail has hung dried twigs from the ceiling, and tied to these twigs are scraps of fabric and trinkets. I know I can't research Ron Clark in here, but maybe I'll find out something about myself, and what I can do with the magic Bones insists is inside me.

It's hard to see with only the light from the lobby, but I can just make out displays of chalices, wooden bowls and tarot cards. I see a knitted Cornish pisky sitting inside a cauldron and next to this a glass case that is supposedly full of wands, but looks more like it contains a load of twigs.

I walk over to another case that is full of books open at random pages. I wonder if any of the books contains a spell that can make lightning happen, but they are full of strange pictures and diagrams, and I don't recognise the language that is used.

Suddenly the room is flooded with light and I spin round to see Abigail standing in the doorway. Sweat prickles my skin and I feel like I've been caught doing something wrong.

Seeing the look on my face, Abigail smiles and says,

'Sorry, I didn't mean to scare you, Sid!'

I smile to hide how nervous I feel. I want to find out what is written in these books, but I can't tell Abigail that I'm looking for a spell to change the weather. So instead I blurt out, 'Are these spell books?'

She nods and comes to join me. 'Although some people would call them a "book of shadows" or a "book of charms". Amazing, aren't they?'

I nod as I look at the brown curling pages. Then, as casually as possible, I say, 'What were these spells supposed to do? Could witches, I don't know, change the weather?'

'I'm afraid most of these spells are more humdrum than that,' says Abigail. She points at something written in a book at the front of the case. 'This one, for example, explains how you can light a candle by uttering the words "*ignis lux*", and the one next to it tells you how to cure a sore throat by spitting on a piece of paper then feeding it to a chicken. The red book at the back has crueller spells in it.'

My mouth goes dry and I feel the hairs on the back of my neck prickle because I already know about one cruel spell that is carved into the doorstep of the Halfway House.

I came in here hoping to find out about myself, but this might be my chance to learn about the Innkeeper.

'What sort of spells are in there?'

Abigail opens the cabinet and takes out the tiny, leather-bound book. A tree is drawn on the front, its twisting roots rise up to tangle with its branches. 'Poisons, recipes for potions that will make people ill, spells that will make cows' milk turn sour.' She shows me a page. 'This one explains how you can use mouse droppings to make a nagging neighbour lose their voice, and the one next to it informs us that "silver snares the dead", whatever that means!'

'Are there any spells in there that can do anything really, really bad?' I ask.

Abigail raises one eyebrow. 'Well, poisoning someone is pretty bad, but I know what you mean. You're talking about murder, aren't you?'

I nod. I couldn't speak right now, even if I wanted to. I feel like all the air has been sucked out of the room as I wait for Abigail's answer.

She closes the book and shows me the tree that's drawn on the front. 'This is an elder tree and it tells us that the witch who owned this book respected the Elder Law. It was believed that a witch could never use magic to take a life, and that if they did they would be punished by losing their powers.'

Relief rushes through me. The Elder Law sounds like an excellent idea. 'Really?'

Abigail nods, but then goes and ruins everything by saying, 'Of course, there are ways around everything. Think about the witch in "Snow White". She wanted to get rid of Snow White so first she hired someone else to do it – the huntsman – and when he failed to do the deed, she went to the trouble of poisoning an apple and giving it to Snow White to eat.'

'So technically she wasn't breaking the Elder Law?'

'That's right, because Snow White *chose* to eat the apple. There are lots of other examples in literature of cunning behaviour being used by witches to cause mortal harm. In "Hansel and Gretel" the witch makes her whole home into a sweet shop to tempt the children to step inside, and in *Macbeth* all the witches need to do to make war break out is tell Macbeth he will be king.'

'So never accept sweets or apples from a witch,' I say.

'Or believe what they say,' adds Abigail with a delighted laugh. 'Come on,' she says, putting the red book back in the case and shutting the door. 'Let's go and find out what terrible name Zen's come up with for the quiz team.'

CHAPTER THIRTEEN

The next morning I find Zen and Bones waiting for me by the giant ice cream.

Zen's got a big grin on his face and he's wearing a thick sheepskin flying jacket over his school uniform. He often turns up wearing clothes from his parents' museum, but this jacket looks far too hot for such a sunny October morning.

'There you are!' says Bones. 'Hurry now. The lad has news, only he won't tell me what it is.'

'I wanted you to hear it too,' says Zen, hopping up and down with excitement.

'Hear what?' I say.

'I've found Ginger!' he cries out.

As we walk towards the bus stop, Zen tells us what he discovered after I left the museum last night. 'I had another look through our Second World War room,' he says, 'but I still couldn't see any mention of a Ron Clark. I was about to give up when something caught my eye.'

'What?' asks Bones.

'This!' says Zen, running in front of us and turning round so we can see the back of his jacket where the word 'Nobby' is printed in fading letters.

'What's "Nobby" got to do with Ginger?' I ask.

Zen wags a finger at me. 'If you knew your history as well as I do, Sid, you'd know that in the past people whose surnames were Clark were often called Nobby.'

'Your mum told you that, didn't she?'

He smiles sheepishly. 'Yeah, she told me when I came down this morning wearing the jacket.'

'But that doesn't mean it belonged to Olive's Ron Clark, does it?' I say. 'There must be loads of Clarks in the world.'

'True,' says Zen, 'but three months ago, to celebrate his one hundredth birthday, a Ron Clark donated this very jacket to our museum. Ron Clark, aka Ginger, is alive and well and living at Sea Breeze Senior Living in Fathom!'

Bones roars with delight and I burst out laughing. I can't believe it. It took us days to solve Bones's unfinished business, but we've found Ginger in under twenty-four hours. 'That's amazing, Zen. It looks like we're pretty good detectives. Well, you are.'

Zen puffs out his chest, making the leather on the flying jacket crackle. 'Thanks, mate, but it was a team effort. Our skills should come in handy after school when we bust Ginger out of his old folks' home.'

'What?' I say, pulling him back by his sleeve.

'Well, that's what we've got to do, isn't it? We take Ron down to the graveyard. Olive sees him, and – BOOM! – her unfinished business is solved and she walks free.'

And with these words Zen climbs, no, *struts* on board the waiting bus.

Bones puts an icy hand on my arm. 'I won't be coming to school with you today,' he says. 'I will stay here in Fathom and do some reconnaissance at Sea Breeze Senior Living.' I must look at him blankly because he adds with a growl, 'I'm going to snoop around the place, Sid. See if I can sniff out Ginger!'

'Got it,' I whisper, then hurry on the bus after Zen.

'Zen,' I say, after we've shown our passes to the driver. 'Are you sure you should wear that jacket to school?'

'Absabloominglutely,' he says, but as we walk further down the bus, Owen Kidd catches sight of it then sees what's written on the back.

'Nice jacket, *Nobby*,' he says sarcastically.

Zen turns up the collar of the jacket, then stares down at Owen. In a deep American drawl he says, 'Watch it, Kidd. Only friends call me Nobby.'

This makes Owen go bright red, but he knows better than to say anything else to Zen who has an answer for everything.

Zen and I take a seat, but before we can come up with a single good idea for smuggling Ginger out of his old folks' home, the bus stops and Mo climbs on board.

This means we can't talk about Ginger, but Mo makes up for it by having a bag of Moam sweets that she shares out. As we drive along the coast road she alternates between eating sweets and taking big gulps from her water bottle. It's enormous and red and has water-drinking slogans written down the side, like, *Good morning!* and *Just another sip!* and *You're doing great!*

We spend the rest of the journey coming up with alternative slogans like, *Massive wee emergency!* which Mo actually writes on her bottle with a Sharpie.

Mo hangs out with us during each break at school and sits with us on the bus on the way home too. It's nice feeling normal for a change and laughing over nothing with a friend, but it does mean that later Zen and I find ourselves standing outside Sea Breeze Senior Living without any sort of plan for getting Ginger out.

'So what do we do?' I say. 'Just walk in there, grab him and then take him to the graveyard?'

'Yeah, something like that,' says Zen. 'Hopefully when Olive sees him she'll know he came back that day and that he's had a sweet life and – kaboom! – the spell will be broken and she'll walk free.'

I look up at Sea Breeze Senior Living. It used to be a hotel and I can still see the faded outline of *Beachview Hotel* painted on the bricks. Net curtains hang at each window with small vases of plastic flowers dotted here and there. A sunroom is attached to the front of the building. It's filled with nodding grey-headed figures who are snoozing or staring at the sea.

'Zen, do you really think they'll let two strange kids walk in off the street and take one of their old folks on a trip to a graveyard?'

He shrugs. 'Why not? Everyone knows that old people and children are good for each other. We're full of life and jolly, and they're full of wisdom. Plus we've got so much in common. They love lazing around, watching TV and eating sweets, and so do we. I bet they'll be thrilled to see us.'

A woman wearing a plastic apron has just walked into the sunroom. She notices us standing outside and glares at us.

'She doesn't look thrilled to see us,' I say. Then I see who's sitting in the armchair behind her. 'Hang on . . . is that Bones?'

The pirate is fast asleep with his legs flung out in front of him and his mouth hanging open. A man with a Zimmer frame walks through his boots and Bones's eye flicker open enough to notice us standing on the doorstep. He jumps to his feet, stretches, then drifts through the window to join us.

'Bones, why were you asleep in there?' I ask.

He shrugs his big shoulders. 'I was simply taking forty winks to keep the brain in good order.' He nods towards the sunroom. 'That glass contraption is quite the sun trap, Jones. There have been moments this afternoon when I almost believed I was in the Caribbean!'

'But did you find Ginger?' I ask.

Bones beams. 'Yes, and he is a marvellous fellow. He has spent most of the day in his room reading a book called *Pride and Prejudice* and eating biscuits.' Bones's attention is caught by something in the garden. 'Look, there he is now, taking the air.'

A tall, extremely thin man is making slow progress around the scruffy garden. His hair is snowy white – there's no trace of ginger now – and he looks like he might be blown over at any moment. When he sees us, he looks confused for a second, then smiles.

'OK. Let's do this thing,' says Zen, turning the collar up on Ginger's flying jacket. 'Chocks away!'

'What? No, Zen! Wait!' I say, but Zen is already hurrying over to Ginger.

'Hello, Mr Clark,' he says when he reaches him. 'Would you like to come for a walk with me and my friend, Sid?'

'Zen!' I hiss, tugging on his sleeve. 'We can't just take him out of here without telling anyone!'

'Yes, you can!' says Ginger in a loud voice. Clearly there's nothing wrong with his hearing. 'I'm not being held prisoner here.' Then he peers closer at Zen. 'What's that you're wearing, young man? I used to have a jacket just like it.'

'This *is* your jacket!' says Zen standing tall. 'My mum runs the Museum of Curiosities and she said I could borrow it for the day. Is that OK? I'm being careful with it.'

For a moment I wonder if Ginger is going to be cross. After all, he donated the jacket to the museum expecting it would be looked after. But then he smiles and says, 'It's good to see a strapping chap like you wearing it. I was only a few years older than yourself when I got my flying stripes. I was so young the other men called me "Boy". I was rather proud of that name.'

'Don't let him get talking,' Bones mutters in my ear. 'Once he starts he can't stop. I've already heard this tale twice today.'

'Mr Clark,' I say quickly. 'Would you like to come on a walk with us to the graveyard?'

His watery eyes turn towards me. 'Why would I want to go there? Bit gloomy, isn't it?'

'No,' I say quickly. 'We love it at the graveyard. Don't we, Zen?' Zen nods encouragingly. 'There are birds and flowers. It's a happy place. Everywhere you look you see signs that people care about each other.' I'm not just thinking about Mum's grave, but of all the headstones with their messages about 'beloved sisters' and 'precious husbands'.

Ginger thinks for a moment, then shrugs and says, 'I might as well come along. They aways put *Sun, Sea and Selling Houses* on at five and I can't stand it.'

Sure enough, the woman with the plastic apron is wheeling a TV into the sunroom.

'Shall I go and tell her where we're going?' I ask Ginger.

He gives a bark of laughter. 'Not likely! She'll never let me go.'

Then with surprising speed he hobbles down the path towards the road.

On the way to the graveyard, Ginger keeps up a steady stream of chatter. It's not really a conversation, more a monologue. He seems to have a story connected to every single building in Fathom. 'That used to be the butcher's. They gave me bones for my dog, Captain. Captain used to roam the streets of Fathom causing mischief and I'm sure most of the dogs around here are descended from him. Oh, hello! The Benbow could do with a lick of paint. You see those window frames? I put those in with my chum, Badger. I went into carpentry after the war. Badger could have been on the stage, you know – he had a lovely voice – but he wouldn't leave Fathom for love nor money.'

Before he can jump straight into another story I say, 'You were stationed here during the war, weren't you? How come you decided to stay?' We're getting close to the graveyard now and before we present him to Olive I'd like to find out what he's been doing for the past eighty years.

'It's a sorry tale with a happy ending,' he says, shuffling up the hill.

Bones snorts. 'I hope it's a short one!'

Ginger carries on. 'I had a fiancé, Olive Buckmore, and she died.' Behind Ginger's back Zen flashes me an inappropriately big grin and a thumbs up. 'Tragic it was. Olive was so young and clever. She's buried in Fathom graveyard and I never left the village because I wanted to stay close to her.'

'Did you marry anyone else?' I ask, hoping that if he did, Olive isn't the jealous type.

Then Ginger surprises us all by saying, 'Oh yes. I married three ladies actually. One after each other, mind!'

Bones roars with laughter. 'Ha! Olive won't be expecting that, will she? Her stuck in that pub for eighty years cause of old Ginger here, and he's off getting married left, right and centre!'

We walk through the rusty gates into the shadows of the graveyard. Olive's headstone is near the entrance and Ginger goes straight to it and sinks down on the bench opposite. I get the feeling he's done this lots of times before, but Olive would never have known because the Halfway House is tucked away on the far side of the graveyard.

'Edna, Rose and Ethel,' says Ginger, ticking his wives off on his fingers. They were all fabulous ladies, but Olive was my true love.'

Suddenly a voice rings out from the lane. 'Ronald! Ronald! Where have you got to?'

Ginger rolls his eyes. 'That's Irena, one of the nurses from the home. She's come to find me.'

'Ronald! Where are you?' shouts Irena, closer now.

Panic rushes though me. Ginger is so close to Olive. If we can just get him over to the Halfway House we'll be able to find out if Zen's Plan B actually works. We'll never have a better chance than this!

'We should hide,' I say.

I'm expecting Ginger to tell me that's a ridiculous idea, but instead he turns and with a gleam in his eye says, 'Good idea. Where?'

I jump to my feet. 'I know the perfect place over by the mausoleum. Follow me!'

CHAPTER FOURTEEN

As quickly as possible, Zen and I guide Ginger round tilting headstones and over the roots of trees. Bones follows at the rear, keeping us updated on Irena's progress.

'She is in the graveyard,' he calls. 'Steady now. She is having a good look round. Make haste! She is coming our way!'

I want to rush, but at the same time I've got to keep an eye out for Old Scratch and make sure Ginger doesn't fall over.

Keeping a tight grip on Ginger's arm, I lead the way over the stream, then we push our way through the long grass until we reach the big oak tree that grows close to the Halfway House. Irena will never find us hidden over here. Sure enough, a minute later Bones reports that she has given up and left the graveyard.

Leaving Ginger resting against the tree with Zen and Bones, I scurry towards the pub looking out for Old Scratch.

'Why's she creeping along like that?' I hear Ginger ask Zen.

'It's how Sid runs,' says Zen. 'She always does it.'

When I reach the Halfway House I peer through the window. Old Scratch isn't there, so I go to the door and pull it open. Sparkly dust billows into the graveyard.

'Olive!' I shout. 'Come quick. We've found him!'

The ghosts jump to their feet, surprised by my sudden entrance, and Olive hurries to the doorway. 'What do you mean, Sid?' she says, peering over my shoulder.

'We've got Ginger! He *did* get home safely that day, and look –' I point to where Zen, Bones and Ginger are standing by the tree – 'he's here in the graveyard!'

Olive's hands fly to her face and there is a collective gasp from the ghosts who have gathered behind her.

'*Ginger?*' she whispers. '*My* Ginger?'

We watch as Ginger walks forward, his hands shaking with each step.

'So that's her pilot,' mutters Holkar. 'Not quite the dashing figure I was expecting.'

Olive either ignores his sarcastic tone or doesn't hear him. Her beautiful face is lit up with an enormous smile and a tear is rolling down her cheek. 'GINGER!' she cries, and without a moment's hesitation, she steps through the invisible barrier and out of the Halfway House.

I'm so shocked that I just stand there with my mouth hanging open. Zen's plan actually worked! We didn't need lightning or a Crunchie. The second Olive's unfinished business was sorted out, the spell keeping her trapped in the Halfway House was broken!

Olive runs towards Ginger, her arms outstretched.

That's when the ghosts still trapped inside the inn start to whoop and cheer.

'She's only gone and flippin' done it!' cries Will.

'Bravo!' yells Beau.

Ginger just looks confused. He can't see the young woman hurtling towards him, or hear the cries of the ghosts, but he can see me and Zen standing there with big grins on our faces.

'Ginger! Ginger! Oh, darling Ginger!' Olive cries, throwing her arms round and through the old man. 'Here you are, safe and sound, you lovely chap. Gosh, I've missed you!'

Ginger can't see Olive, but he must be able to feel her because he starts shivering. He's obviously freezing, but he doesn't turn to leave this dark corner of the graveyard. Instead he stands a little taller and a smile spreads across his face. 'Have you noticed how the sun finds its way between the leaves?' he says. 'What a magical spot you two have brought me to!'

And for a few minutes neither of them move. They seem content to stand there, Olive's face buried in Ginger's chest, the sunlight dancing over them.

Then with a sigh Ginger says, 'I suppose I should think about going home. They usually put the news on at six, and we have a crumpet.'

'Yes. Let's go,' says Olive, and the two of them walk back through the graveyard, Bones and Zen following close behind. Olive doesn't even glance back at her best friend, Peg, as she walks alongside Ginger, her arm slipped through his, fussing and urging him to, 'Go slowly now, old chap. Watch out for the roots!'

Peg watches her leave. 'I can't believe it,' she whispers. 'My pal, Olive. Gone . . . just like that!'

Her face is a perfect mixture of happiness and despair.

And as I'm looking at her I see something strange: one of the freckles disappears from her nose.

I blink, sure I must have imagined it, but on the very tip of her nose, where the freckle used to be, there is now a tiny pale space.

Then I remember what Will said to me, that something 'funny' was going on. Was this what he meant?

Like the other ghosts, Will has pushed his face close to the barrier.

'Will,' I say, crouching down. 'What did you mean when you told me something funny was going on in the Halfway House?'

He glances at the other ghosts, but they are all watching Olive walk away.

'This,' he says, and he taps the little finger of his left hand against the barrier. At first I don't understand what he means, but then I see that the very tip of his finger is missing. It's a strange, unsettling sight.

'It's been fading bit by bit,' says Will, his voice a whisper. 'And now it's gone. The others say it's always been like that. They don't like me talking about it.'

'Why?'

He frowns, biting his chapped lips. 'Cause it's scary, isn't it? Fading away means turning into a wraith.' His big eyes well up with tears. 'And I can't turn into a wraith. My mum's waiting for me on the other side!'

Out in the graveyard Bones shouts, 'Hurry up, Jones!'

The ghosts start calling out to Olive.

'Goodbye, sweet Olive!' shouts Beau. 'Never forget me!'

'Nor me niether!' yells Peg.

I grab Will's fading hand. The cold burns my fingers and creeps up my arm, but I don't let go. 'Don't worry, Will. I'll work out what's going on.'

He smiles. 'Thank you, Sid. I knew you'd believe me.'

Then I have to let go of his hand and close the pub door, shutting out the sunlight.

I catch up with the others by Olive's grave. My mind is racing because of what I've just seen, but I can't talk to Zen and Bones about it, not while Ginger is here.

He's staring down at Olive's marble headstone.

'She was a fine girl,' he says after a moment. 'You know, she trained to be a spy before she became a land girl.'

Olive steps in front of him. 'Do you remember? They

kicked me out because of my heart. They said I couldn't jump out of an aeroplane. Lucky for me or I would never have met you.'

'We had such fun,' continues Ginger.

'Didn't we!' says Olive.

'Picking blackberries.'

'Dancing.'

'Walking on the hills.'

They're both smiling, lost in the past. Then Ginger gives a shake of his head and says, 'News and crumpets,' and shuffles towards the gate.

'I'll see him home,' says Olive, walking by his side. 'We've got so much to talk about!'

'Meet us at the Cockle!' I call after her, but I'm not sure she's heard. Her head is bent close to Ginger's and she's whispering in his ear.

CHAPTER FIFTEEN

We follow Olive and Ginger back to the old folks' home, just to make sure Ginger returns safely, then go to the Cockle to wait for her. Already a cluster of clouds is drifting up and down on the horizon and seems to be forming into a shape.

Quickly I tell Bones and Zen what I just saw at the pub and what Will told me about his finger.

'I am sure that bit of finger has always been missing,' says Bones. 'The lad has probably forgotten. You know how the Halfway House can make you forget.'

'I know,' I say. 'And I did wonder that myself, but I definitely saw Peg's freckle disappear.'

Zen's not convinced. 'Peg's got hundreds of freckles.

How can you be sure?'

'Because I was looking right at her face when it happened! It was there one minute, and the next it was gone. Will thinks there's more dust floating around too. Could the ghosts be fading away?' I don't like saying this horrible thought out loud, but it's the only explanation I can think of. Out at sea, clouds bunch together then billow out again.

Bones shakes his head. 'No. That is impossible. Time stands still in that tavern and if it didn't, all the ghosts would have turned into wraiths by now. I think Will has got muddled and you have made a mistake, but that is easily done. Peg Tiddy has more freckles than there are stars in the sky.'

'I guess,' I say.

Zen nudges me. 'Forget about the missing freckle, Sid. We should be celebrating. We just got another ghost out. Soon the Halfway House is going to be empty!'

I let myself smile. He's right. This is a brilliant moment. Another ghost is free and we know for certain that Plan B works. Just then Olive comes strolling down the lane.

'Hello, chaps!' she says, flashing one of her dazzling

smiles and dropping down on the bench next to us. 'Sorry I took so long. I saw a television and wheelchairs that moved on their own like motor cars. Oh, and there was cream that squirted out of a can already whipped, and something brown called Nutella that Ginger spread on his crumpet!' She laughs then gazes out to sea. 'I say, what on earth is that funny object out there?'

'It's a plane,' I say. 'It's come to take you to the other side.'

'My goodness,' says Olive, shading her eyes. 'It looks like Ginger's Lancaster bomber. I always did want a ride in it!'

'What you have to do next is walk to the end of the Cockle,' says Bones, pointing the way. 'Then go down the steps and walk out across the sea. It might sound funny, but my crew and Dai managed it so I'm sure you will too.'

But Olive isn't going to be rushed. She smiles and looks around, then spots a couple sitting outside the Benbow and cries out, 'What in *heaven's name* are they eating?'

'Nachos,' I say.

'They have something else that they eat a lot of these

days called *fish and chips*,' adds Bones.

'Oh, I know all about fish and chips, darling,' says Olive. 'I grew up on them.'

'I'll wager you have never heard of bubble tea,' says Bones, proud to know more than Olive about the modern world.

Chatting to ghosts in the sunshine is nice, but I'm starting to worry that Olive's plane will leave without her. Plus when Old Scratch discovers another of his ghosts is missing I don't want to be down here on the seafront. There are far too many dark lanes and alleyways around here.

'Olive, shouldn't you go?' I say.

Olive smiles then says, 'Actually, I've decided to stick around, just for a while.'

Zen groans. 'Not another one. What's the point of freeing ghosts if you don't cross over to the other side? I bet it's amazing over there, Olive. There are probably loads of American GIs wanting to dance with you, and they'll be no rationing. You can eat as much spam as you like!'

Olive crosses her legs and adjusts the straps on her dungarees. 'That does sound jolly, Zen, but a therapy whippet called Lucy is visiting the old folks' home tomorrow and I can't miss that.'

'Seriously?' says Zen. 'You're passing up on paradise for a dog called Lucy?'

Olive gives us a mischievous grin. 'OK, it's not just that. I don't want to leave until you've got Peg out. She's my chum and you don't just abandon a chum, do you? The moment she's out, I promise I'll go.' Then she jumps to her feet.

'Where are you going?' I say.

'Back to the Halfway House. I need to let Peg know I'm still here. She probably thinks I left without saying goodbye!'

And with that she strides away from us, back towards the graveyard. Moments later, the plane on the horizon breaks up into little clouds that fade away to nothing.

CHAPTER SIXTEEN

I'm smiling when I let myself into the model village. It feels amazing knowing that we've got another ghost out. Even if I did see Peg's freckle vanish and Will is right about his finger, it's not the end of the world because Plan B works. From now on we don't have to wait for lightning to free the ghosts. I hear seagulls calling out from the rooftops and I smile, letting this brilliant feeling wash over me.

Then I realise that there is one thing that could make this moment even better: a Crunchie! I can see Dad moving around inside the kiosk so I decide to ask if I can have one.

'Dad,' I say, as I throw open the door, 'can I have a . . .'

The words slip away from my lips because the man standing in front of me isn't Dad . . . It's Old Scratch!

Old Scratch's fingers curl into fists as he stares at me with wild eyes. I don't scream. I'm so shocked I can barely breathe. He smiles, revealing a row of small brown teeth, and my stomach flips with fear. I back away, reaching for the door handle.

He moves so fast that I don't stand a chance.

Grabbing hold of my shoulder, he shoves me out of the way and slams the door shut. I open my mouth, but before I can scream he clamps bony fingers across my mouth. I wriggle and kick, but he just lifts me off the ground. He's so strong I soon realise there's no way I can escape.

'Listen to me!' he snarls in my ear.

I twist and turn and lift my feet up to bang them on the floor, but he just holds me higher so that my feet are dangling. I can't move, or make a sound; his grip is like iron. All I can do is fix my eyes on the door that leads to the cottage and desperately hope that Dad comes out.

'I warned you, Sidonie Jones,' he hisses in my ear. 'Didn't I tell you bad things would happen if you kept visiting the Halfway House? Well, those bad things have already begun.'

I throw my weight from side to side, but he squeezes me even tighter.

'You think I'm the villain, don't you?' He laughs bitterly. 'I can feel you shrinking from me like I'm a monster. But ask yourself this: who made me this way?' He waits for a moment then rasps two words in my ear, '*The Innkeeper* . . . Now you have your monster!'

I finally stop struggling. My heart pounds and my legs shake, but I keep quiet because I want to hear what he's going to say next.

'The Innkeeper does not like people who get in their way,' Old Scratch says. 'They will crush you, Sidonie Jones, just as you might crush a fly buzzing about your face. Do you understand?' He waits until I nod my head, then he shoves me away from him and reaches for the door handle.

'I don't believe you,' I blurt out. 'There is no Innkeeper. You're just saying that to scare me!'

Old Scratch's eyes narrow as he stares down at me. 'Believe what you like, but hear this: those who meddle with the Innkeeper do not live to tell the tale!'

Then, after giving me one final unblinking stare, he turns, yanks open the door and strides out of the kiosk.

I stumble after him in time to see him disappearing down the lane . . . But he could come back. I turn and run towards the cottage, fumbling for my keys, but the door is open.

'Dad!' I yell, as I burst into the kitchen. 'DAD!'

There is no answer, but I can hear the TV on in the front room. Quickly I lock the door behind me and find Dad fast asleep on the sofa with a blanket pulled over his shoulders.

'Dad!' I say, shaking him awake.

His eyes fly open. For a second he looks at me, confused, then he smiles and yawns. 'Sorry, love. I didn't know where I was for a moment. I took some medicine for my headache and it must have knocked me out. I can't seem to shift this cold.'

His cheeks are flushed and when I put my hand against his forehead it's hot and clammy.

Suddenly he groans. 'I haven't even shut up the model village . . . Hey, what's the matter with you?'

I can't tell Dad what just happened. If I say that I found man in his kiosk he might call the police, and what good would that do? I'd have to lie to them and the thought of doing that makes me feel sick. Plus if Dad thinks a stranger has been lurking around the model village he'll stop me from going out on my own, and that's no good. Despite everything Old Scratch said, I'm determined to keep helping the ghosts.

So I force myself to smile and say, 'I didn't know where you were, that's all. I was worried. Do you want me to lock up?'

He nods. 'Would you mind, Sid? I've got the worst headache.' He flops back and that's when I notice how thin he has got. His cold has made him lose his appetite.

'After I've locked up I'll make us some food,' I say. 'Is beans on toast OK?'

But Dad has already shut his eyes. I pull the blanket over his shoulders, tucking him in. Then I see something that makes me stop and stare. A couple of glittering specks of dust are drifting through the air above Dad. I reach forward, but they vanish before I can grab hold of them.

It looked like the dust that floats off the ghosts, but why would there be any in the cottage? Before Old Scratch went into the kiosk, did he come here and stand over Dad? I tell myself that it must have come off my clothes, but I just don't know.

Feeling slightly wild and reckless, I walk into the kitchen, grab a tin of beans from the cupboard and dump the contents in a pan. I click the gas on, shove some bread under the grill then unlock the back door.

In the few minutes that I've been inside, dusk has fallen. The moon is already out, lighting up the tiny buildings and shining on the pretend sea. Dad left the electrics turned on and waves wash up and down the fake beach, making a gentle swooshing sound.

I glance into the dark corners of the model village. I feel scared, but I feel something else too. I'm angry. How dare Old Scratch come into this place that belongs to me and Dad? How dare he scare me like that? If he thinks he can bully me into giving up on the ghosts, then he is in for a big surprise.

CHAPTER SEVENTEEN

I'm quiet during dinner, but Dad is too distracted by his cold to notice. As I think over what Old Scratch said and did, he coughs and sneezes into a piece of kitchen roll. In the end he abandons his beans on toast and takes himself off to bed. 'Night, Sid,' he says, as he shuffles up the stairs. 'Don't stay up too late.'

The second I hear his bedroom door close, I pick up the phone and ring Zen. In a whisper, I tell him everything that happened.

When I've finished he lets out a big sigh then says, 'That must have been terrifying, Sid, and I think I owe you an apology. It sounds like there really is an Innkeeper.'

'Maybe,' I say, trying to remember everything

Old Scratch said to me. 'All I know for certain is that he was desperate to keep us away from the Halfway House. I think he'd have said anything to make us give up.'

After a moment Zen says, 'But we're not going to, are we?'

'No way. Not when we've just worked out how to get the ghosts out without lightning.'

'Good,' Zen says and we talk for a bit longer, agreeing not to tell Bones or the other ghosts what happened. If we do that then we'll have Old Scratch and the ghosts trying to get us to give up.

'Be careful, Sid,' says Zen before he cuts the call.

With Dad upstairs in bed the house feels quiet and the fear I felt earlier comes creeping back. Keeping my eyes away from the dark windows, I make some hot chocolate then go up to my room to work on my map. I know this will make me feel calmer. It always does.

I spread my map out across the floor then grab a pencil. My map might be full of pictures, but I can always find space to add more. I begin by pencilling new dots of sand on to Fathom's beach. Then I change to a darker green pencil and I work my way around Fathom's streets, adding things here and there until I find my way to the graveyard.

I start drawing leaves around the Halfway House. Soon a multitude of green surrounds the inn. Then I notice that the leaf pattern I'm drawing is just like the one Sally has tattooed on her wrist. 'Earth, water, fire, hear my spell,' I whisper, as I draw the three looping leaves then add a stem.

Strange, I think, and I sit back to see if I've drawn the pattern anywhere else.

Suddenly I realise that it's everywhere – around my bedroom window, twisting around the edge of the model village, all over the graveyard. I must have been drawing it for days without realising it. Zen and I have visited the Black Spot Cat Café a lot over the past few months so I guess I must have seen it there, either on Sally or on one of our drinks, then started adding it to my map without realising it.

I decide that it looks good and I use it to add more leaves to the roof of the Halfway House. As I draw, I let my mind wander inside the building and down the stone steps that lead to the cellar. Questions start to fill my mind. *Is there really an Innkeeper? Why does Old Scratch collect the*

ghosts' dust? What does he do with it once he goes down those stairs?

I'm sure the answer lies in the cellar.

I'm lost in these thoughts when a dark figure steps through my wardrobe door.

I yell, throwing down my pen and wriggling backwards, but then I see that the figure has bright red nails and is wearing dungarees. 'Olive, you terrified me!'

'Sorry, old girl,' she says, plonking herself down on my bed. 'I've had the most marvellous evening! Ginger got out his old photographs and we had a lovely time looking through them. I know he can't see me, but I do wonder if he knows I'm close. He even said, "You always did look smashing in yellow, old girl," and he said it out loud, as if he knew I was sitting next to him!'

'Did you see Peg?' I say.

'I popped in, but I won't be visiting tomorrow night. Old Scratch always turns up on a Friday evening so I'll be staying well away.'

'What, every Friday?' I say. 'How come you never told us?'

She shrugs. 'You and Zen always visit during the day.

There didn't seem the need.' Then she tells me how Peg is getting on without her. 'Apparently Radulfus misses me terribly. He placed his nubbly head in my lap, Sid, and looked up at me with his big eyes. It broke my heart!' Then she gives me one of her biggest smiles and says, 'I say, Sid, is there any chance you could free Peg next?'

I laugh. 'You're only saying that because she's your friend.'

'That's true, but she's got ever such an easy problem to solve compared to the others.'

Then she starts listing the ghosts' unfinished business, explaining why each one is more complicated than Peg's. 'Think about it, Sid. Holkar needs to solve a murder – tricky. Beau wants to hold up a stagecoach. Bless him. They don't even exist any more! Emma . . . honestly, I haven't the foggiest what her unfinished business is, but it's got something to do with Wayne. Mei wants to find her plane that was lost at sea – impossible! And that leaves Will and his thing for stroking a kangaroo. You see, Sid, Peg is the obvious choice.'

'But she can't remember what her unfinished business is! When I first started visiting she said she needed to find her lost cheese, but now she's not sure she got that right.' It's not surprising Peg's confused. The longer the ghosts are in the Halfway House, the more they forget, and Peg's been in there for over four hundred years.

'Ah!' says Olive, delighted. 'Well, this afternoon I told her that she's got to pull her socks up and have a jolly good think if she wants to get out of that place, and now she says it's not her cheese she's after, but her book of charms.'

Book of charms . . . I know I've heard those words before. For a moment I'm not sure where, but then I remember the conversation I had with Abigail at the Museum of Curiosities.

'She wants to find her spell book,' I say. 'Why didn't she tell us before?'

'She says it just came back to her, but between you and me, Sid, I think she wanted to keep it a secret. Apparently witches guard their spell books with their lives and they're not supposed to go around blabbing about them. Anyway, do say you will give it some thought, darling Sid.'

She gazes up at me with her big brown eyes and I remember Peg's disappearing freckle. Bones and Zen think I imagined it, but if I didn't then perhaps it would be a good idea to free her next.

'A book will be easier to find than cheese,' I say. 'It won't have rotted away for one thing.'

Olive bounces on my bed and claps her hands with delight. 'I'll take that as a "yes". Thank you, Sid!'

'Tomorrow is Friday,' I say, 'so we can spend the weekend looking for Peg's spell book – if it still exists.' I start putting my pens into my schoolbag, then I see my homework diary and groan.

'Whatever is the matter?' asks Olive.

'Zen and I have a history test on the Second World War tomorrow. We were supposed to revise, but instead we freed Ginger!' *And I bumped into Old Scratch*, I add in my head.

'In that case, I shall come to school with you,' says Olive. 'I can whisper answers in your ear; I'm an expert on the war.'

'That should work,' I say. 'Zen and I are in different classes, but our classrooms are next door to each other so you can drift between them. Poor Zen. He's probably trying to revise right now. He hates doing badly in tests.'

'I'll go and tell him the good news!' says Olive, and with that she jumps off my bed and runs through my bedroom door.

As I fold up my map, I wonder what Zen will think when Olive suddenly appears in his bedroom. Then I think about something else.

Old Scratch is expecting me to stay away from the ghosts and the Halfway House, but what if I do the opposite? Olive said that Old Scratch always turns up on a Friday evening. I imagine hiding in the cupboard by the fireplace, waiting until he's done his dusting, then following him down into the cellar. I might finally get an answer to some of the questions that are buzzing around my head.

But would I really dare to do it?

Yes, I think, as I put my map in its holder. *I would.*

CHAPTER EIGHTEEN

I wake up the next morning to find Olive sitting on the end of my bed.

'Time for school!' she says, her dark curls bobbing around her cheeks. 'Oh, Sid, I can't wait to see all the things you've told us about: the pasta station; the magic whiteboards that teachers write on with their fingers; the naughty girls and boys with their white socks. *And* I'm going to get a ride on a bus. What larks!'

Olive hovers around me as I get dressed, telling me that my uniform is as dull as ditchwater and that I could do with a touch of rouge on my cheeks. As I knot my tie and find a matching pair of socks, I find it almost impossible to believe what happened in the kiosk yesterday. Everything feels so normal. This is backed up when Dad knocks on my door to tell me that he's feeling a bit better and has made pancakes. It's like last night was a bad dream.

I go into the bathroom with Olive following close behind.

'You can't stay in here,' I say when she perches on the edge of the bath. 'I want to go to the toilet.'

'Oh, Sid, don't be such a prude. Girls always go to the lav together. It's what chums do.'

'Not this girl,' I say.

'Fine,' she mutters, then she walks through the wall and into Dad's bedroom. A second later, she sticks her head back into the bathroom. 'Sid! Your father is standing on one leg in his *underpants*!'

'He's doing yoga,' I say. I know because I can hear the calming voice of his instructor. 'He tries to do it every day. He gets the videos off YouTube.'

'Yoga?' she says. '*YouTube*? Gosh!' Then she disappears back into Dad's room.

Olive chatters away through breakfast and refuses to leave my side even when I'm doing my teeth. It's a relief when we finally meet Zen by the ice cream.

'You all right?' he asks, giving me a meaningful look.

'I'm OK,' I say, then I change the subject by asking Zen what he thinks about freeing Peg next.

'It's definitely worth a shot,' he says.

Bones doesn't get on the bus today, so Olive takes his seat in front of us. As we're trundling along the coast road, chatting about Peg's book of charms, I warn her that she'll need to move when Mo gets on.

'And remember we can't talk to you when she's around,' I say.

'Roger that,' says Olive. 'Don't forget I'm trained in undercover surveillance, Sid. You won't even know I'm on the bus!'

The bus slows down and Mo gets on. Straight away she pulls a foil packet out of her big bag and shares out some muffins she's made.

'Hey, Sid,' she says through a mouthful of crumbs. 'Can I come and see your model village tomorrow?'

I'd love to show Mo round the model village – I think she'd love it – but we're spending the weekend looking for Peg's book of charms.

'I can't tomorrow,' I say. 'I'm sorry.'

Mo's face falls. 'No worries,' she says. 'It was just a thought.'

I feel terrible, especially when she goes red and takes her water bottle out of her bag and starts gulping it down. I'm sure she's disappointed.

'We'll do it soon,' I say. 'Maybe next weekend?'

Mo clicks the lid on her bottle and smiles. 'I'd love that.'

Olive meanwhile has found another seat and is sitting next to a lady who has a baby on her lap. As Mo, Zen and I talk about *Minecraft* and axolotls – Mo has one called Pinky – Olive chats to the mum and baby, apparently not caring that they can't see or hear her. I do wonder about the baby, though. When Olive starts blowing raspberries at him, he bursts out laughing and tries to grab her nose. Maybe the baby has *the gift*, I think, as I sink my teeth into one of Mo's still warm chocolate muffins.

We have history first thing and for our test we have to choose a question and write our answer as an essay. I decide to write about 'Life on the Home Front', as I'm sure this is what Olive will know most about.

I'm right. She hovers by my side barely drawing breath as she describes rationing, fashion and blackouts. I scribble away, but every five minutes she has to drift through the wall to help Zen in the next room.

When this happens I pretend to read over my answer, but really I'm just waiting for her to come back.

At the end of the lesson, Miss Khan says that as we've got a few minutes spare she'd like to hear what we've written. 'Sid,' she says. 'Why don't you go first? I noticed you carefully checking your work.'

The rest of the class turn to look at me.

'Oh, marvellous!' says Olive who has just swept back into the room and plonked herself down in an empty seat. 'Do read out what you've written, Sid. It's jolly good.'

'Oh . . . I don't think it is jolly good, I mean, good,' I say to both Miss Khan and Olive.

A few of the students snigger, but Miss Khan beams encouragingly and says, 'I'm sure it is. Off you go.'

So I have no choice but to read my strange, rambling essay out loud.

'*Obviously everyone had to keep their chins up on the home front during the Second World War and do their best to help the brave chaps fighting against Hitler,*' I say. '*This meant they had to eat an awful lot of carrots. You see carrots were cheap, there were lots of them and, as everyone knows, they helped you see at night, which was super useful if one*'

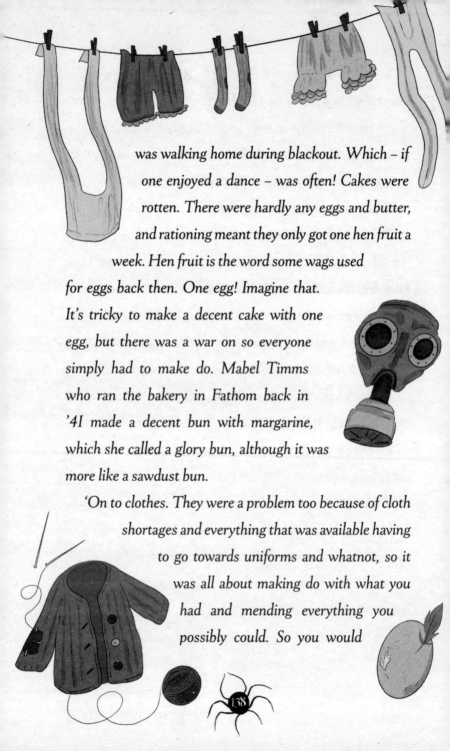

was walking home during blackout. Which – if one enjoyed a dance – was often! Cakes were rotten. There were hardly any eggs and butter, and rationing meant they only got one hen fruit a week. Hen fruit is the word some wags used for eggs back then. One egg! Imagine that. It's tricky to make a decent cake with one egg, but there was a war on so everyone simply had to make do. Mabel Timms who ran the bakery in Fathom back in '41 made a decent bun with margarine, which she called a glory bun, although it was more like a sawdust bun.

'On to clothes. They were a problem too because of cloth shortages and everything that was available having to go towards uniforms and whatnot, so it was all about making do with what you had and mending everything you possibly could. So you would

unravel dishcloths and knit them into splendid cardis, and make woollies look ace by replacing the sleeves with striped ones made of odd bits of yarn. Also your knicker gusset could be reinforced with a piece of sturdy cloth, although, as you can imagine, they looked hopeless.'

I finish speaking just as the bell rings. For a moment the classroom is utterly silent. Miss Khan and the students are staring at me open-mouthed.

'Marvellous!' says Olive, applauding enthusiastically. 'I couldn't have said it better myself.'

Then Miss Khan shuts her mouth, smiles and says, 'Well done, Sid. A fascinating essay, if a little informal at times.'

CHAPTER NINETEEN

After school we find Bones waiting at the bus stop so we go straight to the graveyard to question Peg.

Of course, Zen and I are extra careful today about checking for Old Scratch. We creep from grave to grave while Bones and Olive drift along behind us. When we see the windows of the pub twinkling between the trees we crouch down behind a monument.

While we watch the Halfway House, looking for Old Scratch, Zen and I whisper about our history tests.

'Most of my essay was about working on a dairy farm,' says Zen. 'It was all about bovine diarrhoea and farmers "flipping their lid because certain girls, like Jessie 'Sweaty' Rogers, couldn't remember to shut the gates"!'

'At least you didn't tell everyone how to reinforce their knickers,' I say.

'No, but I did tell them how to make bras out of parachute silk,' says Zen.

'That's enough chatter about undergarments,' says Bones. 'Shall we approach? I am sure it is safe. There is no sign of the rogue.'

I put my hand on his arm and the cold sweeps through me. 'Just . . . one more minute,' I say. 'We need to be careful.'

Bones looks at me sharply. 'Why so cautious all of a sudden, Jones?'

Zen comes to my rescue. 'Better safe than sorry,' he says. 'We freed Olive yesterday so Old Scratch will be furious.'

Bones's eyes narrow even more. 'That may be true, but I think it is safe now.'

So the four of us creep forward, and after peering through the window I open the door.

The ghosts rush over, greeting us with their usual enthusiasm.

'Hello, darlings,' says Olive, strolling inside and giving Peg a hug.

Meanwhile Bones keeps well back from the door. 'I do not know how you can bear to go inside that place,' he mutters.

'Us land girls are obviously made of tougher stuff than pirates,' says Olive, making Peg cackle with laughter.

Zen and I stay on the doorstep, ready to run the second the cuckoo pops out or we hear footsteps on the stairs. As an extra precaution I ask Will to sit close to the door and to listen carefully. Then, when we are all settled, I tell Peg that we're going to try and sort out her unfinished business next. As I speak I watch her carefully, keeping a close eye on her freckles, but they all seem to be staying safely attached to her face.

'Can you remember where your book of charms is?' I ask.

'Shhhh!' she says. 'It is a mighty powerful book, Sid, and I would not like it to fall into the wrong hands.'

'Why do you need to find it?' asks Zen.

Peg looks shocked by his ignorance. 'Why, everyone knows that a witch must not be separated from their spell book. On death it should be buried with its owner, or destroyed, only mine was lost. Knowing my book is lying abandoned makes me hurt right here.' She thumps her chest making dust spill out of her. There's so much floating around today that it drifts out of the pub door, making me sneeze. Peg carries on. 'If you are to get me out of this place, you must find my book and bury it with me.'

'*With you?*' I say. 'Like, literally . . . *in your hands*? Can't we just bury it close to your grave?'

Peg laughs showing wonky brown teeth. 'Scared of old bones are you, Sid Jones? You're a funny sort of witch.'

I groan. Not this again. 'I'm not a witch!'

She waves away my words with one warty hand. 'Yes, yes, we know. I suppose I don't need it to be buried with me. I just need to see it, then you can throw it in the sea, or destroy it. I won't need magic where I'm going.'

Zen says, 'We can decide what to do with it once we've found it. Where do you think it is?'

Quickly I take out my notebook and as Peg talks I write down everything she says.

'Well, as you know, I've forgotten a lot because of bein' stuck in here. For over one hundred years it were just me and Old Scratch.' A small, furry head pops up next to her. It's Radulfus, Peg's goat. He rubs his horns against her hands and bleats.

'Yes, yes, I know. I had you too,' says Peg, 'but they were long, lonely days, make no mistake, and durin' that time I forgot where I placed my book of charms. The only thing I know for certain is that I hid it with my cheese.' Then a look of alarm crosses her face. 'But I can't remember where I hid that!'

'The more I talked to Sid and Zen, the more I remembered,' says Bones. 'So why not start by telling us about your cheese?'

'It all began when Lottie Prentice told everyone I was a witch,' she says.

Zen frowns. 'But you *are* a witch.'

Peg shrugs. 'Yes, but I'm a kind one, a blessings witch. I used my magic for kind deeds.' She waves her hand through the air as if she's holding an invisible wand. '*Shrivel and waste, you perilous pest!*' she says in a sing-song voice. 'That was my second-best spell. It's how I got rid of weeds on my mother's cabbage patch.'

'Tell us about Lottie Prentice,' I remind her.

'Oh yes! She accused me of bein' one of the wicked sorts of witches. Now us blessings witches do good stuff like makin' flowers bloom extra big and breakin'

bad spells other witches have done.' Peg pauses to make sure I've got all that down, then she moves on to the next, shocking part of her story. 'But Lottie Prentice started goin' round tellin' people I gave her WARTS! She always were a liar. What actually happened was I made her a poultice of mice droppings and fennel seeds to get *rid* of her warts. Anyway, I were so annoyed with Lottie that I stole her cheese. My goodness, she were proud of it, always going on about *my cheese this* and *my cheese that.*'

Holkar sighs deeply, but Peg doesn't even pause in her story. 'Then one day I was walkin' past her house and I saw her famous cheese sittin' under a scrap of muslin and, God forgive me, I pinched it!' Peg doesn't look like she wants God's forgiveness. She's grinning at the memory. 'Next thing I know Lottie has gone and told the vicar I'd given the cheese to Lucifer. What a load of codswallop! The vicar said to prove I hadn't given it to Lucifer I had to take him to the cheese d'rectly, and that's where we were all off to – me, Lottie Prentice, Radulfus, the vicar and half the village – when it happened.'

'What happened?' I ask, looking up from my notebook.

'I got trod on by a cow!' Four hundred years after the event and Peg still looks outraged. 'To be truthful, the cow trod on Radulfus first, and then she trod on me, but the next thing I knew I was as dead as a doornail and wanderin' around Fathom, desperate to find my book of charms.'

'Which was hidden with your cheese?' I say.

Peg nods eagerly. 'That's right!'

Then Zen says, 'Think carefully, Peg. Where did you hide your cheese?'

Peg screws up her face. 'To begin with I buried it, but then I thought better of it – on account of worms – so I dug it up and put it –' suddenly her face lights up – 'in my hidey-hole where I hid all my precious things!'

I feel a rush of excitement. 'And where was your hidey-hole?'

'I don't know!' she wails, flopping against the invisible barrier.

This feels like we're going round and round in circles, but then Zen says, 'Hey, Sid, you've got a place where you hide stuff, haven't you?'

I nod. 'Under a loose board at the bottom of my bed.'

'I hide things in an old tin Dad gave me,' says Zen. 'It's on top of my wardrobe.'

146

Olive laughs. 'I used to swipe my big sister's bottles of scent and my mum's toffees and hide them inside my teddy bear.'

'Bedrooms!' I cry, making everyone look at me. 'All our hidey-holes are in our bedrooms so perhaps Peg's was too.'

'In my experience,' says Holkar in his clipped, precise voice, 'a child's home is their world and their bedroom, where they dream and play, is the centre of that world.'

'Well, I don't know nothin' about that,' says Peg. 'But I did have a fine home and a room where I slept with my three sisters. It were cosy when all of us were curled up together on our mattress with the coals glowin' in the fireplace.'

'Where did you live?' I ask, wondering if there's any chance Peg's house is still standing.

Peg has no problem remembering this. 'Two up from the Benbow. My father built it himself and we had *glass* in our windows.'

I have an exciting thought and take my map out to see if I'm right.

Ivy trails over it as I hold it out to show Zen and Bones. 'Look, two up from the Benbow is the Black Spot Cat Café

147

and it's one of the oldest buildings in Fathom. I bet that's where Peg used to live!'

'What is a cat café?' asks Peg.

'Well,' says Bones, and then he launches into a detailed explanation, naming all of Sally's fifteen cats and describing their personalities.

Peg listens carefully, her eyes wide, and it's while I'm watching a smile light up her face that I see another of her freckles disappear. This time it's one on her cheek. I'm just wondering if I should say anything when Will jumps to his feet and cries out, 'Scratch!'

A moment later the cuckoo pops out.

Fear pushes all thoughts of freckles out of my mind. All I can think about is the way Old Scratch stared at me in the kiosk. If he finds me here the day after he warned me off, I don't know what he'll do.

'Get out of there!' I hiss to Olive. The moment she's out of the pub, I shut the door and we run back through the graveyard.

The others follow me and we don't stop running until I get to my grandad's fishing hut.

Then, with shaking hands, I take the key from under a stone, unlock the door and we bundle inside.

It's dark and gloomy in the fishing hut. It takes a moment for my eyes to adjust. Then I see Grandad's boat surrounded by lobster pots and crates, and beyond that shelves stacked high with varnish, paint and tools. It smells delicious, of oil and the sea. Usually I love being in here, but right now I can hardly take it in. I'm too busy thinking about Peg's freckles.

'Gosh, what a marvellous hideout!' says Olive, gazing at the fishing nets and buoys that hang from the ceiling.

I lock the door behind us and pocket the key.

Zen pulls himself up to the prow of Grandad's boat, *Old Buoy*, while the rest of us sit on upturned crates. Through the window the sun is sinking towards a mackerel-coloured sea. It's beautiful, peaceful and it certainly doesn't match how I feel. I have to sit on my hands to stop them from shaking.

'So,' says Bones, folding his arms and staring at me. 'I think it is time you told me what is going on.'

'What do you mean?' I say, but I'm given away by the blush that is creeping over my face.

'You have never run like that from Old Scratch before,' he says. 'You have locked us inside here and now look at you: you are quaking and look like more like a ghost than Emma!'

'It's true, old girl,' says Olive kindly. 'And Zen doesn't look entirely innocent. The two of you have a secret. Spit it out.'

Zen and I look at each other. For a moment I consider lying, but I've never been much good at that.

So instead I take a deep breath and tell them everything that happened last night.

When I've finished, Bones is agitated. He shakes his big head and scowls. 'This is a rum business, make no mistake. Perhaps the old villain was telling the truth and there is an Innkeeper, or the whole thing could have been a pack of lies. What does it matter? Clearly he means to cause you harm, so from now on the two of you must stay away from the Halfway House!'

'We can't stay away now,' I protest. 'It's more urgent than ever that we get the ghosts out. At the Halfway House just now I saw another of Peg's freckles disappear!'

Bones opens his mouth to speak, but I get there first.

'Don't even think of saying I imagined it because I didn't, and that's not all. Will said something has changed

150

and I think he's right. Things are starting to disappear from the ghosts and there is loads more dust floating around than usual.'

Olive frowns. 'But, Sid, ghosts don't fade in the Halfway House. It's a timeless tavern!'

'I know what I saw,' I insist, then I turn back to Bones. 'I know you won't like this, Bones, but I can't stay away from the Halfway House. In fact, I'm going back as soon as I can, and I'm going to go into the cellar.' *Tonight*, I add in my head.

Bones jumps to his feet. 'No!' he bellows. 'It is too dangerous. Have you taken leave of your senses, girl?'

I stand up too and raise my chin. 'You are always telling me that sometimes we must sail into a storm.'

'Yes, a *storm*,' he shouts, 'not a cellar that lies below an enchanted inn that happens to be the lair of a very wicked man!' Then he crouches down so his face is close to mine and I can smell smoke and the sea oozing from his wet clothes. 'On no account are you to set foot in that cellar, missy. Even if I was willing to go into the Halfway House – and let me make this clear, *I am not* – how could I protect you? My hands are useless.'

151

To prove his point, he attempts to grab one of Grandad's lobster pots and his fingers slip straight through it.

Just like I thought, he's never going to be persuaded, so I say, 'Fine, let's talk about Peg's book of charms. We need to work out how we can get upstairs at the Black Spot Cat Café.'

After looking at me for a moment longer Bones nods, but while Olive, Zen and Bones talk about mounting night-time raids, causing distractions and gathering intelligence, my mind stays firmly fixed on the door at the back of the Halfway House. Eventually we fix on a plan and call it Operation Cheese – because we know Peg would hate us to mention her spell book – and we agree to meet outside the café tomorrow morning just before it opens.

Zen and I leave Bones and Olive at the fishing hut and step into the cool evening air. We walk home quickly, sticking to the busier lanes of the village, talking about Operation Cheese, but before Zen goes into the museum, he looks at me and says, 'You're planning on going into the cellar, aren't you?'

'I have to,' I say. 'And I'm going to do it tonight. Please come with me.'

Zen groans. 'Do I have to?'

'If you don't, then I'm going on my own,' I say.

He shakes his head. 'The things I do for you, Sid Jones.'

'I gave you *the gift*, didn't I? If you come with me tonight, then you'll have paid me back.'

Zen smiles. 'It's a deal.'

CHAPTER TWENTY

It's easy to come up with a plan to go to the Halfway House. On Fridays Dad goes with Zen's mum and the rest of their team to the pub quiz, and Zen comes round to my house to keep me company.

Tonight will be no different, only instead of playing *Minecraft*, the second Dad goes out we're going to the graveyard. It doesn't matter how long we're in the Halfway House because time doesn't move in there. We'll only be gone for half an hour. Our parents won't suspect a thing.

It's the perfect plan until Zen's dad decides he wants to go to the quiz too and it's agreed that Zen and I are old enough to babysit Zen's sister, Skye.

I can't say no, not without sounding suspicious, so I find

myself being dropped off at the museum by Dad.

'Sorry, Sid,' says Zen after our parents have gone. 'But maybe it's for the best. Perhaps Bones is right and it is too dangerous to go into that cellar.'

I don't say anything, but all the time we're playing with Skye and reading her stories, my thoughts stay on the cellar. I know that tonight is the perfect opportunity to go in there. It's much better to follow Old Scratch after he's done his dusting because there is more chance that we'll see what he does with his bottle, but as every second ticks past, I know the opportunity is slipping away from me.

In the end, I wait until Skye is fast asleep, then I tell Zen I'm going on my own.

Of course he tries to persuade me out of it, but I'm determined.

'If you're not back in half an hour then I'm telling Bones!' are the last words he says to me as I slip out of the museum.

My footsteps ring out on the cobblestones as I creep past the Admiral Benbow. Laughter seeps from inside, along with the sound of loud conversations and the smell of chips and beer. I hurry past. The sky is clear and full of stars, and to my right the sea is a barely moving sheet of inky blue.

Not quite believing what I'm about to do, I run up the lane and into the graveyard. Stone angels watch as I take the route I know so well, crunching over gravel and slipping on wet leaves. It's dark and I'm totally alone, and I feel cold and scared but also determined. For so long Old Scratch has had the upper hand, but all that could change tonight.

Soon I'm creeping up to one of the candlelit windows of the Halfway House.

Inside I see Will slumped on a chair, his face resting in two grubby hands. The other ghosts are dotted around the room. They look particularly sad tonight. I guess they are dreading Old Scratch's visit. My eyes move to the door to the cellar. It's shut. Old Scratch isn't here . . . but he will be soon.

I go to the door and reach for the handle. But then fear gets the better of me and I hesitate. *Can I really do this?* Instinct makes me touch my map. As usual it's in its holder under my jumper. I feel its familiar hard edges and hear it crackle. It makes me feel safe and it gives me the courage I need to open the door.

CHAPTER TWENTY-ONE

'You're bloomin' brave, Sid,' Will whispers.

I'm crouched in the cupboard, waiting to pull the door shut the moment Old Scratch comes up the stairs.

'Or perhaps "bloomin' foolish" would be a more apt description,' says Holkar.

The six ghosts left in the Halfway House are gathered round me. Even Emma is drifting backwards and forwards, her huge black eyes fixed on me. They're all so curious about what's down in the cellar that only Holkar has tried to talk me out of it.

'Do you know why I ended up in here?' he asks. 'I'm a detective who dug a little too deep. I'm sure you've heard of the saying, "Curiosity killed the cat"?'

'I'll be careful,' I promise. 'I just want to see what he does in there and then I'll come straight out.'

'We have had a wager going for over one hundred years about that cellar,' says Beau. 'I say he has barrels of fine wine and jewels down there.'

'Nah, it's old clocks,' says Peg.

'I think it's dead bodies!' says Will, grinning with excitement.

His words make me wonder if this is a terrible idea after all, but I don't have time to change my mind because just then the wooden doors on the cuckoo clock spring open and the bird starts to call.

The ghosts scurry back to their normal seats and I squeeze myself further into the cupboard, closing the door behind me. Then I put my face to the crack in the wood and get ready to watch everything that Old Scratch does.

The door slams open so fast that it bounces off the wall. Then Old Scratch steps into the room. He's on his own and his dog is nowhere to be seen. He stands very still. His coat, hair and skin are all the same yellowish colour of bone. He's so pale that he seems to glow in the darkness. His eyes slide from ghost to ghost and I realise that he's counting them, checking they are all here.

Next he tugs the silk handkerchief from his pocket and starts to dust, only today it seems to make him furious. He swipes the handkerchief over the tops of tables and around the clocks, pausing to force the sparkly golden dust into a bottle. Every now and then he peers at the bottle before scowling and shoving it back into his pocket.

After half an hour he's done.

He goes to the cellar door, but before he leaves he gives the ghosts one last hard stare. 'Remember, I am always watching you,' he says in a dry snarl. Then he is off, slamming the door behind him and stomping down the stairs.

I wait for a few minutes then creep out of my hiding place.

The ghosts jump off their benches and chairs and walk with me to the cellar door. Will slips his hand into mine. It's like my fingers have been wrapped in an icy glove.

'Sid,' he says. 'You know you can change your mind. None of us will think you are a coward.'

'I'll be back before you know it,' I say, more to reassure myself than anyone else.

Will squeezes his fingers even tighter, but I wriggle free and open the door. A flight of stairs leads down into darkness. The air that washes over me is so cold it takes my breath away. It smells of damp earth and stagnant water.

'I wish I could accompany you,' says Beau, 'but, alas, magic keeps me from fulfilling my gentlemanly duty.' To prove his point, he reaches forward until his hands touch another invisible barrier covering the door.

'Well, I 'ain't sad I can't go down there,' says Peg, eyeing the stairway. 'It's darker than the devil's pie hole and it smells worse too!'

'Please tell me that a pie hole is a mouth,' I say.

This makes Peg roar with laughter, which gives me the courage I need to step into the darkness and shut the door behind me.

CHAPTER TWENTY-TWO

It's like I've been buried under the earth. Darkness clings to me and it creeps inside me too, making it hard to breathe. I force myself to take a few long, deep breaths, then I pull out the matches and candle that I brought from home. A torch would have been easier, but Zen and I have discovered that things that run on electricity never work in the Halfway House. We don't know how Old Scratch makes his more modern clocks work.

With trembling fingers I strike a match and light the candle. Just like they taught us at primary school, I've put the candle in a circle of cardboard. Partly this is to protect my fingers from hot wax, but it will also stop any telltale drips of wax from falling to the floor. I don't want Old Scratch to ever know I've been down here.

Then I start to walk down the stairs.

The staircase is made of huge slabs of stone that take me further and further underground. Each stone has a dip in the middle. I'm not surprised. Old Scratch has been walking up and down these stairs for over four hundred years. I put my feet where his have trodden and move forward as quietly as possible. Old Scratch rushed out of the pub. He looked like he was in a hurry to get somewhere, but even so he could be lurking round the next corner.

I'm expecting the staircase to open out into a cellar, after all, that's what the ghosts have always said is below the pub – but I quickly realise that this isn't going to happen. The staircase curves, then straightens out, then curves again, going deeper underground, and the air gets even colder. It's smellier too. Under the damp I can pick up the woody tang of cloves. It's Old Scratch's rotten Christmas pudding smell and it makes me feel slightly sick.

Eventually the staircase opens out into a long passageway. I can't see where it ends, the candle only casts enough light for me to see just beyond my feet, but I keep walking.

It seems to go on forever. The hairs on my arms stand on end, prickling my skin and my heart hammers. Once again, panic threatens to overwhelm me and I wish Zen was here with me, but more than anything I wish Bones was by my side. He always seems to know what to do in situations like this: dangerous ones.

As I keep walking forward, I try to imagine what he would say.

Hide, I think.

So I look around for a hiding place, just in case.

Slabs of stone line the walls and ceiling. Except for the odd hollowed-out space in the wall, the passageway is empty. But I've noticed a change. I can see a dim green light up ahead and soon I can make out a door. It's standing slightly open and the faint light falling through it shows that plants have begun to grow in the gaps between the stones. Moss and ferns jostle for space, hanging from the ceiling and covering the walls in a patchwork of green. I press my fingers against the soft springy moss. Then I hear trickling water.

I don't know what exactly is beyond the door, but I need to be careful in case Old Scratch is there.

I blow out my candle, then feel my way along the mossy wall until I reach the door. As quietly as possible, I lean forward and peer through it.

I'm at the bottom of a huge circular pit that's crammed full of plants and trees. Birds rustle and call out from the branches and hidden insects chatter. Flaming torches are attached to the walls.

From their light, and the light of the moon, I can see three other doors leading out of the pit. At first I wonder if this pit I'm standing in might be a quarry, but it's too elegantly built for that. The stone walls are smooth and perfectly curved, the doors are carved, and there is a staircase that winds its way up the wall. It hasn't got a railing and the steps are just slabs of rock jutting out of the wall, defying gravity.

I want to get a closer look so I step through the doorway and, keeping my back against the wall, I inch my way round the pit until I'm at the bottom of the stairs, then I duck behind a craggy tree and peer round its trunk.

From here I can see that the pit is big – about the size of our field at primary school – and pacing around in the centre is Old Scratch. My heart lurches at the sight of his pale bony face and hunched shoulders.

I watch as he walks up and down, pausing occasionally to shoot a glance towards the top of the pit. I wonder if I should run back to the door and get out of here, but I don't want to go until I've found out what he is doing, and who he is waiting for, because he's obviously waiting for someone.

I watch as Old Scratch takes a watch on a chain out of his top pocket, glares at it, then shoves it away again. I press myself against the tree. I'm well hidden and I'm sure he won't hear me because water is falling from somewhere up above, thudding down on the steps, leaving behind a slick trail of algae.

But even without the tangle of plants and the gushing water, I'm not sure Old Scratch would notice me. He seems lost in his thoughts as he paces up and down, a scowl twisting the skin on his forehead.

Suddenly he lifts his head and stares at the top of the pit.

And that's when a voice hisses in my ear, 'Do not make a sound!'

CHAPTER
TWENTY-THREE

Cold sweeps over me and then I smell smoke and the sea.

I turn round and find Bones standing just behind me.

'What have I always told you, Sid Jones?' he whispers. 'You must have eyes in the back as well as the front of your head when you are around Old Scratch!'

'You came and found me!' I whisper, and I'm so happy to see him that his frown vanishes and he smiles.

'It was Zen who told me what you had done. I went along to the museum for a chinwag and he was going out of his mind with worry. Said you'd been gone for over an hour.'

'That can't be right,' I say, confused. 'It only took me a few minutes to run to the graveyard and time stands still once we walk inside the Halfway House.'

Bones interrupts me. 'It doesn't matter if you were missing for a few minutes or an hour, I'm glad Zen told me. You don't head into danger without a pal by your side, Jones. Haven't I taught you anything?'

I put my finger to my lips, reminding him to keep quiet, and that's when I realise what I've made Bones do. 'You had to go inside the Halfway House,' I say. 'I'm sorry, Bones!'

He shakes his big head and water drips to the floor. 'It is me who should be sorry. You and me, Sid, we're shipmates, and shipmates stick together. Olive said something similar about Peg. I should never have let you come here alone.'

'So we can stay?'

'I would say it is too late to leave,' says Bones, glancing at the staircase, and that's when I realise that a figure has appeared at the top of the pit.

I can't tell if the person is a man or a woman. Their face is hidden by the hood of a cloak that trails behind them and they are wearing some sort of mask. Their feet are bare and their hands hang by their sides.

They start to walk down the stone steps. The staircase must be slippery from the water, but each step the figure takes is certain and bold, and it brings them closer to the bottom of the pit and the place where we are hiding.

'We need to get out of here!' I say.

I'm about to creep towards the door, but Bones holds me back. 'No. It is too late. If we run for the door, they will see us. We need to hide.'

His eyes dart around then he points towards the space beneath the slabs at the very bottom of the staircase. Ivy has grown over them making a leafy cave. 'That should keep us hidden,' he whispers.

We drop to the ground and crawl forward. I have to push my way between the leaves, but Bones simply drifts through them. Then we huddle under the stone stairs. The ground under my feet is soggy and leaves tickle the back of my neck, plus Bones is so close to me that I'm freezing. I clamp my mouth shut to stop my teeth from chattering and try to ignore all thoughts of spiders and worms as I wait to see what will happen next.

The footsteps get louder. They echo around the pit. Then the cloaked figure walks down the steps immediately

above our heads and sweeps past our hiding place. Through the leaves I catch a glimpse of the mask. It's made of brown leather stitched together and has a sort of beak. Then I realise it's a plague mask. I've seen one just like it in Zen's mum and dad's museum.

The figure seems to be treading a familiar route through the overgrown plants, and soon they come to a stop directly in front of Old Scratch. Then they stand in silence, the folds of their cloak blowing in the breeze. *Like a phantom*, I think with a shiver.

Suddenly a strong hand shoots out from the cloak and an oily deep voice asks, 'Well? What have you got for me?'

Old Scratch pulls out the bottle of dust. It gleams in the darkness. The figure snatches it from him and the bottle is shaken from side to side. The gold dust swirls.

'I need more.' The voice is cold, hard. 'I don't want a speck of lumin left behind.'

Old Scratch's eyes widen. 'So we're really leaving this place?'

The cloaked figure steps forward. Now their faces are centimetres apart. Old Scratch leans back, trying to get away from the beak of the plague mask.

The voice rings out, echoing around the pit. 'You have left me no choice. I have lost half my lost souls because of your weakness, and yet that girl still roams the streets of Fathom!'

Old Scratch opens his mouth to protest, but he doesn't get the chance. Fingers reach out, grabbing hold of his jaw.

'Don't give me your excuses. Because of you I have had to untangle the magic that surrounds the Halfway House and find a new prison. Soon I will have to find lost souls to fill it. I have discovered the perfect place. It is far north of here – remote, ancient, seeped in magic and misery – but it pains me deeply that I am having to do all this because of your cowardice.'

My mind whirrs as I try to make sense of what I've just heard. Is this the Innkeeper? It must be. They say that the ghosts belong to them. But what do they mean when they say that they have had to 'untangle the magic' of the Halfway House?

'I tried to stop her,' whines Old Scratch.

'*Tried*,' the masked figure mimics Old Scratch's whine and squeezes his face even harder. 'You failed, and now I have had to take matters into my own hands.'

Old Scratch is shoved to the ground. Then after a final dissatisfied shake of the bottle, the figure hisses, 'Meet me tomorrow. I need more.' Then they turn to go.

'Wait!' Old Scratch's voice is desperate. 'What about my payment?'

The cloaked figure swings back to face him. 'What . . . this?'

This time another bottle is pulled from a hidden pocket. It's smaller than the one that was filled with dust. It is drop-shaped with a long neck and a cork in the top. The bottle is swished from side to side and the effect on Old Scratch is instant. He lunges for the bottle, but it is held out of his reach.

'Give it to me!' Old Scratch's voice is desperate. Sweat gleams on his ashen face. 'I earned it, didn't I? I look after that miserable place, day in, day out, and I have done for years!'

'To get lumin you must work!' The words are spat in his face.

Old Scratch clutches his hands in front of his face. 'I do work!'

The Innkeeper puts the bottle away, then like a snake

174

striking, grabs hold of Old Scratch's coat, pulling him close. 'No, you do not. My tavern has been discovered and my lost souls have been stolen under *your* watch!'

Old Scratch is thrown back and he slips and slides in the mud. He staggers to his feet and backs towards one of the three other doors leading from the pit. 'I've got a good mind to walk away from you and your ghosts and never come back!' he shouts.

A horrible laugh bursts from inside the cloak. 'You would never do that. You are as tied to me as those lost souls are tied to the Halfway House.'

'Where's my dog?' Old Scratch asks.

'Gone! After what you did, what did you expect?'

Old Scratch slumps against the door. 'But . . . she is my only companion!'

'She *was* your only companion. Didn't you hear what I said? She's gone. Now stop snivelling.'

With a cry of frustrated rage, Old Scratch wrenches open the door, but before he can leave, the cloaked figure has one final thing to say.

'I've got a message for the girl. Tell her that I've been watching her for some time. Let her know that I'm coming for her!' The words are hurled at Old Scratch's back as he disappears through the door. They swirl around the pit. They find me where I am huddled under the stone staircase, and they make me tremble with fear.

The cloaked figure stands very still. A lone moth flies past, drawn to one of the flaming torches. Water trickles. Something crawls up my hand and I flinch, snapping a twig under my foot.

Then two things happen at once. The Innkeeper's hand shoots out, crushing the moth, and their masked face turns to where we are hiding.

CHAPTER
TWENTY-FOUR

The pit is alive with sound: insects scuttle, branches brush against each other, water splashes. Could the Innkeeper – because I'm sure that's who the hooded figure is – really have heard the twig snap under my foot?

Next to me, Bones sits utterly still. Neither of us dare to speak or move. We're trapped in our hiding place and all we can do is stay as still as possible and hope the Innkeeper goes away.

But like a cat who has caught a glimpse of movement, the figure starts to prowl around the pit. I don't know who or what is underneath the cloak, but they are clearly strong.

They shove aside brambles and break branches that are in their way. Their bare feet squelch into the wet ground as they jump over boulders and force their way through thick weeds.

Bones looks at me and gives me the tiniest of nods. He can't speak, but I understand what he's saying. He's warning me that trouble is heading our way. Our hiding place is good, but only as long as no one looks too closely, because just a few strands of ivy hide us from view.

As the Innkeeper moves closer my heart flutters in my chest. I wish we'd found a better place to hide. Some of the plants down here are huge – tree ferns that stretch towards the top of the pit, giant rhubarbs with leaves bigger than me – but the ivy covering the steps is thin and sparse.

Desperately I try to think what I can do, because it is me that needs to do something. Bones might be big and brave, but he can't move or touch anything. Plus he can get away if he wants to. It's me who is the problem, and me who needs to do something before the Innkeeper gets any closer.

It's obvious I can't fight them – I've just watched them pick up a boulder and hurl it into a bush – and I can't make a run for it either because I'd never make it to the door.

The Innkeeper moves even closer and I press back into the wall of the pit, wishing that the leaves were thick like they are around the Halfway House and Dai's grave, like I've drawn them on my map.

It comes to me in a flash . . . Did *I* make that happen? Zen and I keep noticing more leaves appearing in the graveyard, and all the time I've been drawing more leaves on my map. Is it Sally's pattern that has made the leaves appear? She said it was an ancient symbol and she hinted that it was a spell. What if she was telling the truth and each time I've drawn Sally's pattern on my map real leaves have grown in the graveyard?

In front of me, the thin strands of ivy tremble in the breeze. Can I really make them grow?

My fingers feel for the edge of my map. I can't draw on it. I haven't got a pen. Plus my map is huge. There's no way I could get it out of the holder without the Innkeeper seeing or hearing me do it. Leaves crunch under the Innkeeper's feet. A branch is broken in two and tossed to one side.

Perhaps I don't need a pen. Sweat prickles my skin. My mouth goes dry. Like a dark, ghostly shadow, the Innkeeper moves closer. I've got to try something! I close my eyes and press a finger against my map. Then, trying to remember exactly what Sally did, I trace the pattern. 'Earth, water, fire, hear my spell.' My lips move as I say the words silently to myself. Then I screw up my face and I think: Grow, leaves, grow. Please help me. Hide us from this bad person! And just like Peg told me to, I try to force magic out of my finger and into the map.

At first all I feel is a tingle, like pins and needles, pricking the tip of my finger. I recognise this feeling. It happened the night I pulled Zen up the cliff. Relief rushes through me as the tingle grows and becomes a rushing swirl of heat, a tangle of electricity buzzing inside me. I squeeze my eyes shut even tighter as I press my finger down on my map, tracing the pattern again and again.

The birds in the pit are getting louder, calling out to each other. I hear them burst from the trees. The trickle of water becomes a cascade and the breeze that has been circling the pit picks up speed. I hear leaves spiralling up into the air.

'Earth, water, fire, help me!' I whisper, out loud now, and I keep tracing the pattern.

Then I open my eyes.

I see the Innkeeper metres away from us. They turn in a circle, staring up at the top of the pit where the wind is whipping the canopy of trees. They are trying to work out what is causing this commotion. *Me*, I think, amazed, as I see their cloak swing out. *It's me.*

Grow, I think, staring hard at the leaves in front of me, my finger tracing the pattern. *GROW!*

Then the leaves burst into life, doubling in size, tripling, quadrupling. Stems snap and tangle round each other. It happens in the blink of an eye and then Bones and I are hidden in a cave of green.

I stop wishing and let my finger fall from my map and I think, *The charm's wound up.*

Bones stares from me to the leaves in amazement. I hear the wind die down then the birds and insects fall quiet.

'Who is doing this?' The oily voice is close by. But a moment later it seems to be on the other side of the pit. 'I said, *WHO IS DOING THIS?*' The words are hurled at the sky.

For a few minutes, the Innkeeper tears through the pit like a beast on the rampage, ripping down ivy, breaking branches and shouting out threats. I know they are looking for us, or rather me, but I feel safe hidden behind my magic curtain of leaves. I nudge Bones and smile. The icy cold of his arm takes away the last traces of fire in my fingertip.

He grins back as the Innkeeper gives a final bellow of rage then starts to climb the stone staircase, their bare feet slapping angrily on each step.

Bones and I listen until the sound disappears completely.

'Not yet,' I whisper when Bones leans forward, ready to push his head out of the leaves.

'You're right,' he says. 'The Innkeeper is cunning. They might be tricking us.'

'You think they're the Innkeeper too?'

He nods. 'You heard them. They said they were having to untangle the magic on the Halfway House.' He thinks for a moment, then adds, 'I wonder what they meant by that?'

I have an idea, but I'm not sure I want to say it out loud.

'And they threatened you,' he says. '*Let her know that I'm coming for her* ... I did not like the sound of that one bit.'

Strangely hearing these words again doesn't frighten me. What just happened has made me feel brave. Protected.

'I can look after myself,' I say, thinking of my map.

Bones runs his scarred fingers through the tangle of leaves hanging in front of us. 'You did this, didn't you?' he says, then he chuckles. 'I always said you were a witch. Do you believe me now?'

'I know that I can make leaves grow.'

'How did you do it?' He looks at me curiously, his face green from the leaves that are hiding us.

'I wished on my map,' I say.

'And you made it happen.' He shakes his head. 'Sid Jones, you are a wonder!'

CHAPTER
TWENTY-FIVE

Once we have pulled our way out of our cave of leaves we hurry back through the tunnel and into the Halfway House.

Straight away, the ghosts gather round us. Emma drifts over our heads, wailing softly.

'What did you see?' cries Peg.

'Were there bodies?' says Will.

Quickly we tell them what happened, describing the masked figure and how Old Scratch handed over the bottle of dust, but wasn't allowed any of the potion in return.

'The Innkeeper called the dust "lumin",' I say, looking at the golden specks floating in the air.

'And they wanted it badly,' adds Bones.

'So the Innkeeper does exist,' muses Holkar, 'but they never set foot in this place, and they wear a mask and cloak. I wonder why they keep themselves so hidden?'

'You've not heard the best of it yet,' says Bones. 'The Innkeeper almost found us in our hiding place, but young Sid here grew leaves and made a storm of wind whirl around the pit, and she did it using nothing more than her finger and her map!'

This fascinates the ghosts and they beg me to do it again.

'I don't think I can,' I admit. 'I *had* to do it then, I had no choice. It was the same when I pulled Zen up the cliff.'

Holkar asks Bones to describe the Innkeeper in more detail and while he does this Peg pulls me to one side.

'Isn't it the most wondrous feeling to do magic?' she says, her eyes wide with excitement. But before I can reply, her expression becomes serious and she prods one icy finger into my chest right where my map is sitting. 'Keep that thing hidden away,' she whispers, staring at me with her bright green eyes.

A lump forms in my throat. 'Why?'

'Because it is your book of charms, Sid.'

I laugh. 'No, it's not. It's just a picture I've drawn.'

'It is somethin' far more precious than that,' says Peg. 'It is something you love and the place where you have scribbled your dearest thoughts. You might not know it, but you have poured magic into that map.'

I think about the hours I have spent working on my map and the memories I've managed to include on it. And I also think about the strange things connected to it. The way I wrote on it moments before Bones was set free from the Halfway House, and how the leaves I drew on it then appeared in real life.

Peg leans forward and whispers in my ear. 'If your book of charms is destroyed, your powers will be destroyed too. Keep it well hidden, Sid.' Her icy breath sends a shiver down the back of my neck. 'Show no one!'

Then she steps back and grins. I smile back, but my smile slips from my face when I see one of her brown teeth vanish in front of my eyes. 'Oh!' I say.

'What's wrong?'

I'm about to say, 'Nothing,' because I don't want to worry her, but I don't get the chance because suddenly a stomach-churning wail comes from the corner of the pub.

I turn to see Emma slumped on the stone floor.

It's a strange sight. Emma's white, see-through body is always floating or drifting through the air, but right now she looks like a puddle of mist.

Cautiously we gather round.

'Egad . . . she looks like she has melted!' says Beau.

'Get up, Emma!' cries Will. He tries to pull her up, but of course his hands slip through her.

Suddenly Peg gasps. 'She's disappearin'. Look!'

Emma is always translucent, but now she is fading before our eyes. It's like watching a picture being rubbed out. The blank spaces where her eyes and mouth should be are open with surprise. She starts her usual cry of *'WAAAAYYYNNNEE!'* but it's fainter than normal and it's getting quieter by the second. She sounds like a balloon deflating.

'What's happening to her?' cries Will, then he bursts into tears.

'I do believe she is turning into a wraith,' says Holkar in a grim voice.

A sickening feeling creeps through me because I know that he's right.

A wraith is invisible. They are trapped in our world for eternity and can never leave. Desperately I try to think of something I can do to stop Emma from vanishing completely. I try to touch her, but I can barely see her now.

'Sid, you're magic. Do something!' shouts Will.

I reach for my map, fumbling under my jumper, but before I've even touched it, Emma gives one last wail then slides towards the doorway. She disappears before she can reach it.

'Emma!' shouts Peg. 'Where are you? Touch us. Let us know you are here!'

But her words are met with silence and no chilly fingers brush against me.

'Did she get out?' says Will, looking hopefully at the door.

'She may have done,' says Bones, 'but it is no sort of

freedom. Emma is a wraith now and there is going to be no crossing over to the other side for her.'

Will blinks. 'What . . . never?'

'The world is her prison now,' says Holkar.

'But . . . why did that happen?' Will stares down at his left hand, looking at the place where his finger used to be.

I know. It's what I suspected when I saw Peg's first freckle disappear, and the Innkeeper confirmed it for me when they said they were having to 'untangle' the magic of the Halfway House.

I look around. At first glance, the inn looks the same – it's gloomy, cold and filled with the sound of ticking clocks – but Will is right. Something has changed. The air glitters with more dust than ever, and when I look at the cuckoo clock I see the minute hand jerk forward. It's the first time I have ever seen one of the clock's hands move in here.

I run to the front door and pull it open. Then I drop to my knees and brush away the layer of dead leaves covering the doorstep. The ghosts crowd behind me, trying to peer over my shoulder.

'What are you doing, Sid?' asks Peg. 'Tell us!'

'I need to be sure that I'm right,' I say.

'Right about what?' growls Bones.

I've uncovered the spell that trapped the ghosts in the first place. It's still carved into the stone doorstep, but a single word has been gouged out, and that word changes everything.

Now the spell reads:

LOST SOUL,
step forth into this
~~timeless~~ tavern
And surrender thyself to me,
by order of the Innkeeper

I can feel the chilly presence of the ghosts pressing into my back. I turn and look up at them. 'The spell has been changed,' I say. 'The inn isn't timeless any more.'

At first the ghosts don't say anything, but then my words sink in and they start to examine themselves, turning their hands this way and that, because if I'm right, they should be fading away too.

'My ring!' cries Beau, holding up his hand. 'It's gone!'

'And so is the tip of Radulfus's dear little ear!' says Peg.

Suddenly Will cries, 'I knew it! I told Sid my finger had vanished and I was right!' Then he gives a cry of frustration and hurls himself towards me and the invisible barrier. The moment he hits it he bounces back into the pub. Then he throws himself on the floor and starts to wail. 'I don't want to turn into a wraith!' he screams. 'I WANT MY MUM!'

CHAPTER TWENTY-SIX

'I was so worried about you,' Zen says when Bones and I rush into the museum. 'You've been gone for more than two hours!'

Instead of going up to the flat where Zen and his family live, we stay in the lobby of the museum. I'm so exhausted I sink down to the floor, resting against a stuffed bear. '*A lot* has happened, Zen.'

We tell Zen everything, describing the pit, our encounter with the Innkeeper, the magic I did, and we end with the horrible moment when Emma turned into a wraith.

Zen can't quite believe it. He wants to know exactly what the Innkeeper looked like, what they said, and how I made the leaves appear.

'I can't believe Emma's gone,' he says. 'She might not have said much, but she was always there and she was Emma. You know what I mean?'

I do know what Zen means. Emma felt like a person, but all that warmth and humanity slipped away from her when she turned into a wraith. I can remember the same thing nearly happening to Bones before we found his treasure.

'And the Innkeeper has changed the spell.' Zen shakes his head. 'It's so unfair.'

'You should have seen the Innkeeper, Zen,' I say. '"Fair" isn't something that bothers them.'

Suddenly Zen's eyes widen. 'You saw how fast the dust came off Dai. The rest of the ghosts will turn into wraiths in days, if not hours!'

'I don't think so,' I say. 'Whatever the Innkeeper has done to the Halfway House, they can't have untangled all the magic. Time is still slower in there than out in the real world. You say that we've been gone for two hours, but it feels like way longer than that.'

Zen looks confused. 'But why does the Innkeeper want to stop the tavern from being timeless? If they really are making a new prison for lost souls somewhere else – because that's what it sounds like they are doing – why not just leave the ghosts alone?'

Bones speaks up. 'I believe it is because of the dust, or "lumin" as they called it. The Innkeeper told Old Scratch they didn't want any left behind.'

Zen looks horrified. 'So the Innkeeper is speeding things up and getting what they can from the ghosts before they leave.'

Bones nods. 'They are bleeding them dry.'

Zen strides up and down. 'We need to solve all the ghosts' unfinished business as soon as we can, right now! But how do we do it?' His panic is infectious. I feel it too, rising up inside me.

Bones puts himself in front of Zen and places his big hands on his shoulders. Zen shivers, but stays where he is.

'Calm yourself, lad,' he says. 'I have been in some sticky situations before and panic can be the undoing of a fellow. We need a plan, and we need to stick to it.'

'Bones is right,' I say. 'We might need to move quickly,

but we've got an advantage now. We know so much more than we did before.'

We agree that while Zen and I keep trying to solve the ghosts' unfinished business, Bones and Olive will find out more about the Innkeeper. Right now we don't know if they are a man or a woman, but we do know that they are tall, strong and have a distinctive deep voice.

'It was dramatic,' I say. 'It gave me shivers down my spine.'

'And they said they had been watching Sid,' says Bones. 'They said they were *coming for her.*'

I think back to the occasions when I've been sure someone is watching me. Was I right? 'I'll be careful,' I say. 'Plus Zen's mum told me that witches have to stick to a sort of code of conduct.' I tell them about the Elder Law and Zen even gets the book out of the case so we can look at it.

'We've just got to hope the Innkeeper abides by the Elder Law,' says Zen, staring at the picture of the tree. 'And you're going to have to watch out for the Innkeeper, Sid, and don't go into any houses made of sweets.'

Despite everything that has happened, this makes me smile.

'It's good that we're going to try to free Peg next,' I say. 'She's already quite see-through. She'll be the next to turn into a wraith.'

'Aye, you are right about that,' says Bones. 'She walked into the Halfway House with just days to spare. Her and Radulfus have always been pale. Her flaming-red hair is the only colour she has.'

Just then we hear laughing voices and a key in the door. Our parents are back from the pub quiz.

'Listen,' I say, knowing we have only a few seconds left to talk. 'This doesn't change anything. Tomorrow we meet at the Black Spot Cat Café. Starting with Peg and Radulfus, we are going to get the ghosts out of the Halfway House, and fast!'

The door bursts open and our parents bundle in, smiling and laughing and smelling of the pub. 'The Stuffed Weasels were triumphant!' cries Dad. 'We won ice-cream sundaes at Mermaids and four packets of salt and vinegar crisps!'

CHAPTER TWENTY-SEVEN

Zen, Olive, Bones and I stand huddled outside the café, watching as Sally shuffles around inside, putting down chairs and arranging cakes. We all arrived early with the same thought in our minds: find Peg's book of charms and get her out of the Halfway House.

'I'm running Operation Cheese,' says Olive. Bones opens his mouth to protest, but Olive manages to shut it with one fierce look. 'You all know your roles. Stick to your cover stories and everything will go tickety-boo.'

The moment Sally turns the sign from 'Closed' to 'Open', we're the first customers inside.

Morning light bounces off the many crystals throwing rainbows on the cats who are dozing around the room.

'Hello!' says Sally, beaming. 'The cats told me you were coming.'

'Cheers for that, guys,' says Zen, stroking his favourite: a tabby with one eye.

'Now what can I get you?' asks Sally, tying an apron round her waist. 'Is it going to be the usual?'

'Actually,' says Zen, as casually as possible, 'can I watch you make scones?'

This is phase one of our plan: distract.

Sally frowns. 'Why would you want to do that? Your dad makes marvellous scones for the museum café. I'd say they were better than mine.'

'Cover story, Zen!' says Olive. 'Remember your cover story!'

But Zen is already on it.

'He does make good scones,' he says, leaning on the counter, 'but he's never shown me how to do it. You see, my dad is massively protective about his baking. He thinks he's the scone boss, Sally.'

Zen has had ages to think of a plausible reason for

198

watching Sally bake, and this is what he's come up with? Luckily for us, Sally is a trusting person

'Put an apron on,' she says. 'All kids should know how to make a proper scone.'

'Ho ho!' booms Bones, who is hovering behind me. 'The caper has begun.'

'It's an *OPERATION*,' insists Olive. 'Sid, initiate phase two: infiltrate.'

'I feel dizzy!' I say, crashing against a pot plant.

'Oh, you poor duck,' says Sally. 'P'raps Zen should take you home.'

'No, no, I'm not that dizzy,' I say quickly. 'I just need to rest.'

'Of course,' says Sally. 'You sit down and I'll get you some squash.'

I shake my head. 'I think I need to rest horizontally. Can I lie down upstairs . . . in a bedroom . . . at the back of the house out of the sun.' I feel my cheeks go red. I've never been much good at acting.

'Of course you can, my poppet,' says Sally, gesturing to the stairs at the back of the café. 'Up you go.'

Just when I'm thinking how well Operation Cheese

199

is going, the bell above the door rings and I turn round to see Mo walk in. Her face lights up with surprise when she sees us.

'Hello!' she says.

'What are you doing here?' blurts out Zen.

It's a bit of a rude question, but Mo doesn't seem to mind. 'Shopping. I got the bus in. Mum asked me to come in here and buy some cakes.'

'Well, I've got plenty of those,' says Sally. 'I take it you three are friends?'

'Oh yes!' says Mo enthusiastically. 'I've just started at Penrose Academy and Sid and Zen have been really nice to me.'

'Well, you've come at the right time because Sid is feeling a bit poorly,' says Sally. 'Would you mind taking her upstairs and tucking her into the bed in the spare room? I'm supposed to be showing Zen how to make scones.'

'Of course,' says Mo, and she puts a friendly arm round my shoulders and helps me up the stairs.

This was so not part of the plan! I have no choice but to let Mo lead me into the spare bedroom, lift a cat off the bed, and tuck a hairy blanket round me.

Bones and Olive follow us into the room, making the temperature drop by about five degrees.

'It's freezing up here,' says Mo, zipping up her coat, then she plonks herself on the end of the bed and starts swinging her legs backwards and forwards. Then, out of the blue, she says, 'I thought you were busy today?'

I go red when I remember saying this to Mo on the bus. She must think I lied to her.

'I am. I mean, I will be later. I'm helping my dad at the model village.'

She nods, and I can't tell if she believes me or not. Meanwhile Bones and Olive have started searching for Peg's spell book, sticking their heads into the walls and down into the floorboards.

Suddenly Mo says, 'If you feel ill, you should drink water. That's what my mum always says.' Then she picks up my bag and looks inside it. 'Don't you have any water with you?'

'Oh, for heaven's sake!' cries Olive. 'You can't help us look for the spell book while she's here. Get rid of her, Sid!'

'Mo,' I say, doing my best not to look at Bones or Olive, 'thanks for looking after me, but I'll be fine on my own.'

'No way,' she says, patting my feet. 'I'm going to keep you company until you feel better. Let's play I spy. I spy with my little eye something beginning with . . .' Her eyes drift around the room, past Bones who is sticking his head inside a wardrobe and Olive who is scowling at her. 'G!'

I turn my gasp of surprise into a cough. 'Sorry, what did you say?'

'I spy something beginning with G. Have a guess. It isn't hard.' Then she drops her voice to a whisper and adds, 'There are two of them and they're ugly!'

Startled I look around the room and that's when I spot two garden gnomes sitting on the mantelpiece. 'Gnomes!' I say.

Mo laughs. 'That's it. Hey, you're sounding better already! Your turn.'

She is clearly not going anywhere. 'Actually,' I say, 'I would like some water. Can you get me some?'

For a minute I think she's going to offer me some of hers. As usual she's got her red water bottle with her, but instead she gets up and heads towards the door. 'OK, but I've got one more for you before you go. I spy with my little eye something beginning with CF.'

I can't see anything beginning with CF so I say, 'I give up.'

'Cool friend,' she says, pointing at me. Then she grins and runs out of the room, calling over her shoulder, 'Back in a minute!'

CHAPTER TWENTY-EIGHT

As soon as I hear Mo going down the stairs I jump out of bed and start searching for Peg's hidey-hole.

'This is definitely Peg's old bedroom,' says Olive. 'She said she could see the sea from her window.'

'It is a pity she cannot remember anything about her hidey-hole,' says Bones, frowning. He shoves his head back under the floorboards. Suddenly he gives a startled yelp and reappears. 'I just stuck my face in a nest of mice!'

'I'm sure it was scarier for them,' I say, then I start to feel and tap my way along the skirting board, not at all sure what I'm looking for.

'There's nothing under the floor except mice and a rusty key,' says Bones.

'And the walls are solid stone,' says Olive. 'I'm not sure where's left to try.'

'Did they tell you about good hiding places at spy school?' I ask her.

'Loose bricks and loose boards,' she says. 'They're both easy to pull out and it's almost impossible to tell if they've been disturbed.'

I stand in the middle of the room, turning slowly, listening for Mo's footsteps on the stairs. Is there anywhere we've forgotten to look? The problem is, the room is tiny and most of the things squeezed in here – a bed, a chair, some shelves covered in books about fungi and birds – wouldn't have been here when Peg was alive.

I feel a draught on my legs and think one of the ghosts has brushed against me until I realise it's coming from the fireplace. It's tiny and plain with a metal grate and bricks lining the chimney. 'Peg said she had a fire in her room,' I say, then a thought crosses my mind and without even bothering to check for Mo I run forward and start feeling around the edges of the dry bricks.

Olive and Bones crouch behind me.

'The girl would have to be feather-brained to hide cheese in a fireplace,' says Bones, but this doesn't put me off. There is something birdlike about Peg, the way she darts around the pub chirping out rude comments.

With a dull scrape, one of the bricks moves a fraction. My heart starts to speed up as I wriggle it backwards and forwards making red dust sprinkle over the fireplace.

'Prise it out, Sid!' cries Olive.

I cling on to the brick with the tips of my fingers and suddenly it comes free and I topple backwards.

'Sid!' Mo's shout comes from the bottom of the stairs. 'I'll be there in a second. Zen is making me decorate a gingerbread cat!'

I can see a hole in the back of the fireplace. Footsteps sound on the stairs. I shove my hand into the black space. My fingers touch cobwebs, dust, bits of stone, paper, then something crumbly. Could it be the cheese? Then they close round leather. I don't have time to see if I'm holding Peg's book of charms. I pull out whatever it is I'm holding and shove it up my jumper. I'm pushing the brick back in place when Mo walks into the room.

She's holding a glass of water. 'What are you doing down there?' she says.

'Mice,' I blurt out. 'I saw one disappear into the fireplace. I was trying to see where it went.'

She pulls a face. 'I'm not a massive mouse fan,' she says. 'When we moved into the bungalow it was infested.'

I take the glass of water, have a sip, then say, 'I feel better now. I'll follow you downstairs.'

'I'll wait,' she says.

'No, seriously,' I say, slightly louder than I was planning. 'I've got to go to the loo and stuff so . . .'

Looking slightly confused, Mo says, 'OK,' then turns and leaves the room.

'Finally!' says Olive, the second she has gone. 'Let's see what you've found.'

I pull a filthy-looking object out from under my jumper. It is a book. It has a leather front and back, and misshapen pages that are sewn in place by thick brown thread. It's so delicate that pieces of the cover crumble away when I open it. On the first page I can just make out an E, an M and a T.

'Elizabeth Margaret Tiddy,' whispers Olive. 'That's Peg's full name. And look. She's drawn a mushroom.'

'No, surely that is an acorn leaf,' says Bones.

But I recognise the picture. 'It's an elder tree,' I say.
'Peg followed the Elder Law.'

'Are you coming, Sid?' Mo calls up the stairs.

Quickly I wrap the book in a plastic bag, put it in my
rucksack, then run down to join the others.

Sally insists that I stay until 'the roses are back' in my
cheeks so I sit at a table and watch Mo and Zen decorate
their gingerbread cats.

Of course, I'm fidgety and bursting with excitement about the book. Zen is too. I've not been able to talk to him, but Bones yelled, 'She's only gone and blooming found it!' the moment we walked down the stairs and into the café.

I'm desperate to show the book to Peg, but first Zen has to add Smartie eyes to his gingerbread cats. He does this quickly, shoving them into place, then says, 'Thanks for the baking lesson, Sally. Come on, Sid. Let's go!'

'Really? You're going already?' says Mo, disappointed.

I get the feeling that if I let Mo down again she's going to stop wanting to hang out with me, and I don't want that. Even though it's difficult talking to the ghosts while she's around, I do really like her. So when Sally asks Mo to help her carry some baking trays into the kitchen, I thrust the plastic bag containing the book into Zen's hand and whisper, 'You take the book. Show it to Peg then destroy it. Just watch out for the Innkeeper!'

'What are you going to do?' he says.

'I'm going to show Mo the model village.' I glance at the door that leads to the kitchen. 'I can't keep making up excuses not to see her. I hate all the lying. I'll do it quickly then meet you on the seafront.'

'In an hour?' he says.

I nod.

Bones has been listening carefully to this exchange. 'Are you sure, Sid?' he says. 'What do you really know about the girl?'

'Not much,' I admit, 'but I know I like her.'

He scowls. 'Just be careful, that's all. Remember, we do not know who the Innkeeper is.'

I burst out laughing. 'Bones, she's tiny. The Innkeeper was taller than Old Scratch!'

He shakes his head. 'That's true, but there's something about her I don't like.'

I feel a flash of annoyance. I spend every spare moment helping Bones and the other ghosts, and he's trying to ruin the one normal thing I have in my life. 'What don't you like about her?' I demand.

'Up there in the bedroom, she looked at me, I'm sure of it.'

It's my turn to shake my head. 'She was playing I spy, Bones. She had to look around the room. And so what if she looked at you? It doesn't mean she could actually see you!'

'I got a funny feeling, that's all.'

Just then Mo comes back into the café with Sally.

She has a box of cakes in her hands and a smudge of icing on her cheek.

I'm not about to let Bones's funny feeling stop me from being friends with Mo so I whisper, 'Well, I like her and I'm going to invite her to my house. While we're doing that you should try and find the real Innkeeper.' And with that I stand up and call out to Mo, 'Hey, Mo. Do you still want to see the model village?'

She gasps and cries out, 'Yes, please!'

CHAPTER TWENTY-NINE

Half an hour later I'm up in my bedroom with Mo and we're eating crisps.

Dad was thrilled when I turned up with Mo. It's been years since I've hung out with anyone except for Zen, and I guess he's happy to know that I've got more than one friend. He was so happy, in fact, that he let us choose anything we liked from the kiosk.

After I'd given Mo a tour of the model village we came up here and now she's examining all the things on my shelves.

'This is so cool!' she says, picking up my hot dog rubber.

'The little sausage comes out!'

'I love miniature things,' I say. 'I guess I get it from my dad.'

'It's you and Zen!' Mo cries, spotting the models that I took out of the model village. 'Your dad is so clever.' She picks up the model of me. 'He's actually knitted your tiny jumper. It matches the one you're wearing today.'

'It's my favourite,' I say. 'He knitted both of them, but he had to do the little one with a pair of tiny knitting needles.'

'It's amazing,' she says, gazing at the model. 'So realistic.'

I feel a rush of pride. Dad's models *are* amazing and it feels good being able to share them with someone else. I know that Zen loves them too, but hearing someone else say it out loud makes me feel proud.

Next Mo moves on to checking out my books. 'I love reading,' she says, looking carefully at each one. 'Which is your favourite?'

We chat about books for a while, and then stationery. It turns out that Mo is a notebook and pen addict, just like me. My ridiculously large collection of gel pens even makes her squeal.

Of course, what I really want to show her is my map.

At one point I touch my jumper and feel it under my fingers, but then I remember how Peg whispered in my ear that I should 'show no one'.

So I force myself to keep quiet about it, even though I'm sure Mo would love it, and instead I show her my Jelly Cat cuddly toy collection. We both agree that the peanut is the best and I make a mental note to get her one for her birthday.

Just thinking that I have another friend I can choose birthday presents for makes me feel happy. I've always had to watch on at school as girls bring in balloons and presents on each other's birthdays. The only presents I've got from Zen have been strange things from the museum that he's wrapped up at the last minute. That's why I've got a stuffed squirrel sitting at the end of my bookshelf with a fake eyeball on its lap.

After Mo has checked out everything in my bedroom, she tells me that she has to go home. Part of me is glad – I'm desperate to find out if Zen has freed Peg – but the past hour has felt so normal that I don't really want it to end.

I walk with her to the entrance of the model village.

'Come round to my place soon,' she says.

214

'I will,' I promise. Then, as soon as I've watched her walk up the lane and out of sight, I yell goodbye to Dad and charge down to the seafront.

CHAPTER THIRTY

The first person I see is Bones. We meet outside the museum.

'Ah, Sid,' he says. 'I was just coming to look for you. I wanted to apologise for my behaviour earlier. I am sorry. I got a shock when Mo's eyes settled on me.'

I look around to check no one is nearby then I say, 'You've been around Mo loads and she's never looked at you before, has she?'

'No, she has not,' he admits sheepishly. 'I worry for you, Jones, that is all.'

I smile, happy to be friends with him again and say, 'Let's go and find out if Zen managed to free Peg.'

But before we've even reached the Admiral Benbow

we hear a scream. Next, a girl with wild red hair, wearing a dirty dress over even dirtier petticoats comes hurtling down the lane. She's closely followed by Radulfus. Zen and Olive come racing after them.

'I'm free. I'M FREE!' Peg cries, as she runs towards us. She zooms straight through a group of tourists then stops outside the pub and spins round, her arms thrown up in the air. 'I'm bloomin' FREE!'

Olive catches up with her and they hug each other. Then they do a dance in the middle of the lane, screaming and giggling.

Peg breaks away to stroke a dog and then kisses Zen's dad who just happens to be passing by.

'Ugh,' says Zen. 'A ghost witch kissed my dad. Gross.'

Of course, Zen's dad doesn't know what just happened. He frowns, touches his cheek, then waves at us and walks into the museum.

'How did you set her free?' I ask Zen.

'I showed the book to Peg. She started crying and stroking it and stuff, and after a few minutes of this she said I could chuck it in the sea.' He smiles and shrugs. 'Then she walked out of the Halfway House.'

217

Fat drops of rain start to fall.

'RAIN!' cries Peg and she turns round and round, letting the raindrops trickle through her face and outstretched hands.

Once Peg has calmed down about the rain and had a go on Tommy's roundabout, we try to persuade her to cross over to the other side. An eagle made of clouds has come to take her away. She's not entirely sure why, but says that she always did 'love a bird with big wings'.

Zen and I aren't really surprised when she refuses to walk along the Cockle then across the sea to climb on to the eagle.

'Nah,' she says, wrinkling her nose. 'I don't fancy it yet.'

Olive claps her hands. 'Jolly good decision, Peg. I want to take you to Sid's model village and the Yo Ho Ho Shake Shack – their Oreo and Skittles milkshakes smell divine – oh, and if you don't mind a bit of a trek, we can walk to the health club on the cliffs and go in the hot tub. Everyone will moan that we're making it cold, but who cares? They can't kick us out, can they?'

They both start to laugh.

Bones tuts, and next to me Zen sighs. 'We're smashing

this freeing-ghosts thing,' he says, 'but getting them to cross over to the other side is a lot harder.'

'I know I said I would leave when Peg was free,' says Olive, 'but there is so much I want to show her!'

And with this she leads Peg towards the Benbow pub.

'Maybe they can help Bones find the Innkeeper,' I say. 'A witch and a spy might be helpful.'

'Yeah, maybe,' says Zen, but he doesn't sound convinced. Possibly because Peg has just squeezed herself into the Bob the Builder kiddie ride outside the Benbow and is yelling, 'I'm drivin' a car with my handsome sweetheart and he's YELLOW!'

'It's a digger, darling,' says Olive, before dragging her off to sniff milkshakes.

CHAPTER
THIRTY-ONE

The next morning, I meet up with Zen, Bones, Olive and Peg at the fishing hut.

I'm the last to arrive because Dad's cold has come back with a vengeance and this morning he couldn't even get out of bed. I thought I might have to stay behind and run the model village, but he decided to close it for the day. That's when I knew he must feeling ill.

The first thing I learn when I walk into the hut is that Will's flat cap had vanished overnight.

'I wish we could free him next,' I say, pacing in front of the window, 'but Dad has told me that the nearest zoo with kangaroos is over two hundred miles away. Even if Zen and I managed to go there and stroke a kangaroo, I don't think it would free Will. He needs to stroke the kangaroo himself.'

Bones nods his big head. 'True. We need to get the lad out of there.'

Zen looks up from his phone. 'My Stormchaser app says there are no storms forecast for at least two weeks.'

I drop down on the nearest crate and feel the edges of my map through my jumper. 'It would be so much easier if I could make lightning,' I say. 'Do you know any weather-changing spells, Peg?'

She bursts out laughing. 'Not likely! But I do know how to brew up a potion to stop hiccups.'

I can't see that helping so we decide to make a list of everything we know about the Innkeeper. We all agree that Zen and I will be much safer if we know who the Innkeeper is.

But after ten minutes of Bones and I thinking over everything we saw in the pit, we only have five items on our list: *owns a plague mask, tall, doesn't wear shoes, the same age or older than Old Scratch, pale skin* and *can do magic.*

'It's not much to go on,' I say. Elizabeth has landed on

my shoulder and I reach up to stroke her chest. It's like my fingers are brushing over snow.

'Think carefully,' says Olive. 'At spy school they taught us about "tells". Unique features about a person that give them away: their manner of walking, speaking, how they pick up a teacup. Have a jolly good think, you two.'

The hut falls quiet. Outside, waves break on the beach and the morning sun shines across Grandad's boat. Radulfus trots around, his hooves clippity-clopping on the wooden boards. Elizabeth nibbles my ear.

I close my eyes and try to remember all I can about the cloaked figure in the pit.

'They walked like a cat,' I say. 'They prowled.'

'What else?' urges Olive. 'Think about their voice.'

'It was low and smooth as silk,' says Bones. It gave me the shivers, and there isn't much that scares me.'

'I've heard it before!' The words fly out of my mouth.

'*What?*' says Bones.

'I don't think I realised until just then, but I'm sure I've heard the Innkeeper's voice before . . . Lots of times.'

Of course, everyone starts to quiz me. Does it belong to someone I know? A teacher? A person who lives in Fathom? But I can't answer any of these questions. All I know is that the voice is familiar to me.

'It's like a tickle at the back of yer brain, isn't it?' says Peg. 'The memory is buried deep, but it will come back to you, Sid.'

'Was there anything else?' asks Olive.

I close my eyes again and picture the moment the Innkeeper turned to look at us. If only I could have seen behind the mask.

'They really wanted that bottle of dust,' says Bones. Then he mimes how the Innkeeper snatched the bottle from Old Scratch.

He does it well – like a child snatching a biscuit – and I can clearly picture the moment the Innkeeper's hand left the folds of their cloak. And this makes me remember something else. 'They bite their nails.'

'So we're looking for a velvet-voiced, nail-biting, dust-lover,' says Zen. 'I reckon it's your dad, Sid, he bites his nails, doesn't he?'

'Very funny,' I say. And it is. It makes me burst out laughing and this feels so good I suddenly realise how scared I've been recently. My laugh almost turns into a cry, but I manage to swallow it down. I'm not sure that I've fooled Zen or the ghosts, though, because they're watching me closely, and Peg gives me a cold pat on the knee.

Outside, clouds are drifting past the window. 'Whoever the Innkeeper is, they're cruel,' I say. 'That's the main thing I remember, and it's why we've got to get Beau, Holkar, Mei and William out of the Halfway House as soon as possible. They're not safe in there.'

'Agreed,' says Bones. 'But who will it be first?'

CHAPTER THIRTY-TWO

'*Me?*' says Mei Huang. 'Really?'

Zen and I are standing just inside the Halfway House. Once again Will is on cellar-door duty and Bones is in the graveyard. Old Scratch has never approached the pub this way before, but we've decided we can't take any risks.

'Yes,' I say, sweeping my hands through the air to try and clear the glittery dust. 'We think that if we find your plane for you, then you might be able to get out.'

Mei Huang stands up and comes to join us.

She is tiny, almost as small as me, and her face is obscured by her tightly fitting cap and goggles.

Like Will she didn't come inside the Halfway House until she had begun to fade away. Now she's standing in front of me I can see that in just the last few days she's lost some buttons from the front of her flying suit and the fingertips from her leather gloves.

'You truly believe you can find the *Bumble Bee*?' she asks, her husky voice full of hope.

'Maybe,' I say. 'If what you say about your plane is true.'

Her hands curl into fists. 'My plane is on Wolf Island!'

This is what Mei has said again and again, but it isn't what our research has told us. I take out one of the articles Zen and I have found about Mei's death. It has the headline '**Aviatrix Dead: Plane Lost at Sea**' and it's accompanied by a smiling black-and-white photograph of Mei. It's hard to believe that the cheeky, grinning woman in the photograph is the woman standing in front of me. Right now, Mei has her usual angry scowl etched across her forehead and her shoulders are hunched.

'Listen to this,' I say.

AVIATRIX DEAD:
PLANE LOST AT SEA

Plucky aviatrix, Miss Mei Huang, claimed her feet would "never touch the ground" when she set off on her round-the-world solo flying adventure. However, her attempt came to a tragic end on Sunday when, just five miles from her final destination, Fathom, she crashed her plane, the Bumble Bee, into the sea while attempting to land at Wolf Island.

Miss Mei Huang was heroically plucked from the sea by the island's reclusive owner, Morgan Starkey, but hours later succumbed to hyperthermia.

Extensive searches have failed to locate the Bumble Bee.

'They didn't find my plane because it was never in the sea!' cries Mei.

'Sid and I have read loads of articles about you,' says Zen. 'And every single one of them says your plane crashed into the sea.'

'So sad,' pipes up Will from the back of the pub. 'You went flying all the way around the world on your own, then came a cropper just before you got back to Fathom.'

Mei glares at Will. 'Yes, thank you, William Buckle. I am aware of how spectacularly I failed.' Then she drops down on the bench opposite me and wags a finger in my face. 'But know this, Sid: I never crashed a plane in my life. Just as I planned, I landed my plane on Wolf Island to refuel. My landing was executed perfectly and the only truth in that story –' she shoves her faded hand through the article I'm holding – 'is that I had pneumonia. I begged that woman, Morgan Starkey, to refuel the *Bumble Bee* so I could fly back to Fathom and complete my round-the-world trip, but she refused. She waited hours before bundling me into a boat and sailing me back to Fathom. Scores of journalists were lined up on the beach waiting to see me land my plane, but instead I was carried ashore.' A silvery ghost tear slips down her cheek. It's clear that the memory is still heartbreaking for her.

'So why did everyone think your plane was lost at sea?' I say.

'Because that's what Morgan Starkey said happened.'

'Why didn't you tell them she was lying?' Zen asks.

'I did!' she cries. 'I tried to protest, but they thought I was delirious. I mean, I was delirious, but not about that. "I landed my plane!" I shouted to the journalists. "Course you did," they replied, giving each other looks, and then they wrote down everything that liar Morgan Starkey told them. They believed a woman who lived like a hermit and collected dead animals over me!' She screws her hands into fists and her leather gloves creak. 'If I can find the *Bumble Bee* on that island, then the world will finally know that Mei Huang *never* crashed her plane!'

She slumps back, exhausted, and glares at the tabletop.

'Unfinished business,' Zen says from his position by the door.

I look again at the article about Mei Huang. There is also a faded photograph of Morgan Starkey. She's wearing a big hat that throws a shadow across half her face.

The only thing I can see is her big, slightly alarming smile.

'Why would Morgan Starkey make up such a strange story?' says Zen.

Mei rolls her eyes. 'Because she wanted my plane, of course. The woman loved collecting things.'

'She's right,' I say, looking at the article. 'It says so here. Apparently she also had Marie Curie's stuffed cat, Napoleon's toothbrush and Queen Victoria's half-eaten fig roll.'

'And *my* plane,' adds Mei angrily.

Soon we've decided we've spent long enough in the Halfway House. Zen and I leave the fast-fading ghosts behind and walk with Bones back through Fathom. Frustratingly Zen and I still have homework to do on top of our full-time job of freeing the ghosts.

As we walk through Fathom's quiet streets we tell Bones what we learned at the pub.

He nods his big head. 'She always did say some woman stole her plane.'

'Stealing a plane is a pretty bananas thing to do,' says Zen.

'Morgan Starkey had Marie Curie's dead cat,' I say.

'Is wanting Mei Huang's plane any weirder than that?'

He laughs. 'I guess not. The problem is, Morgan must have died years ago and that means someone would have inherited her island and everything on it. If she did steal the *Bumble Bee,* what are the chances of it still being on the island?'

We agree that this is a problem, so when we get to the museum Zen and I put off our homework for a little bit longer so we can find out more about Wolf Island. It doesn't take us long to find a book in the museum shop called *Mysterious Fathom,* that has a whole chapter on Wolf Island.

Zen and I sit in a window seat to look through it. Bones hovers over our shoulder.

'Listen to this,' Zen says, then he starts reading from the book. '*Wolf Island, located less than five miles from the village of Fathom, is a place steeped in mystery. The manor house, built by reclusive millionaire Morgan Starkey in 1910, was destroyed by fire in 1958. Now the charred remains lie alongside the island's crumbling airstrip, gardens and outbuildings. Little is known of the current owner, a distant relative of Starkey, and for now the island lies*

abandoned, frozen in time. Curious readers should note that the island is privately owned and there is no public access.'

Zen grins. 'If the island is "frozen in time", then I bet there's a chance that Mei Huang's plane is there!'

I nod. 'The house might have been destroyed by fire, but the plane wouldn't have been inside it.'

Zen closes the book. 'I say we ignore the bit about there being no public access to the island.'

Bones makes a scoffing sound. 'It's no crime to have a snoop around an island if no one is living there.'

I look out of the window. I can just see Wolf Island, a blurry lump on the horizon. Five miles doesn't sound like much, but from here the island looks very far away. 'How would we even get there?' I say. 'We'd need a boat.'

'We've got a boat!' says Zen. 'Your grandad's boat is just sitting there waiting to be used.'

Bones furrows his brow. 'Are you two truly saying you want to sail that rusty old bucket to Wolf Island?' He stares hard at me and then Zen. Then he grins, showing all his wonky teeth. 'What a magnificent idea. I shall be your captain for the voyage!'

CHAPTER THIRTY-THREE

There are many potential problems with our Wolf Island plan, but Zen and I are so excited by the idea of sailing there and looking for the *Bumble Bee* that we ignore or make light of them all. And Bones encourages us to do this.

We know that time is against us, and that Mei is fading fast, so each day after school we rush to the fishing hut where we work on getting the *Old Buoy* seaworthy. Luckily before Grandad retired to Spain he spent hours looking after his boat so there isn't much to do. As we work, Bones hovers over us, giving us advice and telling us where we need to sand a bit more off and what needs a lick of varnish.

'You missed a spot!' is his regular cry, or rather roar, because he's always outraged when we don't do the job as well as he thinks we should.

Every now and then he leaves us to help Peg and Olive search for the Innkeeper, but they haven't found a single lead.

This is disappointing, but I'm too distracted by the thought of getting the boat shipshape to worry too much about the Innkeeper.

By Thursday the *Old Buoy* is ready and we make plans to sail to Wolf Island after school tomorrow. We've chosen Friday because there's a twenty-four-hour disco happening at school and we've managed to convince our parents that we're keen to take part. Zen's dad has even tried to teach us some dance moves.

Zen is helping Bones to check the sailing conditions on his phone when he gets an alert from his Stormchaser app.

'There's a storm forecast tomorrow morning,' he says, 'and there's an eighty-three per cent chance of lightning!'

'That means we can free Mei Huang!' I say. 'It will be much easier to find her plane if she's with us.' But my excitement at our good fortune with the weather quickly fades when I realise that once again we won't be freeing Will. Yesterday Olive visited the Halfway House and reported that his nose has become a smudge.

We talk about this for a while, but agree that no matter how much we want to free Will, he's actually safer in the Halfway House. There must still be some magic hanging over the place because time passes more slowly in there than it does in the outside world. If we set him free and we don't have a kangaroo ready for him to stroke, or nearby, it would be disastrous for him.

'So it's decided,' says Zen. 'Tomorrow morning we free Mei Huang, then straight after school we sail to Wolf Island. We camp, then the next morning we find the *Bumble Bee* and sail back as soon as we can.'

Put like this the plan sounds simple, but there is one problem.

'I hate lying to my dad,' I say.

'Of course you do, darling,' says Olive, who is sitting on the prow of the *Old Buoy*. 'When I was training to be a spy I told my parents I was selling hats on Oxford Street. It never sat comfortably with me.'

Since Olive and Peg heard about our plan, they've

got fully behind it, although only Peg is coming with us. Olive has volunteered to stay behind to keep an eye on the Halfway House.

'It's the sailing bit Dad wouldn't like,' I say. 'Although I went out enough times with Grandad to know what I'm doing.'

'And we've got life jackets,' says Zen, popping his head out of the cabin. 'And a radio, and the weather is supposed to be perfect once the storm has blown over. Plus we're only going a few miles.'

'And don't forget that you have me as your captain,' adds Bones. 'Many in the Caribbean considered Ezekiel Kittow to be the canniest captain around.'

'Good point,' says Zen. 'If Sid tells her dad that we're being captained by a three-hundred-year-old ghost who sank his ship, I'm sure he'll be fine about it.'

'Shush!' I say to Zen, because Bones still finds it difficult to think about the night his ship went down.

'No, the lad is right,' says Bones. 'I did sink my ship, but do you know why? Because I took a risk and I didn't stick to my guns. I will never let that happen again. If I say it is not safe to sail, then we don't sail. And if I say we need to raydeehoo for help, then that is what we do. When we set sail tomorrow, you will be in the safest hands.'

His words do reassure me, and there is a part of me that can't wait to sail off to Wolf Island. Despite all the searching Bones, Peg and Olive have done, we still don't know who the Innkeeper is. They've been in and out of almost every house in Fathom, but they haven't found any plague masks, or long black cloaks hanging in wardrobes, or discovered anyone pouring over a spell book.

I've been looking out for the Innkeeper too. I'm constantly glancing over my shoulder to see if anyone is following me, but there is never anyone there. Zen has wondered if the Innkeeper has given up, but I know that when they said they were coming for me, they were telling the truth.

At least when we sail away tomorrow I can leave my worries about the Innkeeper far behind me, if only for a few hours.

CHAPTER THIRTY-FOUR

The next morning, I leave for school earlier than usual, telling Dad that I'm helping get the hall ready for the disco.

He's sitting at the kitchen table sipping another Lemsip. I think he's drinking more Lemsip than coffee these days.

'Disco?' he says, frowning.

I tighten my grip on my rucksack that contains all the clothes I'll need to camp out at Wolf Island. 'I told you about it,' I say, keeping my voice as breezy as possible. 'Zen and I are taking part. We'll be back tomorrow afternoon sometime.'

He nods. 'I remember now. Sorry, Sid. I feel like my brain is stuffed full of cotton wool.'

I'm about to walk out the door, but I hesitate. Dad looks really bad today. Pale, with dark circles around his eyes. 'Are you OK, Dad?' I ask, and my stomach flips with worry. I don't know what I would do if anything happened to Dad.

He chuckles. 'Of course I am! I've just got a cold that won't go away. I'll go and see the doctor if I still feel rubbish after the weekend. It's strange. I keep feeling better, then something else crops up. Today it's this hand.' He wiggles his right hand in the air. 'I've got pins and needles in my fingers.' He frowns then smiles. 'Sorry, love. You don't want to listen to me moaning. You go and get ready for your disco. I'm so pleased you're getting involved with stuff at school. To be honest, Sid, I used to get a bit worried seeing how much time you and Zen spent in that graveyard!'

I force myself to smile, but I have to throw my arms round him to hide the guilty look on my face. 'See you tomorrow,' I say.

'Have fun, Sid.' He squeezes me tight.

I run down the lane and see Zen already waiting for

me at the ice cream. Behind him I can see waves breaking over the Cockle and the boats in the harbour are tipping from side to side. The storm we were promised has already begun.

I wave at Zen and that's when I notice the dust glittering on my hand.

'Look at this,' I say, showing Zen my hand. Then we notice I have dust on my other hand too.

Zen runs his finger over my palm and now his finger is shining. 'Weird,' he says. 'Have you been patting any ghosts?'

'No, just my dad,' I say.

But we don't have time to think about where I picked up the sparkly dust because at that moment a clap of thunder echoes across the bay and the first drops of rain start to fall. We're going to have to hurry if we're to get to the graveyard before the lightning comes.

Bones, Olive and Peg are already there, waiting for us, and they've told Mei Huang what we're planning to do.

I walk to Mei's grave, shove a Crunchie on top of it, then after looking around and checking to make sure no one else is in the graveyard, I get out my map. Elizabeth lands on

Mei's headstone and watches me closely, her head tipped to one side.

I get out my red pen then force myself to slow down and think about what I'm about to do. I have to concentrate if I want the magic to work.

Zen is standing next to me. He doesn't speak, but it's reassuring having him by my side. I hear another growl of thunder. It builds up, growing in intensity, until I can feel it right inside me. Then the tingling starts in my fingers. I start to trace Mei Huang's initials on my map and seconds later lightning flashes to earth. The graveyard is flooded with light. I force myself to concentrate and to keep writing the initials MH again and again, until I hear excited cries coming from the Halfway House.

Zen shakes my shoulder. 'Sid, look!'

When I look up, Mei is striding through the long grass towards me. Possibly for the first time since I met her, she's smiling. I jump up and she wraps her arms round me, giving me a quick, horribly cold hug. 'Thank you,' she says, then she lets go of me and fixes her eyes on Wolf Island. 'Let's find my *Bumble Bee*!'

'*Bumble Bee! Bumble Bee!*' cries Elizabeth.

It takes me, Zen and the ghosts quite a long time to persuade Mei Huang that there's no way we can sail to Wolf Island right now.

'Look at the waves, woman, and the wind!' cries Bones. 'Do you want these children to be harmed?'

'Look at *me*!' she snaps back, holding her hands out. It's clear that she's fading fast. The tips of her gloved hands have gone and her palms are white. The goggles that once hid half of her face now look like they are made of mist. Even her dark eyes have become grey.

'I promise we'll go to Wolf Island as soon as we get back from school,' I say, and eventually she agrees to go with Bones, Olive and Peg to wait for us at the fishing hut.

As Zen and I rush to catch the bus to school, she calls out to us, 'Hurry back, please!'

School drags by painfully slowly. Mo wants to know why we aren't doing the twenty-four-hour disco and quizzes me endlessly about what I'm planning to do this weekend. I don't get a second to talk to Zen alone, and it's only after school, when Mo gets off at her bus stop on the coast road that we can finally speak.

'At last!' says Zen. 'Mo does not leave your side, Sid.'

'I know, but she's gone now, and look at the weather, Zen. It's perfect!'

The bus is trundling down the hill towards Fathom. The sea is a deep turquoise blue with only the odd wave dotting the surface.

'I can't believe we're actually doing this,' Zen says, then he glances at me and grins. 'Wolf Island here we come!'

CHAPTER THIRTY-FIVE

Our excitement is nothing compared to Mei Huang's.

She's waiting for us at the bus stop and all the way to the fishing hut she trots by our side, urging us to 'move faster' and to 'stop dawdling'.

Bones is in a jolly mood too.

'This jaunt is just what we need,' he says when we find him with Peg and Olive in the fishing hut. 'A trip on the ocean will take our minds off gloomy thoughts and invigorate our spirits.' He waves a hand towards the window. 'Excellent sailing conditions, don't you think? Calm but with a nice puff of wind to blow us on our way.'

'The boat's got an engine,' I say. 'We don't need wind.'

'Pah, I never needed no engine.'

'Please stop talking,' cries Mei Huang who has already climbed inside Grandad's boat. 'We must go!'

The *Old Buoy* is ready for the trip. We've sanded her down, checked the fuel and packed her full of food and camping equipment. But before we can leave we need to check there is no one around. Luckily the fishing huts are tucked away from the main beach, plus Fathom's sea shanty choir is singing at the Benbow tonight and most of the choir is made up of fishermen and women.

Once we're sure the beach is deserted, Zen and I haul open the doors of the fishing hut, letting light flood over the *Old Buoy*. Then we use the winch to drag the boat down to the water's edge. The ghosts can't help, but that doesn't stop them from giving us plenty of advice.

'By heaven, it will be dark before you get her to the water,' cries Bones. 'Put your backs into it!'

'Yes, do buck up, you two,' adds Olive. 'You're being awfully slow.'

'Seagull!' yells Peg, helpfully chasing a baby seagull over the sand.

'*Rum! Bum! Bully!*' screeches Elizabeth, joining in with the chase.

Mei Huang doesn't say anything. She's still standing on the prow of the *Old Buoy*, hands on hips and her eyes fixed on Wolf Island.

We're just nudging the *Old Buoy* into the sea when a shout rings out from the top of the beach. Someone is calling my name. I hear Zen groan and when I turn round I see Mo running across the beach towards us.

'What's she doing here?' says Zen.

'Shh,' I say. 'She'll hear you.'

Mo reaches us, red-faced and out of breath. 'I saw you from the lane,' she says. 'What are you doing with that boat?'

'And what were *you* doing in the lane?' Bones snaps.

Of course, Mo can't hear him, and she just stands there smiling at us, waiting for one of us to reply.

'We're going for an evening sail,' I say, as if this is something Zen and I do every Friday. 'We love sailing. Don't we, Zen?'

'Oh yeah,' he says. 'Absolutely.'

'My mum's at the fish and chip shop. I thought I'd come and look for shells while we were waiting, but, look, I found

246

you two instead!' She looks delighted by this coincidence and stands there, beaming at us. Then her eyes light up and she says, 'Hey, can I come with you? I can give my mum a ring and tell her. I'm sure she won't mind. Not if you're experienced sailors.'

Zen shoots me a panicked look that I understand. Mo can't come with us. She'll have to ask her mum and dad and they might tell our parents. Plus how can we look for the *Bumble Bee* if she's with us?

'What about your fish and chips?' I blurt out.

Mo shrugs. 'I'd much rather hang out with you two than have fish and chips.'

'But won't your mum be cross?' asks Zen. 'Wasting food like that.'

'No, she'll just be pleased I'm making friends.' Suddenly Mo's smile falters. 'You don't want me to come, do you?'

I glance at Mei Huang. I can see straight through her to the shifting sea beyond. We have to sail to Wolf Island today. It's our only chance to save her.

'Tell her that the two of you don't want her with you,' hisses Bones.

'No!' I say.

Mo looks shocked. 'Why?' she says. 'Don't you like me?'

My cheeks go red and I feel terrible. 'No. Yes! I mean . . . of course we like you, but you can't come with us.'

'Why not?' Now Mo has red cheeks too and I have the horrible feeling she might by about to cry. She looks from me to Zen then says, 'You know, sometimes you two aren't very nice to me. You're always rushing off after school to do homework, but you never invite me, and I practically had to force my way into Sid's house. If you don't want to be friends with me, I wish you'd just say it, because you're making me feel like an idiot!'

This is awful. Mo can't even look at me or Zen. She stares down at the wet sand and I see her brush a tear off her cheek. Of course she's right. Zen and I have been so busy helping the ghosts that we haven't had time to be a proper friend to her.

'For shame,' says Peg. 'The poor mite is crying!'

That's when I decide I need to tell Mo the truth. Well, part of the truth. 'Listen,' I say. 'We'd like you to come with us, but we're staying the night on Wolf Island and our parents don't know.'

'*Wolf Island?*' she says, shocked. All her tears are gone

in a flash. 'But you can't go there. It's miles away!'

'Only five,' I say. 'Our parents think we're at the disco. It would actually be fun if you came with us –' Bones gives an exasperated sigh when I say this – 'but if you ask your mum and dad, they might ring our parents and then we'd get in loads of trouble.'

Mo thinks about this for a moment, then a cunning smile appears on her face. 'Leave it to me,' she says, then she pulls out her phone and dials a number. 'Hi, Mum,' she says, then there's a pause. 'No, I said a spring roll and mushy peas, but listen, don't worry about getting any food for me, I've just bumped into Sid and, guess what, she's asked if I can stay the night at her place! Isn't that brilliant? Please say it's OK?' She frowns as she listens to her mum, then she grins. 'Amazing! Thank you, Mum! Don't come checking up on me, will you? I'm not a baby. I know. It's fine; she says I can borrow a toothbrush and stuff. I love you too. I'll ring before I go to sleep. Thank you, Mum . . . Thank you!' Then she puts her phone into her pocket and looks at us as if she can't believe what just happened. 'I can come!' she cries.

CHAPTER THIRTY-SIX

The *Old Buoy* is a small fishing boat, and she feels even smaller with three ghosts and me, Zen and Mo on board. Luckily Elizabeth is flying over our heads and Radulfus has stayed behind with Olive, but even so it's a squash. Of course, Mo doesn't know what a squeeze it is. She stands next to me at the wheel exclaiming about the light sparkling on the water and the 'gorgeous' blue of the sea and only occasionally complaining about how chilly she feels. It's chilly because Bones keeps bumping into us. He's just too big to keep out of our way.

'My apologies, Sid,' says Bones when he points out a cormorant and sticks his hand through my head.

'Are you OK, Sid?' Mo asks when she sees me shivering.

'Fine. The sun's going down, that's all,' I say, then Mo insists that I wear her fluffy white hoodie.

Eventually Bones joins Mei Huang on the prow of the boat and I start to relax. The conditions are perfect and we should be at Wolf Island in no time. It will be dark in an hour or two so we'll set up camp as soon as we arrive then hunt for the *Bumble Bee* in the morning.

Really everything would be perfect if Mo wasn't with us. For a few minutes I actually consider telling her what's going on. I could probably get her to believe that there are three ghosts on the boat, especially if I got them to touch her and make her cold. But then I decide it would be a selfish thing to do. To make my life easier I would be putting Mo at risk from the Innkeeper. Zen nearly died because of me. I can't let that happen to someone else.

So I keep quiet. Somehow we'll have to find a way to look for the *Bumble Bee* without Mo working out that something funny is going on.

'It's a real island!' cries Mo, laughing.

We're getting close to the island now. We can see sandy beaches fringed by overgrown trees. On the far side of the island, over the tops of the trees, we can just see what's left of the burnt-down manor house.

Mei turns to look at me from the front of the boat and a smile spreads across her face. 'The *Bumble Bee* is here, Sid,' she says. 'I know it.'

CHAPTER THIRTY-SEVEN

'I can't believe we've got this whole island to ourselves!' marvels Mo. We've dragged the boat up the beach and unloaded our stuff. Bones, Peg and Mei Huang have disappeared into the trees to explore.

'We're the kings of Wolf Island!' yells Zen, then he grabs a handful of sand, throws it over his head and starts running along the beach. Laughing, Mo and I follow him and suddenly I feel so happy and free, being here with my friends, and being so far away from Old Scratch and the Innkeeper.

We head inland, searching for a good place to pitch

our tent. As we go, Zen tells Mo about Morgan Starkey. 'She was a recluse who lived in the big old house on the other side of the island with her butler and maid and her collections.'

'What did she collect?' asks Mo.

'Loads of stuff,' says Zen. 'Stuffed animals, fig rolls, stuff that belonged to famous people.'

'But it won't be here now, will it?' says Mo. 'Not if her house burned down.'

'I guess not,' says Zen, but of course we're very much hoping Mei's plane is still hidden on the island somewhere, and tomorrow we're going to try and look for it without Mo realising what we're up to.

We put up our tent in a clearing set back from the beach. We get it wrong to begin with, but in the end we work out which poles go where. Mo might be small but she's the only one who can wrestle the stubborn tent poles into place.

Then, after we've unrolled our sleeping bags and found some blankets for Mo, we make a fire on the beach and sit round it while the sun sets. Above the trees, we can just see the burnt remains of Morgan Starkey's abandoned house.

The blackened bricks stand out against the bright orange sky. We eat sandwiches and toast marshmallows and the ghosts drift back to join us, Mei sulking because she hasn't found the *Bumble Bee*.

When Mo goes off to get more firewood, I whisper to Mei, 'Don't worry. If it's here, we'll find it. I promise.'

'It *is* here,' Mei Huang snaps. 'Where else could it be? That thief Morgan Starkey might have had an airstrip, but she couldn't fly.' She looks so furious I decide not to point out that someone else could have flown the plane off the island, and I certainly don't dare to mention that she could have got it wrong, and that maybe she did crash into the sea and Morgan saved her life.

When Mo comes back she drops the firewood in a pile, sits down for a moment, then jumps up to get more.

'Your young friend is like a jack-in-the-box,' says Bones, the moment she's gone.

'She's being helpful,' I say. 'She probably feels bad that we're having to share all our stuff with her.'

Bones frowns and scratches his beard. 'And a little nervous too, I think.'

I sigh. 'Why won't you leave her alone, Bones?

Maybe she's scared of the dark. She started biting her nails as soon as the sun went down. Or perhaps she's never been camping before and it's freaking her out. There's no big mystery!'

Bones's frown deepens. 'If she is scared of the dark, then why does she keep going off into the gloom of the trees?'

'To do wees?' suggests Zen. 'She does drink a lot of water.'

But still Bones isn't satisfied. 'Something is troubling her,' he says. 'Have you noticed how she lugs her bag around with her as though it contains jewels?'

'She hasn't got it with her now, has she?' I say, pointing at Mo's rucksack, which she's left by the fire.

'Let's find out what's in there,' says Zen, and before I can stop him he's leant over and peaked into Mo's bag. 'Sorry, Bones. It's just her water bottle and pencil case.'

'Who's Bones?' We turn round to see Mo standing in the shadow of the trees clutching a pile of twigs and broken branches.

'Sid,' says Zen. 'When we were little we made up nicknames for each other and Sid was Bones.'

'Oh yeah?' says Mo, dropping the wood by the fire.

257

'What was yours?'

'Buff!' he says, flexing his muscles. Then sheepishly he adds, 'Sorry I looked in your bag, Mo. I was being nosy.'

She smiles. 'I don't care . . . *Buff*!'

I give Bones an 'I told you so' look, then we go back to toasting our marshmallows and throwing pebbles in the sea until eventually it gets so cold and dark that we bundle into the tent.

All of us. Even Elizabeth.

'This is the first time I've ever been camping,' says Mo. 'I didn't realise it would be so cold.' Then she gasps. 'Hey, we should tell ghost stories!'

This makes Bones roar with laughter and then Elizabeth gets overexcited and starts screeching, '*RUM, BUM!*' but Mo doesn't know all this is going on and talks over them, telling us the ghost story of Morgan Starkey.

'Legend has it,' she says, making her voice deep and mysterious, 'that the ghost of Morgan still wanders her island, looking for interesting things to add to her collection . . . And what could be more interesting than three children sleeping in a flimsy tent?' Even though I know she's making this up, a shiver runs down my spine.

'Apparently, if you listen carefully, you can sometimes hear the crunch, crunch, crunch of her ghostly footsteps as she hunts for new specimens.'

Of course we instantly fall silent. Although Mo doesn't know it, I'm now thinking of the Innkeeper creeping around the pit with bare feet.

Then I hear a quiet *tap, tap, tap*.

'What's that?' I say.

'Morgan Starkey!' says Mo in a spooky voice.

'Nah, it's probably spiders,' says Zen. 'This is the first time we've used the tent this year and spiders like wandering about at night.'

'I love a little spider,' says Peg cheerfully.

Next to me Mei shudders and says, 'I don't. I detest them.'

'Me too,' says Mo.

Everything in the tent goes deathly quiet. Did Mo really just reply to Mei? Can she hear her?

'What do you mean, Mo?' I force myself to say.

Mo wriggles round to face me. 'I'm like a spider. I like wandering about at night. The dark has never scared me.'

Relief floods through me. 'Me neither!' I say.

Mo carries on telling us about the wicked things Morgan gets up to when she's out haunting her island and then Zen takes over with a ghost story of his own about a phantom fart.

'No one can see it,' he says, 'or hear it, but everyone can smell it!'

Mo cackles with laughter and Bones whispers in my ear, 'For a moment I thought your young friend had *the gift*.'

'The phantom fart smells of baked beans and cheese!' shrieks Mo. 'It's in the tent with us right now! Run for your lives!'

'But I believe I was mistaken,' Bones adds.

CHAPTER THIRTY-EIGHT

The next morning I'm woken up by a ghost poking on icy finger into my forehead.

'Sid . . . *Sid*!' hisses Mei Huang. 'Get up. We need to find the *Bumble Bee*.'

Bones and Peg have already gone off exploring, but Zen and Mo are fast asleep. I shake Zen awake, then reluctantly wake Mo up too. What we're about to do would be so much easier if she wasn't around.

We crawl out into bright sunshine and quickly send messages to our parents, telling them we're having a great time at the disco and that we'll be home this afternoon.

Mo, of course, says that she's having a great time at my house.

Then we share the last of our food – a tin of pineapple chunks, chocolate Mini Rolls and some warmish milk.

We're just finishing when Bones and Peg come crashing out of the trees. 'This island is a rum sort of place,' says Bones. 'Half of it is overgrown, the other half is full of statues and strange follies. If we are going to find that aeroplane, we should start looking.'

Without bothering to pack up our camp we set off.

Still thinking we're just here to explore, Mo suggests we start on the far side of the island then work our way towards the manor house. 'That way we won't miss any cool stuff,' she says, leading the way through the trees.

It's good that she's at the front because it gives the rest of us the chance to look for the *Bumble Bee*. But we don't see anything remotely plane-like. I'm not sure what I expected Wolf Island to be like. Smaller, perhaps, and less overgrown, but soon we're surrounded by entwined trees and plants. The closest thing we find to a plane is a rusting bicycle half-submerged in a pond.

There are little tracks leading in different directions, which Mo confidently tells us are badger paths. She seems to know a lot about nature, which isn't surprising as her dad is a gardener.

'Look at this,' she says after we've pushed through a glade of bamboo.

She's standing in front of a statue that's completely covered in ivy except for a woman's face that's poking through the leaves.

'Creepy,' says Zen. But I don't have time to pull away any of the ivy because Mo is off again, plunging into the long grass.

Soon it becomes clear that the island isn't completely wild and that we're exploring what was once a very smart garden. We discover more statues, empty weed-filled ponds and benches blanketed in moss, but definitely no planes.

'We need to go closer to the house,' complains Mei. 'That's where the airstrip is.'

'We'll get there soon,' I whisper. 'At least this way we know we've checked everywhere.'

'I don't know about that,' says Mei. 'I feel like we are going round in circles.'

Mei is walking next to me. In the gloom of the trees

I can clearly see the dust pouring off her, and when she pointlessly tries to swat a cobweb out of the way, her whole hand vanishes, only to reappear a few seconds later.

I pick up the pace. We need to find her plane quickly, but I soon find myself almost walking into Mo who is dawdling.

She seems to be losing her enthusiasm for exploring.

'Let's go towards the house now,' I say.

She nods, but then something catches her eye. 'What's that?' she says, leading us to a tall gate covered in ivy. When she gives it a push it swings open. 'Shall we see what's inside?'

Please let it be a plane, I think, but instead we step into a walled garden full of twisted trees.

'Look, apples!' says Zen 'This must have been an orchard.'

Mo reaches into the nearest tree and plucks an apple from a branch. 'Anyone want one?' she asks.

'Definitely,' says Zen. 'I'm starving.'

Mo throws him an apple, but I shake my head. I don't want to lose the taste of my chocolate Mini Roll.

For a few minutes we explore the orchard. Mo and

Zen crunching apples, the ghosts drifting off in different directions.

I look at my watch. It's nearly midday. We're going to have to go back to Fathom soon. I'm just about to suggest we go to the burnt manor house when Peg bursts through one of the walls, her bright red hair flying out behind her.

'You have got to come and see this,' she says. 'I have discovered a house made of *glass*!'

CHAPTER
THIRTY-NINE

'I think we should visit the manor house then go,' says Mo when I say that I want to explore behind the wall. 'I told Mum and Dad I'd be back soon.'

'I know,' I say. 'Don't worry. I won't be long.'

Before Mo can protest, I run back through the rusty gate and find a path that leads behind the orchard. The ghosts have already gone on ahead, drifting through the wall, and I'm desperate to catch up with them and see the glass house for myself. I'm excited. Before Peg went back through the wall, she said it was massive, easily big enough to hide a plane inside.

'Wait for me!' calls Zen, and Mo has no choice but to follow us.

'I'm going to be in so much trouble if I get back late,' she grumbles. It's the first time I've heard her moan about anything.

I turn a corner and skid to a halt. A huge greenhouse rises up in front of me. It has a big, arched door and curling ironwork rising to form a domed roof. The only reason we didn't spot it from the orchard is because it's covered in vines.

Suddenly Bones pops his head out of the door. 'Hurry now, you have to see this!'

I step through the door. It's like walking into a miniature jungle. Palm trees rise from the ground, their leaves spreading over my head, and twisting vines loop between them. The air is humid and sticky, and there is a powerful smell of crushed leaves.

I walk along a narrow path. In a sunny corner I find an armchair with a bottom-shaped dent in the cushion. Mice have nibbled at it and stuffing spills on to the floor. A delicate cup and saucer rest on the arm. The cup is full of green mould and a teaspoon rests on the saucer, tied to the cup by a delicate tendril of ivy.

I'm just stepping over what looks like a wicker wheelchair when Zen and Mo catch up with me.

'So cool,' whispers Zen, staring up at the ceiling. It's covered in thick, twisting stems that look furry. They hang down, brushing against us like the fat legs of spiders.

We split up and I take an almost invisible pathway, squeezing through a tangle of plants. Some have black berries that look like fat beetles. Another has bright red pea-like seeds. I don't recognise many of the plants. There's one with blue flowers that might be a delphinium and another that looks like cow parsley, but I can't be sure. I run my fingers over a seed pod that's spiky and bright green. 'There are some weird plants in here,' I say.

No one replies. I'm not even sure they can hear me. I'm at the very back of the greenhouse. I find a bench and I sit on the cushion of moss that covers it.

Green light falls on me. I can hear tiny, sucking oozing sounds, as if the plants are growing every second. The smell of wet leaves is overwhelming. Then I see another cup, only this one isn't a delicate cup and saucer. It's a black mug with the Marmite logo stamped on the side. I pick it up. There is a puddle of cold tea at the bottom.

It's not mouldy. In fact, it looks like someone left it here recently.

My heart beats faster. Who could have left it here? Are they still on the island? Suddenly I want to get out of this greenhouse and back on to the boat, but we can't do that. Not until we've found Mei's plane.

My mouth goes dry as I put the mug back down. I force myself to stay where I am on the bench. I've got to calm down. Quickly I reach my hand under my jumper and pull out my map. Almost immediately I feel better. I hold it tight in my hands. I can see Fathom's streets that I drew with a technical pencil and little pencilled dots of sand on the beach.

I take a couple of deep breaths and my heart slows down a little. I decide to add Wolf Island to the map. I can't draw all of it, but I can at least get the shape right and mark where we camped last night, and roughly where we are now. I lean on the bench and draw a blobby island shape just off the coast of Fathom. It only takes a few minutes of drawing for me to start to feel like myself again.

'Hey, Sid!' Zen's voice rings out from the other side of the greenhouse. 'We should go. There's nothing here.'

I know what he's really saying: the plane isn't here.

Suddenly I hear Peg yelling, 'Do not touch that!' followed by a crash and the sound of shattering glass.

I push my way through the plants until I find Zen sitting squished inside the wicker chair with his knees up by his chin. Bones and Peg are hovering next to him. They obviously can't pull him out. Zen looks wide-eyed and shocked. All around him are shards of glass.

'What are you doing in there?' I say.

'I'm not sure,' he says, frowning. Peg told me not to touch a plant, and the next thing I knew I felt dizzy and I crashed down on this chair. The seat must be rotten because I fell through it. He starts to laugh as I grab his hands and help him up.

'Why is there glass everywhere?' I say.

'The chair crashed into one of the panes,' says Zen.

'The lad is lucky he didn't bring the whole place down,' says Bones.

Just then Mo appears from behind a banana plant. She takes in the glass and Zen's startled look. 'We should go,' she says. 'This place isn't safe.'

'Good idea,' I say, and we pick our way over the broken glass towards the door.

271

I feel a cool hand wrap round my wrist. It's Peg and she's holding me back. I let the others walk ahead then whisper, 'What is it?'

'I need to tell you why I told Zen not to touch the plant.' She looks at me with her bright green eyes. 'Sid, every plant in this place is poisonous!'

CHAPTER FORTY

Peg is still holding tight to my wrist. An icy cold flows through my arm. 'What do you mean?' I whisper, looking at the plants that surround me. 'They're just flowers.'

'Hemlock, foxglove, wolfsbane.' Peg points at the plants closest to us. 'All these flowers can kill, Sid! And look –' she points to the metalwork above the door where we are standing. The rusting iron has been twisted to form two triangles, one inverted on top of the other – 'that is the alchemist's sign for arsenic, a most deadly poison. I believe we are standin' in a poison garden, Sid. Most likely the very air is putrid!'

As soon as she says this I feel my throat tighten. The moist sappy air does have a bitter tang. 'Why would someone plant a garden full of poisonous plants?' I say.

'P'rhaps to make medicine,' says Peg. 'Tiddly bits

of poison can be useful. Or there may be a more wicked explanation.'

Outside, Mo calls out, 'Sid! What are you doing?'

Leaves brush against my legs and arms. The oozing sound that I heard earlier has intensified. I feel something tickle my leg and suddenly I'm desperate to get out of a place that I know is less abandoned than it appears. 'You go ahead,' says Peg. 'I will have a closer look at these plants and see if I can discover why they are being grown.'

'Thank you,' I say, then I rush outside, happy to be free of the cloying air.

I don't think I'm going to be able to tell Zen about the Marmite mug or the poisonous plants, but when we're walking along what's left of the runway, close to the ruined manor house, Mo offers to go back to our camp and pack up our stuff.

'You two check out the house,' she says. 'I'll get everything into the boat then we can leave as soon as you get back.'

She looks nervous and I understand why. It's nearly midday and we really should be going back to Fathom. We are all going to be in big trouble if we don't get home soon.

'Good idea,' I say, then Mo sets off, heading towards the beach where we camped last night.

Zen and I follow the runway until we reach an overgrown garden and the ruins of the manor house. As we walk I tell Bones, Mei and Zen about the poison garden and the Marmite mug I found. None of them seem as bothered by it as me. Mei just wants to find the *Bumble Bee*, Bones is distracted by the weather, which he claims has become windier, and Zen is, well, just distracted.

Peg catches up with us just as we reach what's left of the house. She has nothing more to report. Just like she thought, the greenhouse is stuffed full of poisonous plants.

I follow Zen as he picks his way over the charred bricks. 'Don't you think it's strange, Zen? Why would there have been a Marmite mug sitting there with tea at the bottom?'

'Maybe someone went poking around, just like us,' he says.

'What? And brought a kettle, a stove, tea bags, milk and a mug?'

He sits down, slumping against one of the low walls. 'They might have had a Thermos flask. Sometimes I leave mugs in weird places.'

This is true. Zen loves tea and if he hasn't finished his morning cup he'll bring it to the bus stop and shove it in a bush to pick up on the way home. Suddenly I notice how quiet Zen is. We are in the ruins of a burnt-down manor house. Scattered across the ground there are charred pieces of pottery, melted lumps of metal and even some scraps of embroidered fabric. Usually Zen would find this place fascinating and be looking for treasure, but instead he's just sitting there, staring at the sea.

'Are you all right?' I ask.

'Tired, that's all,' he says, then he pulls himself to his feet and says, 'Come on. The plane isn't here. We might as well go.'

Bones and Mei join us. 'I do not like the look of the weather,' says Bones. 'We should set sail immediately.' He can't quite bring himself to look at Mei as he says this.

She stomps ahead of us to where a huge front door would once have stood. The door frame is all that remains. She stands there, surrounded by burnt bricks, then gazes across the island. 'The *Bumble Bee* is here,' she says. 'We just need to find it!'

We crunch our way towards her, stepping on and

over blackened beams and crumbling bricks. I trip over something, and when I glance down I see an eye staring up at me.

My heart leaps with surprise, but when I crouch down I realise I'm looking at a fragment of a painting.

I pull the painting free from the mud and weeds. It's faded, damp and cracked, but it has somehow survived the fire and the elements. It shows the corner of a woman's face. I can see a curving, cat-like smile, one brown eye, and the edge of a bonnet.

'Look at this,' I say, going to the doorway and showing the others what I've found. 'Do you think this is Morgan Starkey?'

'Too old,' says Zen confidently, then he points at the bonnet. 'That's a French hood and it's short. Anne Boleyn made them popular, so this woman, whoever she is, was alive around four hundred years before Morgan Starkey.'

I can't take my eyes off the picture. I gaze at the face and at the easy smile that doesn't match the slightly narrowed eyes. 'It's strange,' I say, 'but she looks familiar.'

Peg glances over my shoulder. 'I don't know about that, but she certainly has a sly look about her.'

I fold the damp canvas and put it in my pocket. Whoever the woman is, it's cool to have found something so old, and for a few minutes it has distracted me from what we are supposed to be doing, or rather, from what we have failed to do: find Mei's plane.

We stand together at the top of the steps, looking over the island.

'We need to go,' I say reluctantly.

'No!' Mei turns and grabs hold of my arm. 'My plane is here, Sid. You two say you're detectives so, please, help me find it!'

I'm about to tell Mei that I'm sorry, that we tried, when Bones mutters, 'Now what might that be?'

I follow his pointing finger to the side of the weed-strewn runway. And there, half hidden by an enormous oak tree, is a low building covered in ivy. A few minutes ago we must have walked straight past it, but from up here its boxy shape is clear to see.

'That's got to be worth checking out,' I say.

'And then we go,' says Zen.

We hurry over and while Zen and I walk round the building, looking for a door, Mei, Bones and Peg march inside. A moment later, we hear a scream of delight, then Mei's pale face appears. 'We've found a plane, only we can't see it properly!'

Next Zen shouts, 'And I've found a door!'

Together we pull leaves away from a huge, sliding door. Soon we're able to push back a rusting bolt. Zen grabs the handle, but he can't open it. I help, digging my feet into the ground and pulling as hard as I can. 'Do you think it's locked?' asks Zen.

'No!' I say, and then, with a rusty squeal, the door starts to slide open.

Zen and I step into what looks like a garage. There are wheels stacked on top of each other and oil cans pushed against the walls. Even though there are no roads on the island an old-fashioned car stands in the corner blanketed in a layer of dust and cobwebs. But that's not what is making Mei jump up and down and shout, 'It's the *Bumble Bee*. I know it!'

Standing in the middle of the garage is a large object shrouded in a dust sheet.

'Pull off the sheet!' cries Mei Huang.

Zen and I grab hold of the heavy cloth and after some tugging manage to drag it away.

And there, shining bright in the gloom of the garage, is Mei Huang's bright yellow *Bumble Bee*.

Happiness rushes through me. Mei smiles, shuts her eyes and rests her face against the nose of the plane. I watch her closely. I love this moment: when a ghost's unfinished business is solved and I see the worry slip from their eyes and colour sweep through them.

But nothing happens.

It's obvious that Mei is overjoyed. Now she's laughing and running round her plane, climbing inside the cockpit and shouting things out like 'She's perfect!' and 'At least that idiot Starkey looked after her!'. But her flying cap is still a dull grey and when she jumps down from the cockpit she becomes a ghostly blur of white mist.

Zen, Bones and Peg look as baffled as me.

'What is wrong with you, girl?' Bones asks. 'You're as pale as milk. Why haven't you got colour back in your cheeks?'

'It doesn't make sense,' I add. 'You said finding your plane was your unfinished business and, look, we found it!'

Mei smiles and shrugs then says, 'I admit, finding the plane is only *half* of my unfinished business.'

My excitement fades away. 'What's the other half?'

Mei's eyes are wide with excitement. 'I must complete the round-the-world trip I began seventy years ago and fly back to Fathom!'

CHAPTER FORTY-ONE

'No way!' I say, as we march back across the island. 'I am not flying an antique plane, or any other plane for that matter.'

Mei tries to block my way, but I walk straight through her, making a wave of cold crash through me. She trots by my side, trying and failing to grab my arm. 'Please, Sid. I'll tell you what to do. It's simple. Like riding a bike!'

'No! I've done some pretty stupid things for you ghosts, but I'm not risking my life in that rusty old plane, even for you.'

Mei gasps. 'How dare you! There is no rust on the *Bumble Bee*!'

I don't look at her. I'm too cross. She tricked us into

coming here. We could have been spending our time getting Will to a kangaroo or finding a carriage for Beau to hold up. Amazingly it turns out that both of these things would have been easier than sorting out Mei's unfinished business.

Realising I'm not going to be persuaded, she decides to appeal to Zen instead.

'How about it, Zen? You like vehicles, don't you? Wouldn't you like to be as free as a bird, soaring through the sky?'

Zen shakes his head. 'I can't fly a plane, Mei, and neither can Sid. I'm sorry. It's too dangerous.'

Abruptly she stops walking and collapses to the ground. 'Then I'm stuck here!' she wails. 'Forever!'

I can't walk away and leave her, no matter how angry I feel.

Bones crouches by her side. 'Come now. You can't expect the kiddies to fly your aeroplane, but that does not mean you will become a wraith.'

'Yes, it does!' she shouts. 'It's already happening, and if I don't fly back to Fathom then I'm doomed.'

'You must not say doomed,' says Peg, trying to hold her hand. 'This is what Olive would call a "sticky fix".'

But Mei Huang won't be consoled. She snatches her

hand away from Peg and buries her head in her arms. Then her shoulders start to shake. I know she would hate us to see that she's crying, but even so I brace myself for the cold and put a hand on her shoulder. 'I'm sorry I got cross, Mei,' I say. 'And I'm sorry we haven't been able to set you free.'

'And you never shall,' comes her muffled voice.

'We found Bones's treasure, didn't we? I'm sure we can think of a way to help you complete your round-the-world trip.'

'Sid's right,' says Zen. 'In fact, I've already had an idea. We can tell someone important that your plane is on this island and I bet they will send someone out here to fly it home. It doesn't belong to this Morgan woman, does it? She stole it so now it must belong to . . . I don't know, the Crown or something.'

Mei looks up. Her goggles are misted with ghostly tears.

'But how long will that take?' she asks. 'Weeks? Months? I haven't got that long, Zen!'

'Perhaps there is another way you can fly back,' I say.

'You could hang off a drone,' suggests Zen.

I really don't think Mei Huang can hang off a drone,

285

even if she is a ghost, but I don't say anything because she's jumped to her feet.

'A drone . . . Is that some sort of light aircraft?'

'Very light,' admits Zen.

I glance at my watch. 'We can talk about this back at the fishing hut. Right now we've got to sail home. If our parents find out we've spent the night here we'll be grounded for life, and then we'll never be able to come back. Please come with us, Mei. We'll think of something.'

'Yes, let's go,' says Zen. 'I'm not looking forward to a bumpy boat ride. I'm not feeling too great.'

I look at Zen. He's slightly bent over and beads of sweat stand out on his forehead. 'Are you OK?' I ask.

'Yeah, I probably ate too many Mini Rolls.'

Mei gazes in the direction of the garage and her beloved *Bumble Bee*. When she turns back to face us I see tears in her eyes. 'I never crashed my plane in the sea!' she says.

'We know,' I say. 'And we will make sure everyone else knows it too.'

And she finally lets us lead her away.

CHAPTER
FORTY-TWO

We walk straight across the island towards our camp.

Mei is marching ahead of us. She's so pale that she looks like a flickering film. Like a ghost, I think, and to calm the panic that rises up inside me I press my hand against my chest. I'm expecting to feel the thick folded edges of my map, but there's nothing there.

The shock makes me stop walking and shove my hands under my jumper. The map holder is empty. When Peg cried out in the greenhouse I did the one thing she told me never to do: I let myself be separated from my book of charms.

I've left my map in the greenhouse!

I feel sick. Without my map I won't be able to free any more ghosts. How could I have been so stupid?

I know why. I barely slept last night and I'm exhausted. But really it doesn't matter why I did it. I've got to get it back. Zen and the ghosts are up ahead and have nearly reached the camp. I'm about to shout out and tell them what I've done, when I see Mo.

She's put our tent and bags in a pile and is obviously waiting for us to help her load up the boat. It's clear we need to go. Grey clouds are gathering in the sky. The journey back to Fathom is short, but we still need to set off straight away.

I can't shout out about my map, not with Mo there, but at the same time I can't leave my map behind. I don't even think I've got enough time to run up and whisper in Zen's ear.

So I make a snap decision. I duck off the path and into the trees, then I find the track that leads to the poison garden. It's five minutes away if I run. I can be there and back in ten minutes. By the time I return Zen and Mo will have loaded up the boat and I can jump on board, my map safely tucked under my jumper, and we can go.

I tell myself they might not even notice I'm missing.

I run fast. I follow the path round the orchard then dash through the rusty doors of the greenhouse. Trying not to brush against the toxic plants, I go straight to the bench.

My map is exactly where I left it: spread out on the moss that covers the bench. Relief makes me burst out laughing. Quickly I put it safely back in its holder. Now I need to get back to the boat so we can go home.

I'm walking down one of the narrow paths when a cloud drifts over the sun. The greenhouse is plunged into shadow and the temperature drops. It feels quieter too, as if the plants have paused in their suckering and twisting and are wondering where the sun has gone.

That's when I hear a faint bubbling noise. I stand still and listen carefully. There it is again. A gentle *pop, pop, popping* sound, and it's coming from somewhere behind me.

I turn and find myself face to face with a wall of climbing plants. Some have purple star flowers, others berries the colour of milk. One is covered in what look like tiny bunches of grapes, only each berry is the colour of black ink. If I didn't know they were deadly poisonous, I might be tempted to pop one in my mouth.

I can still hear the sound, but there doesn't seem to be anything causing it. I decide that the greenhouse must have some sort of drainage system underground. I'm about to go when something stops me in my tracks. Golden dust is drifting out from between the leaves. I reach out and stare at what I've caught on my fingers. It's ghost dust. I'd recognise it anywhere.

Pulling my sleeve down so that it covers my hand, I reach into the leaves. I don't touch glass or a wall. My hand just keeps going. There must be another room behind this tangle of poisonous plants. Squeezing my eyes shut I take a deep breath, then push my way through the leaves.

CHAPTER FORTY-THREE

What is this place?

I'm in a windowless room that looks like an ancient science lab. The glittering dust I saw seeping through the leaves is heavy in the air and swirls around me as I peer at the shelves lining the walls. They're filled with jars and bottles. I can see dried flowers in one and another is stuffed full of hair. The next jar has a symbol scratched into the glass. When I wipe the dust from the surface I see tiny, jelly-like balls suspended in an amber liquid. It looks like bubble tea. But then I notice that each of the balls has a dot in the centre. They're eyes!

Horrified, I step back, banging against a table. Then I find out what is making the bubbling sound. An experiment is set up. There are large test tubes attached to clamps, and flickering candles burn beneath jars. A collection of stoppered drop-shaped bottles also sit on the table alongside a large leather book.

I pick up one of the bottles and hold it close to the candle. It contains a clear liquid with glittering specks of gold floating through it. The label reads: *Luminos.*

My heart leaps. The Innkeeper called the ghosts' dust 'lumin', and this potion seems to contain the dust. I'm sure it's identical to the bottle the Innkeeper dangled in front of Old Scratch's face. But what does it do?

And that's when I realise the danger I'm in. The last time I saw one of these drop-shaped bottles the Innkeeper was holding it. Does this lab belong to the Innkeeper? Could this whole island belong to the Innkeeper?

I feel hot and then cold. I have got to get out of here and warn the others, but then I see something that freezes me to the spot.

Lying on the table, among dried leaves, a box of matches and a half-eaten packet of Hobnob biscuits, is a tiny model of a man. I'd recognise him anywhere. It's my dad.

I pick him up and a sob bursts
out of me. Someone has done
something to the model. His hands
are missing and so are both his feet.
I start to search through the mess
on the table, thinking that if I can find
the missing bits, I can mend him.

I don't see any tiny feet or hands, but
I find something much worse: more
models. Zen's sister, Skye, is here
and so are his mum and dad and
Sally from the café. None of them
have their hands or feet cut off,
but now I know I was right. The
model of Dad wasn't lost or taken by
children. Old Scratch or the Innkeeper
took it and at some point they went back
and took these other models too.

I really do have to find the others and
warn them that we've stumbled into a
very dangerous place. Before I leave I
take one of the bottles labelled

Luminos and slip it in my pocket. Perhaps Bones or Peg will be able to tell me what it is.

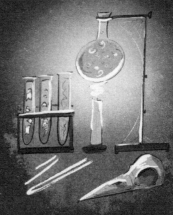

I run to the curtain of leaves. I'm about to push my way through when I hear footsteps on one of the gravel paths in the greenhouse. For a second fear keeps me frozen in place, but then I realise that the footsteps are heading straight towards me. I have to hide!

My heart races as I look around the room. Next to me, I spot a huge cauldron. I don't stop to think. I grab a cloak that's draped over a stool, climb inside the cauldron and pull the cloak over my head.

Seconds later I hear the leaves being pushed aside. I wrap my arms round my knees to stop them from shaking and squeeze my eyes shut. Then I try hard not to think about the fact that I'm sitting in a cauldron.

For a moment there is silence and I can sense that someone

is looking around the room. Then I hear more footsteps followed by the scratch and flare of a match being lit. Next I hear a *crunch, crunch, crunch* sound and I'm sure something is being ground in the mortar.

Curiosity makes me open my eyes and raise my head a fraction. The cloak slips to one side and I can see through a small gap into the room. A candle flickers on the table. In the dim light I can see a figure bent over the table. In one swift movement, the figure reaches for the model of my dad, breaks off a bit of his arm, drops it into the mortar and starts to grind.

I feel sick to my stomach. I cover my mouth to stop myself from crying out, but I must make some sort of sound because the figure spins round.

It's Mo. Relief floods through me. I smile and I'm about to stand up and give myself away when I remember what I've just seen.

Mo just broke a piece off my dad's model and started grinding it into a powder. I heard her walk straight into this room. And now she's casually lighting another candle and taking a biscuit from the packet on the table.

As she munches on the biscuit, she sprinkles some of

the powder from the mortar into one of the bubbling jars of liquid. Instantly it explodes into a puff of glittery smoke that travels along one of the glass tubes. I see Mo smile.

Desperately I try to think why she might be doing these things. Perhaps she came looking for me, heard the bubbling sound and found the room. Maybe she started to explore and began playing with the things she found. She might not have known that the model was of my dad. *Please let this be true*, I think as panic squeezes my chest.

But what I see next tells me that this isn't true at all.

Without warning Mo slams her hands down on the table and hunches forward.

Then she starts to transform in front of my eyes.

It happens so fast it's like watching a speeded-up film. Mo's skin becomes paler, then lines tug down the corners of her mouth. Her hair loses its bright red colour, gradually becoming grey. Then her body starts to contort.

With a groan of annoyance, Mo kicks off her trainers then arches her back. Her muscles and bones push against her skin as if they're trying to escape.

Part of me screams, *Help her!* But I don't move from my hiding place because Mo doesn't seem at all shocked by what is happening to her. In fact, she just looks mildly irritated.

Suddenly she flops forward, her hair covering her face. She snaps her head to the left then to the right. Then calmly she stands up and brushes her now long grey hair away from her face.

It's still Mo standing in front of me, but it's Mo grown up. In the last couple of minutes she's aged by years.

She is now a tall woman with an icy stare and strong hands. Mo's baggy clothes have stretched to accommodate her extra foot of height. She glances around the room, then reaches across the bench, grabs a cloak and throws it over her shoulders.

Even though she isn't wearing the plague mask, I know that I'm staring at the Innkeeper.

CHAPTER FORTY-FOUR

Bones was right all along.

I stare at Mo, no, *the Innkeeper*. I can't take my eyes off this woman who is both familiar and a stranger to me. I watch as she starts to busy herself with the potion she's brewing, closing a valve, opening another, tipping the contents of a small vial into the bubbling mixture.

I've got to get out of here. I have to get back to the others so we can sail away. I need to warn them that the enemy has been by our side all along. Not only that, I invited her to the island with us!

But I can't go anywhere. I can barely breathe without

revealing my hiding place. And Mo seems in no hurry to leave. She turns her attention to the models on the table. This time she picks up the model of Skye and her strong hands fold round it. She's about to snap it in half.

'NO!' I scream, throwing off the cloak and jumping out of my hiding place.

Mo staggers backwards with shock. Clumsily I clamber out of the cauldron. But before I've taken even one step towards Mo, she's slammed her hand down on the leather book on the table and started to whisper some words.

I can't hear what she's saying. She points in my direction with her free hand and hisses the words louder and faster. I step backwards. That's when I feel something tickle my neck. Too late, I realise Mo is saying the words of a spell. I glance down and see that the plants covering the entrance are reaching for me, twisting their tendrils round my ankles and winding their way round my waist. I struggle, twisting from side to side, but instantly they tighten, snaring my wrists, yanking my hands back, binding them together. In a matter of seconds I'm trapped, entangled in ivy which feels as strong as chains.

Mo stops speaking and lets go of the book.

'You're a witch,' I say, my eyes travelling from the book and back to Mo.

She raises an eyebrow and smiles, something I've seen her do so many times before at school. 'Takes one to know one, Sid.'

Her voice is louder, like a purr. Just like in the pit, I recognise it, only I don't know where from.

Mo picks up a bottle of Luminos and swishes it from side to side. 'You gave me a shock, Sid, but I'm pleased you're here. You are about to witness something truly incredible!'

She pulls the cork stopper off the bottle, pours the glittery contents down her throat, then licks her lips and grins. 'Are you ready?' she says.

This time her transformation is slower. Gradually her hair darkens and her skin gains more colour. Whatever she just drank – the stuff called Luminos – is reversing her age. The veins on her hands shrink and her eyes become brighter. Mo seems to be relishing what is happening to her: running her hands through her hair, stretching her arms, flexing her fingers as, second by second, she becomes younger. Her head hangs forward for a few seconds and when she looks up a pretty young woman with silky brown hair is staring back at me. I recognise the face from the scrap of portrait I pulled from the rubble of the fire and from somewhere else.

'You're Molly Noon,' I say. I've seen this woman on the countless yoga videos Dad does, and on the packaging for her candles and herbal tea bags. I even saw her on breakfast TV once.

'Yes!' She seems delighted that I've worked it out. 'I've had many names over the years – Morgan Starkey, Molly Noon, Mo – but my given name is Morgan Gundred Noon.' Her face creases with mock concern. 'Would you feel more comfortable if I looked like Mo?'

Without waiting for me to reply, she pulls the stopper off another bottle of Luminos and gulps down half of the contents. The first thing to change is her hair. Like ink spreading across the page it turns from brown to bright red, then she rolls her head from side to side as her muscles contract. She's shrinking and soon the Mo I know so well is standing in front of me swamped in a black cloak.

'Ta-da!' she says with a grin.

'The ghosts' dust makes you younger,' I say.

She swishes what's left in the bottle from side to side. 'Almost. It's the potion – Luminos – that I make out of their dust that makes me younger. I invented it. Aren't I clever?'

It's so strange hearing these boastful words coming from Mo's mouth, but then I realise this is the real Mo. She's been acting the whole time, saying and doing exactly what she thought I wanted her to say. I think about her love of axolotls and books, her sense of humour and her shyness. She faked it all for me, and I fell for it.

'Jones!' The shout comes from the greenhouse. 'Jones, where are you?'

It's Bones. Relief surges through me that it's him and not Zen.

'I'm in here!' I yell, and a moment later he bursts through the leaves. His head swivels from left to right, looking from me to Mo then back again. He takes in the vines wrapped round my body and Mo standing there with a smug smile on her face.

'I'm sorry, Bones,' I say. 'I should have listened to you.'

CHAPTER FORTY-FIVE

When Bones realises what Mo has done to me he leaps into action. He rages at her to let me go then tries to grab hold of her, but his hands can't do a thing. They don't even seem to make her cold.

'I knew it!' he says. 'I knew it the moment you crashed into me on the bus but didn't shiver. You've been able to see us the whole time, haven't you?'

She does one of her sly smiles. 'I can't tell you how unbearable it has been ignoring your constant chattering, but I only slipped up once, last night in the tent. You see, I do actually hate spiders!'

'Let Sid go!' roars Bones.

'Or what?' she says. 'Will you swish your useless hands through me again? Accept it, Ezekiel Kittow, you can't do a thing to help your little friend.'

'Yes, he can,' I say, then I look at Bones. 'Go and tell Zen what's happened. Tell him that Mo, the Innkeeper, Molly Noon and Morgan Starkey are all one person. Tell him that she's been making a potion from the ghosts' dust to stay young. Tell him that she's got me tied up in here and to call the police.'

'They'll never believe him,' says Mo.

'It doesn't matter,' I say. 'They'll still come. You don't ignore a phone call about a child being held prisoner.'

I'm expecting Mo to look worried or try to stop Bones, but she just shrugs and says to Bones, 'Do what she says. Go and tell Zen everything.'

Bones looks at me. 'Are you sure?'

'Yes!' I cry. 'Go!'

The moment he's gone I have only one thought: keep Mo talking until help arrives, so I say, 'Was everything a lie?'

She thinks for a moment. 'Almost. I do have an axolotl. Six actually. I sell a tranquillity candle made from the algae in their tank. It glows a magnificent green as it burns.' And then she is off, boasting about her 'powerful magic' and the fact that she's the only witch to ever discover the secret of life: the ghosts' dust or 'lumin' as she calls it.

As she's talking she strides up and down the room, occasionally fiddling with a test tube or adding ingredients to one of the bubbling jars.

Suddenly she stops and stares hard at me. 'Perhaps now you understand why I was so furious when you freed my ghosts from the Halfway House. You were stealing *my life* from me, Sid!' The fury comes so fast it's a shock.

'You really need their dust,' I say.

'Yes, I need their dust!' she cries. 'Without it I can't make Luminos and I will wither away and die. The ghosts' dust has kept me and my pathetic son alive for over four hundred years.'

'Your son?' I say, interrupting her.

'Yes, Old Scratch is my son.' Suddenly she grins. 'It must seem strange hearing me say that.'

It is strange, but I'm starting to realise that the person standing in front of me isn't Mo. It's the Innkeeper.

'I gave him that name,' she continues. 'He was such an irritating child, hanging off my skirts, whining for attention.'

She scratches a nail along the table three times. 'He was annoying like a scratch, see?'

'But he was useful for collecting the ghosts' dust,' I say. I glance towards the wall of leaves. How long will it take for help to come?

She shrugs. 'I suppose he managed that, until you came along and set Kittow free.' She scowls. 'And you freed him just when I needed more dust than ever. My potion was magnificent – you have seen the evidence of it with your own eyes – but over the years I perfected it until I could not only make time stand still, but reverse it as well.' Her eyes grow wide. 'Sid, can you imagine what people would pay for that? Not good, honest, hard-working people, of course, but exceedingly rich people who believe they have the right to buy anything.'

'But what about the ghosts?' I say. 'Don't you care what you've done to them?'

She looks at me like I've lost my mind. 'No, of course I don't, and I don't care for you either. When you set the pirates free and my supply was halved I wanted to break your neck.' She says this casually and I remember the night on the cliffs when Zen nearly fell off.

'It was you who rearranged the stones on the cliff, wasn't it?'

She nods. 'It was all I could do. Even a witch of your limited skills must have heard of the Elder Law. That's why I was forced to become your friend. If I couldn't hurt you with my hands then I knew I would have to do the next best thing and destroy your spell book.'

I remember how desperate Mo was to be invited round to my house and how carefully she looked at all the books in my bedroom. Then I glance in the direction of the greenhouse again. Bones will be back at the camp by now and I know Zen still had battery left on his phone. He will have called the police. They should be on their way.

This thought makes me bold enough to say, 'But you never found my spell book, did you?'

Her head snaps up. 'No.' She steps towards me and grabs hold of my face, just like she did with Old Scratch. She squeezes it, digging her fingers into my skin. 'I've a good mind to make you talk, but there's no need now. When you told me that you were visiting this island, *my island,* and not telling anyone, you gave me a gift, Sid. I knew you would never be going back.' She pushes my face away.

'You were wrong about that, weren't you? The police will be on their way. They might send a helicopter. That would get here in minutes. There's even a landing strip on your island!'

She bursts out laughing. 'You don't get it, do you? The police aren't coming, Sid. No one is coming.' She reaches into the bag she always carries around and pulls out Zen's phone. Smiling she wiggles it from side to side. 'Zen isn't ringing anyone.'

'When he realises his phone is missing he'll go in the boat! He's probably halfway to Fathom by now!'

She gives a gasp of exasperation as if I'm an idiot. 'There is no boat. I sank it when I went to pack up the camp, and even if there was I very much doubt Zen would have the strength to climb on board.'

'What do you mean?'

'Think about Snow White, Sid.'

I know she's playing games with me, but I still have to do what she says. Then I understand. 'The apple,' I whisper. Nausea rushes through me as I remember Zen crunching down on one of the apples we found. 'But you ate one too!'

'I ate *an* apple, but not one from my orchard. I'd never

310

be so foolish. I've been watering those trees with a tincture of the *papaver acris* for years. It's a powerful poison. First comes tiredness and nausea, then a loss of consciousness. Death follows soon after. I'd say your friend has an hour or two at most.'

'NO!' I shout, twisting and turning, trying to break out of the vines. Zen isn't getting help. He's been poisoned, and I can't do anything to help him.

Mo watches me, clearly enjoying my distress. 'You know, the poison is wickedly efficient, but the antidote is cobnuts. *Cobnuts!* So simple, and yet you won't find a single cobnut on this island. Obviously it's going to take you longer to die.' She stares at me with her clear brown eyes. 'I'd put you out of your misery, but' – she shrugs – 'sadly my hands are tied by the Elder Law we must all abide by – as a witch I'm sure you understand.'

'You're just going to leave me here?'

'That's right. I wonder who will go first? You, Zen, Mei Huang? Or maybe your father?'

She picks up the model with its cut off hands and feet.

'You've been making him ill, haven't you? Please don't do anything else to hurt him!'

'I had to steal this myself because my pathetic son refused to. Your father made them with such care and love that I've been able to use them to harvest even more lumin.' She wiggles the model from side to side. 'I've been taking a tiny piece off at a time – draining your dad's life force drop by drop – but there's no need for discretion now, is there?' She starts to move around the room, throwing things into her bag. In go all the models that she's stolen from the model village, then she wraps up the bottles of Luminos and puts them in too.

'A mysterious illness is about to befall the good folk of Fathom, Sid. Your lovely dad is about to get very poorly indeed. He probably won't even realise you're missing. I doubt he'll ever wake up again.' She thinks for a moment then adds, 'I might go missing too. I've overstayed my welcome in Fathom. Molly Noon and Mo can mysteriously vanish, along with two local children.' She does a mock sad face and says, 'So tragic.'

Her rucksack is heavy now. She drags it on to her shoulders and tightens the straps. She's getting ready to leave.

'Please,' I say desperately. 'Don't hurt my dad or Zen.

It's me who made all this happen.'

At the curtain of leaves she pauses, looking at me thoughtfully. 'You know, you would have made a magnificent witch, Sid. My son never had a magical bone in his body, but you?' She puts a cool hand on my cheek. 'You're potential is quite incredible. I could have taught you to control the wind, the rain and the sun, to make poisons that could kill in an instant, but instead you're going to wither away on this island. What a terrible waste.'

She pats my face and smiles. 'Time to go,' she says brightly, but she can't quite bring herself to leave. 'There is one thing I would love to know. Where is your book of spells, Sid?

For a moment we stare at each other. My map burns where it's hanging under my jumper. I force myself to stare straight back at Mo. I can't let her know it's there. My map is my only hope.

'You're not going to tell me, are you?'

'Never,' I say.

'Then die with your secret,' she hisses, and then she pushes through the leaves and is gone.

CHAPTER FORTY-SIX

For a few minutes panic crashes through me, stopping all logical thought.

I twist and turn, thrashing from side to side, but if anything this only makes the plants wrapped round my body pull even tighter. Sweat trickles down my back and my heart races. I have to get out of here!

Then I hear the crackle of my map under my jumper. Magic. It's my only hope.

I can't touch my map with my finger like I did in the pit, and even if I could I don't know any spells . . . Or do I?

I try to remember what I saw when I was looking at the spell books in the museum. But they were so confusing, written in a version of English that was impossible to read.

Then I think of Peg. I'm friends with a witch. Suddenly I wish I'd asked her more about magic, got her to teach me some spells. I freeze. She did tell me about one spell. She said she used it to get rid of weeds on her mum's cabbage patch. What did she say? *Shrivel and waste, you perilous pest?*

It's got to be worth a try.

I stare at the tendrils wrapped round me then say, '*Shrivel and waste, you perilous pest!*'

Nothing happens. I don't even feel the tiniest spark of magic bubble inside me. But I won't give up. I think about Peg's other piece of advice; that I need to squeeze the magic out of me. The magic worked in the pit because it was a matter of life and death, and so is this.

I close my eyes and start to whisper the spell.

'*Shrivel and waste, you perilous pest . . . Shrivel and waste, you perilous pest . . .*'

As I say the words I remind myself why I am doing this. Zen is dying. Mei Huang and the ghosts still trapped in the Halfway House are about to turn into wraiths. The Innkeeper is planning to hurt my dad and so many other people in the village. This has to work!

The heat explodes from where my map is resting close to my heart. It shoots through my body, fizzing to my fingers and toes. It makes the hair on my head tingle. I squeeze my eyes shut as I shout, '*SHRIVEL AND WASTE, YOU PERILOUS PEST!*'

The stems and leaves explode from my body, scattering across the room in a mist of green. It happens so suddenly and violently that for a moment I just stand there, my hands still clamped together behind my back. Then I realise I'm free and I have one thought: *Zen.*

I find him curled up on the beach, Mei Huang, Bones and Peg by his side. Elizabeth flies over our heads screeching her unhappiness.

'Sid . . . I don't feel so good,' Zen says, clutching his stomach.

I can't think of an easy way to say this so I blurt out, 'You've been poisoned, Zen.'

He nods, wincing. 'I guessed. Bones told us about Mo. It was the apple, wasn't it? That was the only thing you didn't eat.'

I kneel by his side. 'I'm so sorry. This is all my fault!'

He shakes his head. 'No, it's all her fault. Mo . . . the Innkeeper, whatever her name actually is.'

'It's Morgan Gundred Noon,' I say. 'And she's over four hundred years old.'

Zen actually manages a smile. 'Course she is. You manage to make one other friend except for me at school, Sid, and she's a four-hundred-year-old witch!'

I smile, but I'm crying too. 'It's a powerful poison, Zen. I'm so sorry.'

He opens his eyes and looks up at me. 'I'm not dead yet. Tell me what she said.'

'And don't miss out a single detail,' adds Bones.

As quickly as possible I tell them everything the Innkeeper said to me. I tell them about the ghosts' dust, lumin, and the age-defying potion she has made out of it, and about my dad and the models. I even say that she's got the models of Zen's family.

'What about the poison?' asks Peg.

I explain that cobnuts are the antidote, and that the Innkeeper said there aren't any on the island. 'She could have been lying,' I say, 'but we don't have time to search and find out.'

'I know where there are cobnuts,' says Bones. 'Sally uses them to make her beer!'

For the first time since I found Zen lying on the beach I feel a glimmer of hope. 'But how can we get Zen back to Fathom? The boat's gone and the Innkeeper has Zen's phone.'

Next to me, Zen groans and curls his knees closer to his chest. I don't need to add that we don't have long. One look at Zen makes that very clear.

For a moment we all watch Zen. There is a faint rumble of thunder out at sea. There are dark clouds gathering too. Has the Innkeeper done this? She said she could control the weather, and a storm is the perfect way to keep us trapped on the island.

I give Zen a gentle shake. 'We're going to help you, Zen. We're going to get you back to Fathom, get some of Sally's cobnut beer into you.'

'How?' he says through gritted teeth. Sweat beads on his forehead and his skin is boiling to touch. I don't think I've ever felt so hopeless.

'I don't know how,' I admit, and I swallow down the sobs that are threatening to burst out of me. 'The thing is, we don't have long, Zen. Less than an hour.'

'I know how we do it,' says Mei. 'We fly!'

CHAPTER FORTY-SEVEN

I haul the wicker wheelchair over a tuft of grass. Zen lurches from side to side, but manages to stay in thanks to the hoodie I've tied around his waist and the back of the wheelchair.

'Nearly there,' I tell Zen. He doesn't reply. His head droops forward.

Bones, Peg and Mei can't help me push the wheelchair, so instead they give me encouragement and lots of advice.

'Hurry now!' urges Bones. 'Watch out for that rut in the earth. Careful, Jones, he is tumbling out!'

I yank Zen back into place and try to go faster.

But the ground is so uneven and the path is overgrown. Zen's breathing is shallow and each time I go over a particularly big bump he groans. Except for this he barely makes a sound.

'Zen?' I give his shoulder a shake. 'Can you hear me?' His head lolls back and his eyes flicker open. I take this as a good sign. 'Look, we're nearly at the garage.' I'm pushing the wheelchair across the weed-strewn runway. 'We'll have you in that plane in no time and then –' I pause, not quite able to believe what I'm about to say – 'I'll fly us back to Fathom and get some of Sally's cobnut beer into you!'

His eyes open for a moment and he whispers, 'I'm not sure what part of that sentence I'm more scared of.'

Suddenly Peg says, 'Look at those trees dancin' around. I feel an ill wind in the air. I believe it's the Innkeeper's doing.'

'Maybe it is,' I say, 'but we can't stop now. We've got to get Zen to Fathom.'

When we reach the garage, Mei Huang goes to check the runway is clear of debris. 'You get Zen into the plane,' she calls over her shoulder. 'Into the front seat. The aviator goes in the back. That's you.'

Me. The aviator. I try to swallow away the fear that's building up inside me. I remind myself that I have no choice. I have to fly this plane.

I push Zen into the gloomy garage and alongside the *Bumble Bee*.

Up close, Mei's bright yellow plane looks alarmingly like a big toy. It's a biplane, which means it has two sets of wings. It also has an open cabin with two seats, one behind the other. Somehow I've got to get Zen into the front seat, which right now seems a long way off the ground.

'Its nose doesn't half stick up in the air,' says Peg, as she surveys the plane. 'How do you reckon on getting Zen up there?'

'I'll do it somehow,' I say, sounding more confident than I feel. 'I pulled him up a cliff, didn't I?'

I climb on to the wing of the plane and open the little flap that acts as a door.

'Zen!' I have to shout to get his attention. 'Do you think you can climb up on to this wing?'

He doesn't reply. I jump down from the plane and lift his face. 'Zen, listen to me. I need you to climb on to the wing then into the plane. Can you do that for me?'

He forces his eyes open and nods his head slowly. 'My whole body feels like jelly.'

'We will help you, lad,' growls Bones. 'Have courage.'

Quickly I untie the hoodie holding him in place, grab him under his arms and heave him up until he's standing. He totters unsteadily, rocking backwards and forwards until he slumps against the wing.

'OK, pull yourself up,' I say.

But Zen is like a badly controlled puppet. His arms and legs flop about as he tries and fails to scramble on board.

'Just shove him in!' growls Bones. 'That's what I used to do when fellows in my crew were too seasick to climb into their bunks.'

'Did you hear that, Zen? I'm going to give you a big shove and get you into that cockpit.'

'Use your gift, Sid,' Zen slurs. 'I need it.'

'I'll try,' I say, 'but I need your help too. We'll do it on the count of three.' I manoeuvre Zen so that he's tipped towards the cockpit then wrap my arms round his legs. 'One . . . two . . .' I crouch down, getting ready to push. 'THREE!'

I squeeze Zen's legs, pushing him higher and higher.

323

'That's it!' bellows Bones. 'Heave him up, Jones!'

At first I don't think it's working. Zen feels like a dead weight in my arms, but then I feel him shooting upwards. My muscles burn. Zen's arms scramble as he tries to grab hold of something.

Bones yells, 'He's nearly in. Shove him, Jones!'

And I do shove him. I feel the burn of magic again – just like I did when I was pulling Zen up the cliff and in the potions room. It's like a bright light that fills me with energy. I hurl Zen forward and he topples into the cockpit like a sack of potatoes.

There's no time to lose. I jump on to the wing and push his legs into place. Before he can slump forward, I do up his seat belt. Finally I grab a leather flying cap that's sitting on the rear seat and ram it on his head. With a groan I jump down from the plane and flop back into the empty wheelchair, panting for breath.

'Well, he's in the plane all right,' says Bones. 'Your gift got him up there!'

And it seems like my gift has given Zen a boost of energy too, because a few moments later he's lifting his head and looking around.

Mei bursts into the garage.

'The runway is clear!' she cries, not even trying to hide the excitement in her voice. 'Let's go, Sid. Let's complete my mission!'

'You mean, *let's save Zen's life?*' I say, not wanting her to forget why we're doing this.

'Absolutely,' she says. 'That's my mission now. Come on, Sid. Chocks away!'

'What?'

'Let's get the *Bumble Bee* back in the air!'

CHAPTER FORTY-EIGHT

I'm standing in front of the *Bumble Bee* wearing a too big leather flying jacket and goggles. Zen is squeezed into the front seat, Mei is in the rear seat, and Bones and Peg are crouched on the wings. Elizabeth is circling the plane and squawking with a mixture of alarm and curiosity.

Everyone is waiting for me to spin the propeller and start the engine. As soon as I've done that I've got to pull away the chocks – the wooden blocks that stop the plane from moving forward – run round a wing and climb into the rear seat. Right on top of Mei.

Not only am I about to fly a plane, I'm going to do it while sitting on a ghost.

'I'm sorry, Sid,' Mei said when she explained where she would need to sit. 'You will only hear my instructions if they are spoken in your ear. The *Bumble Bee* is a magnificent machine, but she's very noisy.'

'Ready?' I shout, my hand on the propeller.

'Ready!' Bones, Peg and Mei call in unison.

'*Rum! Bully!*' cries Elizabeth.

Zen doesn't shout. He just wiggles his fingers to show that he's heard.

I glance along the weed-strewn runway. It seems too rutted for this ancient plane, but Mei has assured me that the *Bumble Bee* is up to the job.

Before I can have second thoughts I pull down hard on the propeller. The engine roars, the propeller spins and the *Bumble Bee* leaps into life, shuddering as if she's desperate to get moving. Black smoke billows from beneath the plane, but this quickly changes to white.

I run to the side of the plane and, just as Mei instructed, I tug the chocks away from under the wheels using the rope attached to them. I was worried that the plane would immediately surge forward leaving me behind, but Mei said it wouldn't go anywhere until I got behind the controls.

'Come on, Sid!' Mei cries, and I dart round the wing and pull myself into the rear seat, jumping straight on top of her. It's like plunging into a bath full of ice cubes. The cold is so shocking that for a second I can't talk, but at least it makes me feel alert. What's harder to get used to is her voice that seems to be coming from inside my head.

'Right, you see those two switches?' she says. It's as if the old flying cap I'm wearing is talking to me. Suddenly a wispy white hand shoots out of my chest and points at switches labelled *BAT* and *GEN*. 'Flick them down.' I do what she says, then I follow her instructions to pull a lever and 'open the throttle'.

Straight away the engine roars, the arrow on a display in front of me spins around, and we lurch forward and start to trundle out of the garage and along the runway. The plane shudders and trembles, matching the shaking of my entire body.

'Is it supposed to do that?' I shout, not bothering to hide the panic in my voice,

'Of course.' Mei's voice is crisp and calm. 'Don't ask

unnecessary questions, Sid, and please try to steer us in a straight line.'

'But I can't see anything!' I wail, and it's true. The nose of the *Bumble Bee* is pointing up in the air and all I can see out of the window is the dark, angry-looking sky.

'Yes, that is a problem with Tiger Moths,' says Mei. 'I used to look out of the side and wiggle the plane from side to side so I could see where I was going.'

'I have to wiggle?' I'm finding it hard enough keeping the plane going in a straight line.

'No. I'll look for you.' Mei stands up, rising out of my body and sticking her head out of the top of the plane like a periscope. Then she starts calling out instructions, yelling so she can be heard over the roar of the engine. 'Left a bit . . . Too much! That's better. Now go right. OK. We're good to go!'

Mei drops back down into the seat and once again an icy coldness sweeps through my body. Then her voice speaks into my left ear. 'Ready to fly, Sid?'

Of course I'm not, but I can't admit that. Zen's head is flopped to one side. I can't even see if he's breathing.

'Yes. Just tell me what to do.'

'Push that lever fully forward.'

I do what she says and the plane starts to pick up speed. The wings wobble and I feel like the whole craft could fall apart at any moment. Perhaps it's a good job I can't see where I'm going because I know this runway isn't long. If we don't lift up into the air soon, we'll crash into the sea.

But flight seems impossible. The plane bounces clumsily along the runway and the engine splutters. My teeth are shaking. My whole body is shaking.

'What's going on, Mei?' I yell.

'Push down harder!' she shouts. 'Harder!'

I do what she says and at that moment the shuddering stops and the plane lifts off the ground and up into the air.

I hear a delighted scream in my ear. 'We're flying!' Mei cries.

And amazingly . . . we are! I follow Mei Huang's instructions, making the plane climb higher into the sky, then banking to the left and catching a dizzying glimpse of Wolf Island far below us. We head towards Fathom, racing over the churning sea, Elizabeth somehow keeping up with us. The wind is still strong. It seems angry, tugging our little plane up and down in the sky and throwing it from side to side.

Mei talks constantly, urging me to 'Tap the wings left' and 'Pull back a touch on the throttle' and because she keeps saying 'That's it, perfect', I lose some of my fear. I'm a puppet and Mei Huang is controlling me: I pull down on levers and flick switches whenever she gives me the command.

I force myself to concentrate on what I'm doing and to ignore the huge drop beneath us, and I try not to think about what I'm going to have to do in a moment: land a plane. I have to stay calm. I have no choice. My life and Zen's depends on it. But then Mei says something that makes the panic come sweeping back.

'I don't like this weather.'

Her voice still sounds calm, but I can detect a trace of worry and that's all it takes to make my hands start to shake and sweat prickle my skin.

The clouds have become darker and rain starts to fall. This wasn't meant to happen. I checked the forecast again and again before we sailed to Wolf Island. We're supposed to have beautiful weather for the whole weekend. Is Mo doing this?

Suddenly I feel very vulnerable in our little plane. The cockpit is uncovered so the rain and wind blow into my face. Under my hands the yoke shudders. I hold it even tighter.

'We need to land!' Mei shouts. It's what I want to hear, but at the same time I'm scared. Just then a gust of wind slams into us and for a moment we're tilting so far to the right that when I turn my head I'm looking straight down at the sea.

It swirls below us, a churning mass of foam and green waves.

'Rudder left!' Mei shouts. 'Too much. Ease off. OK. Prepare to land.'

When we were crossing the island with Zen in the wheelchair we talked about this moment. The tide is out, so the place we call the secret beach with its wide stretch of sand is the perfect spot to land a plane. But when I imagined doing it, I didn't think we'd be battling the wind and rain.

Mei must be able to feel my fear because she says, 'Sid, I've landed the *Bumble Bee* in storms before.'

'I haven't,' I whisper.

Suddenly her hand appears through my stomach and ghostly fingers pat my knee. 'Trust me,' Mei says, followed by, 'Pull back on the throttle. Now.'

I must yank the lever back too hard because the plane suddenly plunges down.

'Ease back,' says Mei, then she starts jumping out of her seat and peering out the roof of the plane, before popping back into my head to give me more instructions.

Soon we have dropped so low that we're racing over the tips of the waves. If that wasn't alarming enough, the cliffs are straight in front of us. Wet sands lies between us and the cliffs. And I can see something else, or rather *someone*.

Standing at the very edge of the cliff, her black cloak whipping around in the air, is Mo, only now I can only think of her as the Innkeeper. She seems to have grown taller and she's wearing the plague mask. One hand clutches her spell book while the other reaches up towards the sky. She's pointing directly at us and as she moves her hand I feel another brutal gust of wind slam into us.

The Innkeeper is making this storm happen. She's doing everything she can to bring down the *Bumble Bee*.

Briefly I wonder how she got back to Fathom, but suddenly we're flying over sand and the cliff face looms in front of us. I push all thoughts of the Innkeeper and her magic from my mind. I have to land this plane. Now!

'Pull slowly on the yoke,' says Mei, a trace of panic in her voice. 'Harder. All the way!'

I want to yank it back, but I force myself to stay calm and ignore the wall of granite racing to meet us. The plane bumps, jerking me up and down in my seat. Up ahead, Zen flops around like a rag doll. Then the plane starts to vibrate and it bounces down on something once, twice, three times.

We've landed! But my relief is short-lived. We're going way too fast, and heading towards the cliff!

'Use your feet, Sid!' cries Mei. 'Brake and turn. NOW!'

To use the foot pedals I have to slide out of my seat and stretch my legs down into the footwell. My toes only just reach the pedals, but I can't see a thing. I squeeze my eyes shut, press down on the brake, yank the throttle left. The next thing I know, an ear-splitting scream fills my ears.

It takes me a second to realise that it's me who is screaming, but I don't stop until the plane swings in a circle and comes to a juddering halt.

I lie flopped in the cockpit, my hands still locked round the throttle. With a cry of delight Mei Huang jumps out of the seat – and me – and clambers down on to the sand.

Slowly warmth returns to my body. I feel dizzy and sick, but I know that flying back to Fathom was only the start of what I have to do. With trembling hands I unclip my seat belt and look over the side of the plane.

The first thing I see is Mei turning a cartwheel across the sand. She's thrown off her cap and goggles, and her hair streams out behind her, silky and black. All her faded pallor has gone. The leather of her flying suit is a rich chestnut brown and a joyous smile is spread across her face.

'I'm free!' she shouts. 'I'm free!'

Dark clouds still hang above us, but they break up to allow a ghostly hot-air balloon to pass through them, before settling on the horizon. It's come for Mei Huang, but she dismisses its presence with a wave of her hand.

'I'm not leaving until this is over,' she says.

CHAPTER
FORTY-NINE

By pushing and shoving and summoning all the strength my map can give me, I drag Zen out of the plane and now he's lying on a pile of seaweed, one foot dangling in a rock pool. I press my hand against his cold clammy forehead.

I'm feeling desperate now. Zen's rasping breath has gone and the only way I know that he's breathing is the slight rise and fall of his chest. His lips are blue. His whole body is floppy. I've got to go and get some of Sally's cobnut beer, only I don't know if Zen can last until I get back.

Then I remember the bottle of potion that I slipped into my pocket. I take it out and see the word *Luminos* written on the label. The liquid inside sparkles in the gloomy light.

Bones, Mei and Peg huddle close round me. The storm seems to have died down and when I glance at the top of the cliff I see that the Innkeeper has gone.

'What's that you've got there, Sid?' asks Bones.

'It's what Old Scratch and the Innkeeper have been drinking to stay alive. It's made from your dust.'

'Are you going to give some to Zen?' asks Mei.

'I need to do something,' I say. 'It will take me twenty minutes to run to the café and then get back here.'

Suddenly Zen's eyes flicker open. I show him the bottle. 'Zen, I want you to drink this.'

He blinks then says in a hoarse whisper, 'I'd rather have an ambulance.'

His words make me want to laugh and cry at the same time. 'Trust me,' I say, desperately hoping that I'm right. 'Because there really isn't enough time to get an ambulance, and even if there was I don't think they'd listen if I told them you'd been poisoned by a witch and needed to drink some cobnut beer.'

He nods. I'm about to uncork the bottle when a force slams into me, knocking the bottle from my hands.

I look up to see the Innkeeper standing at the foot of the cliff. She must have emerged from one of the tunnels that leads on to the beach.

She's not Mo any more, that much is clear. She has grown older and now she is taller and the hand reaching towards me is large and strong. She still has her spell book clutched to her chest.

I scrabble for the bottle, grabbing hold of it. I'm about to put it to Zen's lips when I'm knocked back again. This time the bottle rolls into a rock pool. I crawl towards it, but the Innkeeper is walking towards me, still whispering her spell, and I feel myself yanked back by the wind. It's so powerful that my feet lift into the air and the next thing I know I've been dumped on my back on the sand.

Bones is hurtling across the beach, heading towards the Innkeeper, but I know there's nothing he can do to stop her. This is down to me.

The Innkeeper – I can't think of her as Mo any more – seems to have forgotten that she's not the only witch on this beach.

I reach under my jumper, grab hold of my map, then jump to my feet.

Bones has reached the Innkeeper. I can see him desperately trying to grab hold of her, but his hands do nothing to stop her. She pulls back her arm, ready to send another blast of wind in my direction, but I get there first.

'*Earth, water, fire, hear my spell!*' I shout, my voice battling to be heard over the wind, then I trace the magical leaf pattern and I whisper my secret wish, '*Get her.*'

There isn't a moment when I have to concentrate, or force magic to spring from my fingers. It happens the moment I say the words.

A wave breaks free from the sea and comes racing across the sand, foaming, roaring . . . It rises higher and higher, heading straight towards the Innkeeper.

She turns to look at it. The wave is huge. '*Get her. Get her,*' I whisper, and the more I say the words, the faster the wave goes and the bigger it gets.

The Innkeeper clutches her spell book even closer. Then she comes to a decision. She turns and runs, disappearing into one of the caves. The wave follows her, smashing at the mouth of the cave, then it is sucked back out to sea.

For a moment I just stand there, clutching my map, but soon it becomes clear that the Innkeeper's gone. For now.

'Sid, come quick!' cries Peg.

I grab the bottle and race to Zen's side. I pull the cork out with my teeth then rest the bottle against his lips and drizzle the glittery liquid into his mouth.

Bones races back to us.

'How fares the lad?' he asks.

'Come on, Zen,' I say, giving him a little shake. 'Drink it!'

I see him swallow. Then he licks his dry lips. Suddenly his eyes open and he gasps and sits bolt upright.

He stares at the beach and then at us. 'Get me some of Sally's beer!' he says.

CHAPTER FIFTY

I hoped the Luminos would give Zen enough strength to hang in there while I ran to the café and back, but it must be powerful stuff because he's able to stagger to his feet and come with me.

The potion seems to have set back the effects of the poison. It's obvious Zen isn't better, but at least he can walk and slowly we make our way across the beach. Zen has to lean heavily on my shoulder, but I don't care. I'm so pleased that I don't have to leave him on the beach with just the ghosts to protect him from the Innkeeper.

We keep plodding onwards. I'm exhausted, both from the wind that's pushing against us and the weight of Zen. Every few steps I glance over my shoulder to check that the

Innkeeper isn't there, but she's nowhere to be seen.

'Maybe she's given up,' says Zen, wincing with each step.

'She will never give up,' I say. 'Look at the weather, Zen. Does this feel natural to you?'

The sky has become a strange yellow colour. The storm has come back with a vengeance and waves are hammering at the Cockle. It's so windy we're struggling to stand upright.

'You think this is her doing?' asks Bones.

'I'm sure, it is,' I say. 'She's furious that we got off the island and this weather feels furious too.'

Peg bursts out laughing. 'And she won't have liked that hiding you gave her on the beach, Sid!'

'No, she won't,' I admit.

I hate to think what the Innkeeper is planning next. I can't stop picturing the moment she swept the models into her bag. She told me she could use them to gather more lumin, but I don't think that's the only reason she wants them. I'm sure she'll use them to punish me and Zen. Why else would she have chosen models of the people we care most about? I just hope we can come up with a way to stop her before she does anything.

But I can't worry about that until I've got Zen to drink some of Sally's beer. It's obvious that the poison is still in his body. In the time it's taken us to walk across the beach he's become weaker again. We stagger up the steps and on to the seafront. Zen collapses on a bench. 'I'm sorry,' he says. 'I need to rest.'

'You stay here,' I say. 'I'll get the beer and bring it to you.'

Zen lets his head flop back and shuts his eyes.

I leave Peg and Mei with Zen, and Bones follows me up the lane.

Fathom is deserted. I can see a few people in shops and cafés, but there isn't a single person on the streets. Plus even though it's a Saturday some businesses are closed. Mermaid's is shut up and so is Tommy's roundabout.

Luckily the Black Spot Cat Café is open.

Bones and I rush inside. The fairy lights and salt lamps are switched on, but Sally isn't behind the counter and there are no customers. Taylor Swift is playing on the radio and an untouched cup of coffee sits on the counter. At least the cats are here. Straight away they jump down from chairs and tables and start meowing and rubbing against my legs.

'Sally!' I shout. 'SALLY!'

There's no reply. I decide that this is one situation where I'm allowed to help myself, so while Bones goes upstairs to look for Sally, I search the fridge for a bottle of her cobnut beer.

They're easy to spot with their yellow home-made labels and I'm grabbing a couple when Bones shouts out, 'You had better come and see this, Sid!'

I take the stairs two at a time and find Sally curled up in her bed, a thick blanket pulled over her shoulders.

'Sally?' I say, rushing to her side. 'Are you OK?'

She doesn't reply. She doesn't even open her eyes. Then I notice a layer of glittery dust hovering over the bed.

'The Innkeeper is doing this,' I say to Bones. 'She's got Sally's model and she's breaking bits off to steal her lumin. This is what happened to Dad!'

'Then we will stop her,' says Bones, 'but first we must get that cobnut beer to Zen.'

I pull another blanket round Sally's shoulders, then after telling her we're going to help her, we run back to the seafront.

Zen is exactly where we left him, with Peg and Mei by

his side. 'Quick, drink this,' I say, twisting the lid off one of the bottles.

He gulps the straw-coloured liquid down, burps, then reaches for the other bottle.

'How do you feel?' I ask when he's drained the last drop.

'Better,' he says. Then he smiles. 'Much better!'

Within minutes colour has come back to Zen's face and his temperature settles down. Soon he's able to sit up properly and look around.

'Where is everyone?' he says when he notices Fathom's deserted streets.

Quickly I tell him what we found at the café. 'It could be that the storm is keeping everyone inside, but I've got a bad feeling about this, Zen. I think the Innkeeper's hurting Sally, and that means she could be hurting other people too.'

I don't say, *like our parents and Skye*. I don't need to.

Zen jumps to his feet. 'I need to go home,' he says.

And I know that I do too, so we agree that Zen will go with Peg and Mei to the museum while Bones and I go to the model village. Once we know what's going on we can come up with a plan.

I force myself to hurry up the lane. My legs feel heavy

348

and I'm starving, but I won't let myself slow down until I've seen Dad.

'It could be a coincidence,' I say to Bones. 'Sally could just be ill.'

'Perhaps,' he says, but I don't think either of us believes this.

As soon as I step into the model village I realise that the situation is worse than I ever imagined.

Dad isn't in the kiosk and every single model has gone: Mrs Ferrari, Roundabout Tommy, even Mrs Neary, my old head teacher at Fathom Primary.

I run up and down the narrow paths, peering into shops and houses. 'They're *all* gone!' I say.

'How do you think she did it?' asks Bones. He's staring down at the now empty model seafront. 'Did she get Old Scratch to do it while we were on the island?'

I shake my head. 'She said he refused to steal the model of Dad. I think she must have taken some last night before she came and found us on the beach and the rest when she left us on Wolf Island. I don't know how she got back to Fathom so quickly, but I bet it has something to do with all the tunnels under the Halfway House.'

'Why didn't your father stop her?' asks Bones.

That's a question I've been avoiding thinking about.

I turn and run into the cottage shouting, 'Dad . . . *DAD!*'

I find him curled up on the sofa. I'm trying to shake him awake when Zen, Mei and Peg burst into the cottage. 'In here!' I shout.

Zen sees Dad and says, 'My mum, dad and Skye are the same, Sid. They're lying in their beds. I couldn't wake them up!'

I shake Dad's shoulder. A cloud of dust rises off him, but his eyes remain firmly closed. 'It's like a curse in a fairy tale,' I say.

Zen nods. 'The Innkeeper has put the village to sleep, only she hasn't just put them to sleep. She's hurting them too. We've got to stop her!'

'I know,' I say. Then I turn to look out of the window.

From here I can just see Orlig House up on the cliffs.

Molly Noon and the Innkeeper are the same person, which means this is the Innkeeper's home. I think about the bungalow at the end of the path. Mo said that was where she lived and that the man in the garden was her dad. But he never even glanced in our direction. I bet he's just some random man who lives in a bungalow near Orlig House. I can't believe how easily I fell for Mo's lies.

I find the window in the tower where I first set eyes on Mo, or rather the Innkeeper. Was she was experimenting with her potion when we saw her? Then I remember the big water bottle that Mo always carried around. Did that contain Luminos? Was she drinking her potion all day at school to make sure she stayed young for the whole day?

Black clouds hang over Fathom and the sea, but the sky above Orlig House is strangely clear. Suddenly I know that whatever the Innkeeper is doing to the models, it's happening up there, in Orlig House.

'We need to get inside Orlig House,' I say. 'We need to get the models back and destroy the Innkeeper's spell book so she can't do any more magic.'

'What about the ghosts?' says Zen. He doesn't mean the ghosts who are with us right now. He means Will, Beau and Holkar who are still fading away in the Halfway House.

'They are at risk,' says Bones. He gestures towards my dad lying in bed. 'If she will treat the living so cruelly, she will think nothing of causing harm to the dead.'

I'm sure Bones is right. One look at my dad tells me that the Innkeeper is trying to get every drop of precious lumin that she can before she goes away, and she's not going to forget about the ghosts in the tavern.

Zen joins me and stares up at the sky. 'If only there was lightning, then you could at least get them out of the Halfway House.'

I put a hand on my chest, feeling my map and I say 'I don't need lightning.'

CHAPTER FIFTY-ONE

The streets are deserted as we hurry towards the graveyard.

'Why don't you need lightning?' asks Zen. 'You had it when you freed the other ghosts. What changed?'

'Nothing,' I say. 'I don't think I ever needed it. It was a coincidence, a red herring. There just happened to be an electrical storm when I freed Bones and that made me think it was important. I bet I don't need a Crunchie or a red gel pen either.'

'You sound mighty sure of yourself,' says Bones. I can't tell if he's impressed by my confidence or suspicious of it.

'I am,' I say. 'I watched the Innkeeper when she did her magic. All she had was her book and some words.'

'Just like you had on the beach,' says Mei.

'Exactly,' I say, and my confidence helps me to walk boldly through the graveyard gates without even checking to see if the Innkeeper or Old Scratch are nearby.

The storm seems particularly bad in here. The trees are being tossed from side to side and the wind howls between the graves. Beyond the sea wall, waves thunder down on the beach, tossing seaweed and sand over the headstones.

Holkar's grave is the closest to the gates so that's where I go first. I don't even consider going to the Halfway House to warn the ghosts about what we are about to do. There's no time. The moment the ghosts are free we have to go to Orlig House and stop the Innkeeper.

I only look over my shoulder before I take my map out. It would be disastrous if the Innkeeper got her hands on it now. 'Watch my back,' I tell the others, then I find Holkar's grave on my map, and without hesitating, without even bothering to use a pen, I use my finger to draw his initials. I press down hard on my map and I know exactly what spell to say.

'*Earth, water, fire, break her spell,*' I whisper. '*Earth, water, fire, break her spell.*'

As I speak, I let the wind push me from side to side, and

I feel the spray from the sea fall on my face. '*Earth, water, fire, break her spell!*' I repeat, louder this time, almost shouting the words.

Suddenly Zen shakes my shoulder. 'Sid, you can stop. It's worked!'

Dazed, I look up.

Holkar is stumbling between the graves with a look of shocked bewilderment on his slim face. Bones roars his approval, but I don't wait for Holkar to join us. Instead, I jump up and run to Beau Fiddler's grave. It's a small stone set flat in the ground. Moss has grown over it, but I pull it away with my hands, then slam my map down. I start to draw over Beau's initials, saying the words that I now know for certain can break the Innkeeper's spell.

It takes less than a minute this time. Suddenly I hear Beau bellowing, 'I am out! Where are you?'

I grab my map and run towards Will's grave. He is the last ghost left. I can't leave him in the Halfway House on his own.

Pressing my map against his grave, I find his tiny headstone and start to draw his initials, whispering as I go.

I'm not sure what first alerts me to the fact that

something is wrong. Behind me, I sense that the ghosts have fallen quiet. I hear Holkar arrive and then Beau, but they aren't crying out happily. They are whispering to the others, and then a chilly hand lands on my shoulder.

I look up to see Bones staring down at me.

'Will has gone, Jones. The Innkeeper has taken him.'

CHAPTER FIFTY-TWO

I fight my way through the weeds towards the Halfway House with Zen and the ghosts following close behind.

It's only when I step inside the Halfway House that I actually believe what Bones has just told me.

It's empty. Will has vanished. Even though I can see there isn't a single ghost left in the pub, I still run around the room, looking under tables and even checking the cupboard by the fireplace.

'Where's Olive?' I say. 'She said she would look after him!'

'And she tried, Sid.' Holkar stands directly in front of me, blocking my path. Then he looks me in the eye and says, 'She shouted and raged at the Innkeeper, and begged

Will not to go with her. We all did. But he slipped his hand into hers and left by his own free will. He has gone.'

Tiredness washes over me and I sink down on the nearest stool.

'Here, eat this,' says Zen, pushing one of his dad's cherry scones into my hands.

All of a sudden I realise how hungry I am and I start pulling off chunks of the scone, stuffing them in my mouth. 'Where's Olive?' I say through a mouthful of crumbs.

'Looking for you,' says Holkar. 'She left the moment the Innkeeper took Will.'

'Tell me what happened,' I say.

'It happened a short while ago,' says Holkar. 'We heard footsteps on the stairs, the cellar door was flung open and a woman burst in. She wore a cloak and had a mask slung about her neck. Of course, I recognised her immediately from your description and identified her as the Innkeeper.' He can't help but sound proud of himself when he says this. 'She looked wild and dishevelled and she marched straight up to Will and asked him if he would like to go with her.'

'Blast it, we told him not to!' says Beau.

'So why did he do it?' I say.

Beau gives a wry laugh. 'Because she told him she had a kangaroo that he could stroke, and the lad believed her.'

'Unfinished business,' says Zen.

The ghosts nod. They all understand its power to control.

At that moment Olive comes running through the door.

'So you've heard?' she says when she sees us gathered together.

I nod. I know that if I say anything else I will cry. The storm is still raging over Fathom, the Innkeeper is hurting all the people that Zen and I care about, Holkar and Beau are fading away, and Will has been taken by the Innkeeper. I swallow down the sob that threatens to burst out of me and push the rest of the scone into my mouth.

'What shall we do?' asks Zen.

I get to my feet. I can't give up now. 'We are going to Orlig House,' I say. 'We will get Will back and destroy the spell book.'

Zen looks around at the ghosts. They are all here, even Radulfus has wriggled his way into the middle of the group and is watching us all closely with his diamond-shaped eyes, and Elizabeth who is perched on Bones's shoulder.

'What . . . *all* of us?' says Zen.

One by one the ghosts nod. Elizabeth cries, *'RUM! BULLY! RUM!'*

'Perhaps not quite all of us,' says Bones, eyeing his noisy parrot, 'but I for one will not be leaving your side, Sid. We are a crew and we must stick together.'

'But, Sid, darling,' says Olive. 'How do we get to Orlig House? It is either a walk along the cliffs or a bus ride on the coast road, and we don't have time to do either.'

'There is another way,' I say, and I look at the cellar door.

CHAPTER FIFTY-THREE

'How long is this tunnel?' whispers Zen. With the exception of Radulfus and Elizabeth, we are all creeping through the tunnel that leads to the pit. 'And how can you be so sure this leads to Orlig House?'

'We'll find out if I'm right in a minute,' I say. 'Look. There's the door.'

Up ahead we can see the green light seeping round the edges of the door, and we can hear the *drip, drip, drip* of water. As Bones and I have been here before we take the lead, ushering Zen and the ghosts forward.

Of course we go carefully, walking as quietly as we can

and stopping every now and then to listen for footsteps. We're not just looking for the Innkeeper but for Old Scratch as well. So far all we've encountered are spiders and one very surprised rat.

Soon we're stepping out of the tunnel and into the pit.

'This is unbelievable!' says Zen, gazing around.

Just like last time, the pit feels alive with plants and insects. Trees tower above us and birds burst from their branches. But there's no time to explore. 'This way,' I say, and I lead us towards the stone slabs sticking out of the walls of the pit.

'What manner of staircase is this?' asks Peg, as we start to walk up.

'A filthy one,' replies Holkar with distaste. He might be a ghost, but he still treads daintily over the green streaks of algae that coat each step.

'It's slippery,' I warn Zen. 'Be careful.'

For a while we are quiet as we concentrate on climbing the staircase, but then, in hushed tones, Holkar and Beau start to tell us about their unfinished business. I understand why they are so keen to share their stories. I might have freed them from the Halfway House, but dust

is pouring off them, making the air around us glitter. Time is running out for them and it seems to be happening even more quickly than usual.

Beau admits that although he was considered 'the most dashing' of highwaymen, he wasn't particularly successful. 'I was too much of a gentleman,' he says. 'And I was, sad to say, most teased for it.'

Zen and I already know this. When we were researching the ghosts' unfinished business we stumbled across a song that was inspired by Beau called 'The Ballad of the Hopeless Highwayman'.

Our footsteps ring out as we walk higher up the staircase.

'But what is your unfinished business, exactly?' urges Olive. 'Spit it out, Beau. Now isn't the time to be coy.'

'I wanted to successfully hold up a carriage, that is all,' he says. 'I wanted to stand in a country lane, bellow "Stand and deliver!" and to be met with obedience and not laughter.'

'Mine is simplicity itself,' says Holkar. 'I must discover who murdered me. I was invited to investigate the theft of a most unusual snuff box – it had belonged to

Admiral Nelson – and in the course of my investigation I was poisoned, only I do not know by who, or how the poison was administered.'

We're getting near to the top of the pit. 'Shh!' I say, putting my finger to my lips.

It's late afternoon, but the dark storm clouds make it seem like night-time has come early. I take the last couple of steps slowly, not sure what I am about to discover.

I breathe a sigh of relief. I'm standing in a wild garden. It's like a giant rockery. Huge boulders are dotted with plants scrambling over and between them. A path winds between the rocks, and there at the end of the path is a lawn that leads to Orlig House.

The ghosts and Zen emerge from the pit and gather round me. We stare at the many windows of Orlig House.

'So that's where the villain lives,' mutters Bones.

'But that ain't fair,' says Peg, summing up how all the ghosts must be feeling. 'It's a flippin' palace!'

It's true. Orlig House is huge, with turrets, arched windows and two towers, one taller than the other. I can't imagine how many rooms there must be inside, but the Halfway House could probably fit inside one of them.

We creep forward until we reach the lawn, then we stick to the shadows. Orlig House is lined with windows, and we know that the Innkeeper could be standing behind any one of them looking out. We can see a large wooden door, but decide it's too dangerous to walk across the lawn towards it, and instead we work our way round the side of the house. It's Olive who finds a smaller door leading into what looks like a library.

I reach forward, ready to try the handle.

'Steady now, Jones,' Bones says. 'Should we not come up with a plan? Heading into battle without one does not sit easy with me.'

'We find Will, we find the models and then we find the Innkeeper's spell book and we destroy it,' I say.

It's not much of a plan, I know, but it's going to have to do.

I don't wait for Bones to reply. I push down on the handle and when it opens with a gentle click, we step inside.

CHAPTER FIFTY-FOUR

'Do you remember how Mo described this place?' whispers Zen.

The two of us are creeping up a huge wooden staircase. It's covered in dust and cobwebs. Plaster that's crumbled from the walls crunches under our feet.

'She said it was amazing,' I reply. 'That there were gold taps, an indoor pool and a chandelier.'

Zen shines the torch on the ceiling. 'She wasn't lying about the chandelier.'

It's hanging at a wonky angle, held up by just two of its four chains. The crystals might have shone once, but now they're dull and tangled together.

'Maybe that's the pool,' I say. Water drips from the ceiling on to the tiled floor of the hallway below. The roof has obviously been leaking for years and the water gathering in a large puddle below is brown and stagnant.

The ghosts have drifted off to different corners of the mansion to look for any sign of Will, the Innkeeper or her book of spells. Zen and I were supposed to wait for them in the hall below, but we got impatient and decided to go upstairs and check out the first floor for ourselves. The whole house is neglected. Gas lamps hiss on the walls casting a greenish light over peeling wallpaper and stained tapestries.

Every now and then the Innkeeper's eyes stare down at us from portraits and photographs. Just like Old Scratch's clocks that fill the walls of the Halfway House, there are pictures of the Innkeeper everywhere. There is no order to them. In one oil painting she's wearing a tight ruff and her jewelled fingers clasp a dog. Next to this is a mottled black-and-white photograph that shows her standing on the deck of a ship wearing a black coat and a huge hat. A little further up the stairs I see a framed article taken from a newspaper. The headline reads **'Molly Noon, the Modest Millionaire'**.

'Modest?' says Zen when he sees this. 'I've never seen someone put up so many pictures of themselves.'

'Look, is this Old Scratch?' I say, pointing at a tiny watercolour portrait of a young man with a gaunt face. His dark hair is swept back from his bony forehead.

'I think so,' says Zen. 'She's not so keen on putting up pictures of her son, is she?'

'Come on,' I say. 'We need to keep going.'

We make our way along the first and then the second floors of the house, peeking into every room we come to. Some are filled with junk – old furniture and piles of mouldering clothes – others look like they belong in a different house entirely. We find one that is painted a dazzling white, with artfully arranged pot plants sitting on wooden shelves. A camera on a tripod and a collection of yoga mats tell us that this is where Molly Noon records some of her yoga videos.

The next room we come to is obviously where the Innkeeper transforms into Mo.

Mo's school uniform and her colourful clothes are heaped in a pile. A table is covered with gel pens, fluffy notebooks and quirky accessories.

Zen picks up a sloth hairgrip. 'You know she bought all this to appeal to you, don't you?'

I nod, running my hands over a fluffy white hoodie. Mo was wearing this when I first saw her in the window. She was probably standing in this very room. There are three identical hoodies dropped on the floor. To the Innkeeper, Mo was just another of her acting roles, and this room is filled with the props and costumes that helped her transform into someone I would want to be my friend.

A thud sounds in a room somewhere above us. Zen and I freeze, looking up. We hear the thud again followed by a muffled voice. I can't be sure, but I think it might be Will.

'Let's go,' I say.

'Shouldn't we wait for the ghosts?' asks Zen.

'There is no time,' I say, and I run to the door.

A suit of armour stands next to a spiral staircase leading to the tallest of the towers. The staircase is dark and narrow, but we know that this is where we need to go and we soon reach a heavy door.

I put my eye to the keyhole.

I can see a round room with candles dotted here and there, and a cauldron spluttering over a fire. It's similar to the potions room on Wolf Island: jars line the walls and a table is covered in vials that are filled with strange-coloured liquids. Ghost dust glitters in the air and a pile of books is balanced on a chair. Could one of those be the Innkeeper's spell book? I try to remember what it looked like – it was large, covered in green leather, with a faded elder tree on the front. A figure walks to the table, making me jump.

It's the Innkeeper.

I hold my breath and watch as she tips the bag she is holding upside down. Objects spill out across the table. Some fall on the floor. I press my face closer to the keyhole and see little arms and legs and tiny smiling faces. It's Dad's models. My heart lurches to see them treated so roughly. Then I see the innkeeper pick one up at random – it's Sally, I recognise her from the green jumper she's wearing – and grab a pair of secateurs.

I have to act quickly.

'Go downstairs,' I whisper to Zen. 'Do something, *anything* to get her out of this room.'

He nods and creeps back the way we just came. I stand up and press my back against the wall next to the door. There's nowhere to hide, but if my plan works and the

Innkeeper rushes straight down the stairs, then she won't notice me standing here.

Zen doesn't hang around. A few seconds later, an almighty crash rings out, echoing up into the tower.

I think Zen might have thrown the suit of armour over the staircase. For a moment everything goes quiet, then I hear footsteps and the door is thrown open.

My heart leaps and I press back against the cold stone of the wall. The Innkeeper flies past me, her cloak whipping against my face.

I wait until she's halfway down the spiral staircase then slip into the room.

I take a few footsteps then remember that the Innkeeper could come back at any moment. I close the door. There's no key, so I drag a heavy chair across the room, wincing as it scrapes over the floor, then I shove it under the doorknob.

It won't keep her out for long, but it might buy me a bit of time.

I'm about to look at the books when I hear a whimper coming from what looks like an alcove. It's covered by a thick curtain. I run across the room and pull the curtain back. A pale shape is slumped against the wall.

'Will? Is that you?'

A white face looks up and two dark hollows fix on me. Slowly the figure nods.

I want to pull Will to his feet and hold him close, but of course I can't do that.

I put my hands on his icy shoulders. 'You've got to get up, Will,' I say. 'She's going to be back in a minute. You need to hide.'

Slowly he shakes his head. 'Can't,' he whispers, then holds up his hands. A delicate silver chain is wrapped round his wrists. There's a chain round his ankles too and they are both attached to a thick metal loop embedded in the wall.

'*Silver snares the dead,*' I whisper, remembering what Abigail read from the spell book at the museum. But it can't hurt me. I grab the chains and wrench them apart.

Will is still too weak to move and he stays where he is, curled up in the alcove.

'Help me, Sid,' he whispers.

CHAPTER FIFTY-FIVE

I'm wondering what to do next when I hear footsteps thumping up the stairs.

The Innkeeper is coming back. I have to find her spell book! Running to the pile of books on the chair, I grab the top one, but it's far too small so I toss it to the ground and look at the next one. That's when the doorknob turns. The door opens a fraction then hits the chair.

'OPEN THIS DOOR!' screams the Innkeeper. As the doorknob is twisted frantically back and forth I search through the rest of the books, but none of them have a green cover or an elder tree on the front. Suddenly there is a crash and the chair is shoved back. I see the Innkeeper's staring face appear at the gap in the door.

She sees me searching through her books, snarls, then hurls her weight at the door.

This time there is a loud crack of splintered wood and the chair clatters to the ground. The door flies open and the Innkeeper bursts into the room, dragging Zen by his neck. My heart sinks when I see her green spell book clutched to her chest.

When she sees me looking at it, she grins. 'A good witch always keeps her spell book close, Sidonie Jones. Don't you know anything?'

She shoves Zen towards me, then raises her hand and points at the window behind us, muttering under her breath. Suddenly the casement window is blown open, smacking against the wall and sending glass flying across the room.

Next the Innkeeper moves her pointing finger from the window to me and Zen. She walks closer to us, continuing to whisper her spell. A fierce wind is sucked into the tower and whips past my face. The next thing I know Zen and I are being dragged by the wind towards the open window.

'This ends now!' the Innkeeper cries, and I feel myself being sucked back by the wind. It's like a hand has grabbed hold of me and is trying to hurl me out of the window.

My legs hit the frame, I wobble, getting a glimpse of a terrifying drop, but I manage to cling on to a long velvet curtain. 'Hold on, Zen!' I shout.

Just before he tumbles out of the window he wraps his arms round my waist and I hold on tighter to the curtain.

'Jones!' bellows a familiar voice. 'Zen! Where are you?'

There are voices on the stairs, a thundering of footsteps, then the ghosts burst into the room. Bones's eyes fly from me and Zen to the Innkeeper who is still muttering her spell. The room is in chaos. The howling wind is spinning paper around the room and pulling bottles off the shelves. They shoot through the air, smashing into each other.

Bones lurches towards the Innkeeper. 'Stop your magic, fiend!' he cries. The other ghosts shout and scream too, but it's like they are invisible. The Innkeeper keeps her eyes fixed on me and Zen and commands the wind to pull us even closer to the window edge.

So the ghosts hurl themselves at her. They run through her body, punch, slap and grab hold of her arms and legs.

Even Will staggers up from his spot on the floor and pummels her with his fading fists.

But their attempts just make her throw back her head and laugh.

'Zen, I'm not sure how much longer I can hold on,' I shout, as the Innkeeper shakes free of the ghosts and walks closer towards us. The wind moves with her, building in ferocity. My fingers start to slip on the velvet.

'Do some magic,' he says. 'Fast!'

Desperately I try to think of a spell that will make the Innkeeper stop, but there are no plants in the room that I can make grow or shrivel. I try to remember what was written in the spell books at the museum and all the things I've seen Peg do. The wind drags me further back and Zen tightens his arms round me. Then I remember that I do know another spell: one that was written in one of the books at the museum.

The Innkeeper is standing right in front of me now. As she speaks she twists her fingers and the wind slams into my body. I glance over my shoulder. Zen is hanging half out of the window. The only thing stopping him from falling to his death is me. Then I hear a rip and the curtain tears.

'Seriously, Sid. Do some magic. Now!' cries Zen.

'Without her spell book?' sneers the Innkeeper.

I stare into her cold, arrogant eyes and I shout, 'A good witch always keeps her spell book close! Don't you know anything?' Then I take one hand off the curtain, grab my map through my jumper and shout, 'IGNIS LUX!' and I pray Abigail was right when she said this spell would light a candle.

A golden spark shoots from my map and lands on the Innkeeper's leather-bound spell book. It bursts into flames. The Innkeeper doesn't throw her book to the ground. She stares at the burning object in her hands and forgets to say her spell. Then several things happen at once. The wind stops, the curtain tears from its fittings, I pull Zen back into the room and we tumble to the ground.

'Quick!' Bones beckons to us and we crawl towards him, away from the window and the Innkeeper with her burning book. Thick smoke fills the room; it burns the back of my throat and makes my eyes stream.

Still the Innkeeper clutches her book even though the flames are rising higher.

'Throw it out of the window!' I shout.

She shakes her head and flames jump from the book to the sleeve of her cloak.

I look around for water as the ghosts and Zen start to shout at her, urging her to drop the book and save herself.

I see that outside the black clouds have turned white. The storm has gone. The Innkeeper's power is fading.

The Innkeeper notices this too. 'My magic!' she cries, hugging her book even closer.

'Please!' I say, reaching to her through the smoke. 'Drop the book and take my hand!'

Instead she holds her book tight, squeezes her eyes shut, and takes one, two, three steps backwards. Her legs hit the low window frame, but she does nothing to stop herself from falling. She falls backwards through the open window in a rush of flames, and then she is gone.

CHAPTER FIFTY-SIX

'We must leave this place now!' orders Bones.

Flames have sprung up on the heavy curtains. They spread quickly, leaping to the ceiling, setting fire to the books on the chair. Glass bottles start to pop and explode.

I step forward to collect Dad's models, but Zen pulls me back.

'The Innkeeper's gone, Sid, and so has her magic. The only thing this fire can hurt is us. We have to go!'

Feeling numb, I nod and I reach out for Will. He slips his hand into mine. I don't care how cold it is. I'm not letting go. Then we run out of the burning room and down the stairs, smoke billowing behind us.

When we reach the landing, Zen says, 'What about

Old Scratch? If he's here, we need to tell him about the fire.'

'The house is empty,' says Holkar. 'We checked every room.'

Zen nods and we carry on down the staircase, but when we reach the hallway with its pool of stagnant water I realise Holkar has fallen behind. I turn round to see him standing halfway down the stairs, staring at a photograph.

I let go of Will's hand and run to him. 'Come on,' I say. 'We've got to go!'

Holkar points at the picture. It's one I saw earlier. The Innkeeper is dressed in a wool coat and standing on the deck of a ship. She's smiling from under the brim of a large hat.

'I met this woman on the train as I travelled to investigate Nelson's stolen snuff box. She was charming company. We went to get tea from the buffet car. When it came she added a cube of sugar to my cup when I didn't ask for one. She stirred it so thoughtfully I thought it bad manners not to drink the tea.'

He turns to look at me. 'The next morning I was dead. *That's* how I was poisoned, Sid. I was murdered by the Innkeeper!'

Colour floods through his body. His skin becomes dark

brown and his hair jet black. The rose tucked into his lapel blooms a delicate shade of pink. He smiles contentedly and offers me his arm. 'My last case is solved,' he says. 'Shall we?'

I take his arm and together we walk out of Orlig House.

We catch up with Zen and the rest of the ghosts on the patio and we all walk across the lawn. Considering how neglected the house was, the lawn is pristine. The Innkeeper obviously had to keep up appearances for the sake of Molly Noon. Elizabeth swoops low over the grass and lands on my shoulder. Radulfus appears from a bush. He trots over to Peg and butts against her.

As we cross the striped green lawn, Zen calls the fire brigade.

'I said that I was walking on the cliffs and saw flames in the distance,' he says.

I look over my shoulder. Now the whole tower is ablaze. Ash drifts down on us like snow. I feel strangely calm. I even glance at the foot of the tower, but the only sign of the Innkeeper is a pile of dust, a scorched cloak and some fragments of burnt paper.

Zen pulls me forward. 'Come on. We don't want to be here when the fire brigade turns up.'

Soon we hear sirens and see the flash of blue lights in the sky. None of us want to go back down into the pit – we've had enough darkness for today – so instead we scramble over a wall and then pick our way across a field. Brown sheep can be seen huddling under a hedge along with one bright white one.

We're too tired to talk. And with Will so close to turning into a wraith none of us can think of anything to say. He's holding my hand again although I can barely feel his chilly fingers.

'Will,' I say, squeezing his hand. 'Tell me about your unfinished business.'

'It was to do with me being a thief, Sid.' Two dark spaces where his eyes should be gaze up at me. 'They said I stole a pair of boots only I thought they were mine for the taking. No one's feet were in them when I took them and I didn't have any. I was thrown in jail, then I had my photograph taken and a man told me I was wicked and was to be sent to Australia. My mum was allowed to visit me and she cheered me right up. She said Australia was a fine place to go where a fellow could make something of himself. She said I would be able to see kangaroos and that their fur was the softest thing in the world and wasn't I a lucky chap to be able to touch such a thing with my own fingers!'

I glance down and see that he's smiling at the memory.

'What happened next?'

'I got sick. Lots of us did because it was rotten in that jail, and I never got to go to Australia and see a kangaroo. I never even got to leave the jail, not in this life anyway. I was wandering around Fathom looking for my mum and that's when Old Scratch found me. You know what happened next.'

My feet feel heavy. I'm not sure I can make it across the field, let alone home. My heart is breaking for Will, but I can't see any way to solve his unfinished business. Even if I marched home and demanded that Dad drive me straight to a zoo, we would never get there in time.

Next to me Zen gasps. 'I do not believe it,' he says. 'Look!'

He's pointing at a sign by the edge of the field. It looks brand new and it reads: 'Coming soon . . . West Coast Wallabies, the wildest wallaby walk-through in the west!'

I look around for the sheep I saw a minute ago. Straight away I realise they're not sheep at all. They're beautiful brown wallabies, although one of them is a dazzling white.

It's time for me to tell one last lie.

'Look, Will,' I say, turning him round and pointing at the wallabies. 'Kangaroos!'

CHAPTER FIFTY-SEVEN

It's hard to persuade Will to leave the wallaby he's chosen to throw his arms round.

The wallaby is unaware that it's being hugged by a ghost and continues to munch the grass with a bored expression on its face. It doesn't even look cold.

'Kangaroos are as good as my mum said they would be!' says Will. 'They're like rabbits, only fatter, and they stay still.' He looks up at me and grins. I've never seen him so full of colour. I didn't even know he had blond hair. Eventually he gives a happy sigh and stands up. 'Come on. I want to see my mum.'

We're just leaving the field when we meet a man wandering along the lane.

I recognise him immediately. It's the man from the bungalow, the one Mo said was her dad.

'What are you two up to?' he says, looking at me and Zen. Next to us the ghosts shift nervously. 'You do know that's private property.'

'I'm sorry,' I say. 'We just wanted to see the wallabies.'

He smiles. 'I don't blame you. Lovely things, aren't they? But I'm afraid you'll have to wait until we're open to visit them again.' He starts to walk on up the lane, looking curiously at the smoke that's coming from Orlig House.

My shoulders sag with relief and Zen pulls me away, but there's something I have to ask the man. 'Excuse me,' I call after him.

He turns round.

'Do you let your children play with the wallabies?'

'I've got a son. He's grown up now, but he likes them well enough.' Then he gives me a friendly nod and walks away.

As Zen, the ghosts and I traipse down the lane I think about Mo, the friend I never really had. The man from the bungalow clearly had nothing to do with her. She just saw him standing in his garden and decided to pretend he was her dad. I can't believe how easily she told lies. I guess if you've been doing it for hundreds of years you hardly realise you're doing it.

Now the storm has gone it's a beautiful evening. The sun has begun to sink towards the sea and the sky is a golden colour. Beau falls in step beside me. 'Looks like it's just me left, Sidonie,' he says. 'I don't suppose we could find a carriage laden with riches and hold it up, could we?'

Beau is smiling as usual, but I can tell he's worried. All the ghosts look so bright and colourful compared to him. In fact, he's the only one who actually looks like a ghost. 'I think it's pretty unlikely,' I say. 'Which is a shame because I'm exhausted and I could do with a lift back to Fathom.'

Just then I hear the throb of an engine and two headlights

swing round the corner. A bus is coming towards us. Zen and I step up on to the verge to let it pass, but then I see the name of the company painted in big letters on the side of the bus: *Stagecoach*.

'Beau!' I shout, pointing at the bus. 'Hold up that stagecoach and demand they give me a lift home for free!'

A smile spreads across his face. 'Anything my lady requires!'

Beau leaps into the middle of the lane, pulls out his pistol and shouts, 'Stand and deliver! This fair lady seeks free passage. Let her on board, do you hear!'

He doesn't see me lift up my hand and wave at the driver, and when the bus stops he's too busy finding me the perfect seat to hear me explain to the driver that we've got lost, and although we know this isn't a real bus stop would he mind giving us a lift home so we can get back to Fathom before it's dark.

'Sid, Zen!' cries Beau, waving from the back of the bus. 'I have found you the finest seats. Come. Rest your weary feet.'

The bus door swings shut and as it trundles down the lane, Zen and I make our way to the back, followed by the ghosts. Beau is already sitting there. His cloak is a rich plum

391

colour and his trousers are bright green. He grins at me and I see his dazzling white teeth. Not a speck of glittery dust floats from him. My shoulders sag with relief. I look at Zen. 'We've done it,' I say. 'The ghosts are all free.'

'Nice work, Sherlock Bones.'

'Thanks, Whatsupson,' I reply and we give each other a weary high five.

We all squeeze on to the back seat together. Will is overjoyed to be on a bus and screams with delight every time we pick up speed or go over a bump. I'm sitting squashed between the window and Bones. I rest my head on the glass and look towards Fathom. There are only a few other passengers on the bus and their eyes are all glued on Orlig House where smoke still pours from the roof.

But my eyes are fixed on the horizon.

The evening is beautifully clear, but some pink-tinged clouds are drifting down from the sky. They settle on the sea. I am so happy to see them and to know that all the ghosts can cross over to the other side. But even so, a tear slides down my cheek.

'Bones,' I say. 'What do you think it's like on the other side?'

'I don't rightly know,' he says, putting his hairy face close to mine so he can look out of the window. Elizabeth, who is back on his shoulder, peers out of the window too. 'But I believe I will soon find out.'

He's telling me that it's time for him to go.

'I'll miss you,' I say. I need to say this now because I don't want to be sad when I say goodbye on the Cockle. I don't want to cry and ruin it for everyone.

'And I shall miss you, Jones. I never dreamed I would have a pal like you. I am so glad that you wrote my name on your map.'

I turn and rest my head on his big shoulder, next to Elizabeth. I should feel nothing except a wave of cold, but for a moment my cheek rests against a warm shoulder covered in rough wool. I smell smoke and the sea and I feel the nibble of a parrot's beak, and I feel very lucky to be here, right now, with my friend, Ezekiel Bones Kittow.

CHAPTER FIFTY-EIGHT

When we get off the coach we walk straight to the Cockle. None of us need to say anything. We all know what happens next.

Together we walk to the end of the harbour, the sea lapping against the high wall. Elizabeth flies over our heads. She seems excited, as if she knows that something is about to happen. '*Rum! Bully! Rum! Rum!*' she cries.

'What do you think it's going to be?' asks Zen.

The clouds keep clumping together and then drifting apart again. It's as if they can't make up their mind about what they should become. At one point Peg is sure she can see an eagle, but what looks like a beak floats up in the air and becomes the wheel of a carriage.

'Why, it's a fine landau!' declares Beau, but the clouds won't stay still for long and soon the carriage has vanished.

We walk down the steps towards the sea. The sun is sinking fast and has made a golden path across the water that leads to the horizon. The sea laps over the bottom steps as I tread carefully, avoiding the seaweed that's been left behind.

The next time I look up the clouds have gathered together into a ship. It has three masts and huge sails that billow in the breeze. The ghosts gasp with delight.

'Why, it is my ship, the *Black Gannet*. She has come to take us away!' declares Bones.

Peg is the first to go. She stands opposite me and gives me a tight, cold hug. 'I feel honoured to have met a witch like you, Sid,' she says, then she reaches a hand out for Will. 'Come on, let us make this last walk together.'

'I am going to see my mum!' is all Will says to me and Zen, although he does yell 'See ya!' over his shoulder, as he and Peg run over the sea towards the waiting boat.

The rest of the ghosts leave one by one.

Holkar bows. Beau kisses my hand. Olive hugs me and Zen at the same time, telling us we're 'super chums'.

I watch them hurry across the sea and I'm surprised to find that I don't feel sad. I am happy that they are going on this last journey together.

Then only Bones is left.

He stands on the bottom step and salutes. He's about to go when he turns back.

'Jones, you asked what I think it is like on the other side. Truly I do not know, but a fellow once told me that the sun is always shining, sweet music and the smell of honeysuckle fill the air, and true friends meet again. I do hope he is right.'

Then he wraps his arms round me and gives me a final hug. I embrace the cold. I breathe in his smoky smell. I never want to forget this moment.

Bones gives me a final pat on the back, tips his hat to Zen, then turns and steps on to the sea. 'Come, Elizabeth!' he calls, and he follows the other ghosts along the golden path towards the ship with Elizabeth flying after him.

Zen and I watch until, one by one, the ghosts vanish into the haze on the horizon. Bones is the last to leave.

Then, with a final dazzling burst of light, the ship goes too.

For a few minutes we stand in silence and watch the light dancing on the sea. Then we turn and walk back up the stairs and on to the Cockle. Now the storm has gone, people have come down to the beach. Dogs and children are running across the wet sand and groups of villagers are standing around talking. Some are looking at the sea, others are turned towards Orlig House where smoke still drifts from the roof.

Then I spot a familiar figure bent over a pile of driftwood.

It's my dad, and Zen's parents are at the water's edge holding Skye's hands. Each time a wave comes they lift her up, helping her to jump over it.

Zen and I stand on the Cockle watching them.

Suddenly Dad straightens up and sees us on the harbour wall. He waves and calls out, 'Come and see what I've found. It's a real mermaid's purse!'

'I bet he's put a pound in it,' says Zen.

It's what Dad always does when he finds a mermaid's purse on the beach.

'If he has, I'm buying us some sweets,' I say.

Then, together, we go to join our friends and family on the beach.

CHAPTER FIFTY-NINE

The next few weeks feel like a dream.

Dad discovers Grandad's fishing boat is missing and puts it down to the storm. I sleep for hours at a time and can't stop eating. In the end Dad bans me from helping myself to Wotsits and Crunchies from the kiosk. Zen and I go to school, explore the beach and spend a lot of time playing *Mario Kart*. Orlig House is boarded up and the internet can't stop talking about Molly Noon. Apparently she's gone missing and no one knows where she is.

Dad doesn't notice that I haven't visited the graveyard in a while. He's too busy making new tiny people for the model village. He says he doesn't know who took them, but from now on he's taking them in every night.

Then one Friday after school, after we've got off the bus, Zen says, 'Shall we go to the graveyard?'

'OK,' I say.

We wander along the narrow paths and jump over the stream. We visit Mum's grave and spend a bit of time tidying it up. Eventually we find ourselves heading towards the darkest corner of the graveyard.

I smile when I see that the Halfway House is still there with its little windows and lantern hanging over the door. If it had turned back into the mausoleum I might have wondered if we had imagined our adventure with the ghosts.

'Shall we go inside?' says Zen, but I'm already marching forward and pulling open the door.

The candles have gone out and so has the fire. The air is still. A few specks of golden dust drift through the air. I stand in the middle of the room and turn round. Then I notice what's changed. The room is silent and the walls are bare. Every single clock has gone.

'Where do you think Old Scratch is now?' I say.

'I don't know,' says Zen. 'I know he was horrible to the ghosts, but his mum was horrible to him. Part of me hopes he's enjoying his retirement somewhere.'

'Maybe he's opened up a clock shop,' I say.

'Or a pub?' suggests Zen, making me laugh. He looks around the low-ceilinged room. 'Do you think more ghosts will come?'

I nod, because I'm sure they will, only this time when a lost soul wanders in here, they will find a comfortable place where they can rest for a while, and when they want to leave, they can.

For the first time in weeks, I put my hand on my map, then I point at the fire and I say, '*Ignis lux.*' Flames spring up in the grate. Then I turn and point at each candle in turn. I don't even need to say the words, I just think them, and the candles splutter into life.

Zen laughs. 'I can't believe I'm friends with a witch. Hey, if a ghost does come in here and needs our help, what are we going to do?'

'Help them, of course,' I say, then we leave the Halfway House.

I know it won't be long before we return.

ACKNOWLEDGEMENTS

Thank you to the magical team at Farshore for helping me write the book that you have in your hands today, and, of course, to Chloe Dominique for her spookily brilliant illustrations. I pictured the world Chloe created as I wrote this book and it was a wonderful place to be.

Find out where it all began . . .

ARE YOU READY FOR
FOR
ROAR?

Believing
is just the
beginning . . .